Cross The Line

Rie McGaha

Publishers Note:
This is a work of fiction. All names, characters, places,
and events are the work of the author's imagination. Any
resemblance to real persons, places, or events is
coincidental.

Marie McGaha ©2011
All rights reserved
ISBN 13: 978-0615510729
ISBN 10: 0615510728

~ ONE ~

"I don't know if I can do this on my own, Daddy." Carrie cried as she forced the jacket sleeve over her father's arm. The Confederate uniform was stiff, but the weight of her father's dead body hindered her endeavor even further.

"Amazing grace, how sweet the sound..." She began to sing, as she buttoned the jacket and clasped the frog hook under her father's chin. She wiped tears from her face and sweat from her brow, then set about tugging on his boots.

"You look *very* handsome, Daddy." She brushed his light brown hair to one side and kissed his cheek.

~ * ~

Carrie Anne Robertson wiped her arm across her brow and sucked a rasping breath into her lungs as she leaned wearily against the handle of the shovel she held. The late summer sun bore down and no breeze could be found. Sweat ran in rivulets down her back, down her front, between her breasts, and her clothing clung wetly to her body. Her hands were dirty and she could taste dust on her lips as she wiped a hand over her face once again. Then she slid to the ground, the shovel clattering hard on the rocks beside her. She cried hot, bitter tears.

Having spent most of the previous day digging the grave in the hot, summer dried ground, and she'd gone to bed aching and exhausted. Blisters covered the palms of her hands and though she was used to hard work, she wasn't used to digging for hours on end. She hadn't even bothered with supper and had barely managed to wash the dirt from her hands and face before she fell onto the bed in a heap. Then, earlier in the day, she'd spent the better part of an hour getting her father's body from the cabin to the grave. He was a big and heavy man alive, but dead, Carrie thought she might not be able to manage him on her own. She'd had no choice either; there was no one to help her for miles in any direction.

Finally, she had gotten her father's horse and tied a rope around its neck, then tied the other end around her father's big chest and dragged his body to the grave. Kneeling on the ground, she'd managed to roll him into the hole she'd dug and spent the entire afternoon burying him. The dirt now covered his body, packed into place but she still had to place large rocks on top to keep wild animals from digging for him later on. Carrie lifted her apron and wiped her face. She took a few deep breaths, blew them out, and then she got to her feet and began the task of rolling the rocks to the grave. When she was finally finished, Carrie stood next to the grave and stared. Her back, arms, and neck ached, and her hands were raw and bleeding.

After a few silent moments she whispered, "Good-bye, Daddy. I love you."

Turning, she walked slowly to the creek behind the cabin. Stripping out of her clothing, she waded into the pool that had been made with fallen trees and boulders a few years before. Sinking into the water, she let it wash completely over her. Then, she scrubbed the dirt from her skin, washed her hair, laid back and floated. She closed her eyes and thought of her father, thought of her mother, and her sisters. All gone now, leaving Carrie alone.

The War Between the States had taken its toll on the country in every way possible but the way it had ravaged Carrie's family left her feeling hollow. Charleston had been hit hard by the war and Carrie's father had already been off fighting the Yankees when they had arrived at the plantation, burning everything in their path.

When Yankee soldiers came to the Robertson house, Carrie's mother told her three daughters to run and hide while she loaded the musket and stayed behind to defend their home. Carrie grabbed Lydia's small hand and pulled her along behind her as she ran out the back door of the house. She could hear her older sister, Marianne behind them but when their mother screamed, Marianne told Carrie to keep going and went back to the house. Carrie and Lydia ran and ran. They hid all night long, watching fire shoot high into the dark skies all around them, and late the next morning, black smoke continued to rise high into the sky, the acrid smell burning their eyes and lungs.

That evening, the pair ventured from their hiding place, more from hunger than anything else, and went back home. What remained of the house continued to smolder, and their mother and sister both lay half-naked and dead in the yard. Carrie didn't know how long she sat with Lydia lying across their mother, screaming and crying. Carrie sat and stared. She looked up when she heard voices and saw their neighbors, Mr. Carter and Mr. Ellis hurrying toward them. Lydia fought when they tried to take their mother from her, and Carrie held her even as she kicked and screamed while the two men buried her mother and sister.

The girls went with them to Mr. Ellis's house, and Mrs. Ellis hugged them both. "Child, it's a miracle our house wasn't burned too, but the fact you two are live, mercy!" Mrs. Ellis said, as she hugged Carrie to her. "Come on with me now, and we'll get you cleaned up. Then we'll get a proper meal in you."

Nearly two months passed before Charles Robertson came home.

He packed the girls on horseback and rode far away from Charleston. They just kept riding and riding until Carrie thought he'd never stop. Eventually they arrived in Memphis where he sold the horses, bought train tickets for them all and once again, they were traveling.

The days were long, the nights longer, and Carrie was so tired, she thought she'd never feel good again. When the train stopped in St. Louis, Carrie hoped they were where they were going to stay for good, but her father just bought more horses and another wagon loaded with supplies. Carrie wondered if they were going so far away they'd never be found.

Finally, after another three weeks, they stopped again. Her father said they were somewhere near Arkansas in the Indian Territory. The hills were beautiful, covered in trees and there were no other homesteads for miles and miles. Carrie wondered if she'd ever see another human being in her life. But that was where her father built a cabin with his own two hands, and they'd lived there now for nearly four years. Although it had been just the two of them for the last three years since Lydia came down with the flu the first year there and died before Christmas.

Charles Robertson was a big man, but after the war and the loss of his wife and daughter, he seemed to be getting smaller. After Lydia died, Charles seemed to be disappearing altogether, and now, Carrie thought, that's exactly what he'd done. Buried in the ground next to Lydia, she hoped they were both at peace. Hoped they'd joined her mother and Marianne in Heaven. Hoped her mother's stories had been true and her family was watching her, looking out for her from high above the Earth.

She opened her eyes and looked at the sky above. What was she supposed to do now? Even if her family was watching from Heaven, they surely weren't offering any advice. Carrie had a little money and she had the cabin. Her father had tried to make a go of the place and there were a few horses, a good milk cow, a dozen laying hens, and a randy old rooster in the yard. There was hay for the animals in the barn he'd built as well.

Her father had spent that first summer after the cabin was built plowing the ground for acres around the cabin, planting hay, winter wheat, and corn. Carrie planted a vegetable garden and spent the time each year to put up as many of the vegetables as she could so they'd have plenty of food during the winter. Her father put in a few apple trees, pear trees, and a few cherry trees, that

10

just this year began to produce enough fruit she'd have to eat long after the season ended.

Her father left weapons and ammunition, and made sure she knew how to use them so she was able to defend herself and be able to hunt. He hadn't been there emotionally for her, she knew, but he'd made sure she would eat. Made sure she could take care of herself if she had to, and, Carrie thought, now she had to.

Carrie squeezed the water from her hair, gathered up her clothing from the bank of the creek and walked back inside the cabin. She combed out her long brown hair, braided it in a single strand down her back, then slipped a camisole over her head and pulled on her drawers. She was alone now, there were no other homesteads for miles in any direction and it was still so hot out, she didn't see any reason to put on a dress while inside. There was no one to see her so indecently dressed, no one to reprimand her for not being a lady at all times. Out here in the wilds of Indian Territory, Carrie felt as if she was the last person on earth.

Carrie cut a slice of bread from the loaf on the cutting board and smeared butter on it; she was hungry but didn't feel like cooking. Daylight began to wane, so she took the bread to her bed and sat down, leaning back against the wall. She could see the sky from the window, watched it turn shades of red and orange as the sun set, and then fade into deeper colors of purple and blue, and eventually black. The stars began winking on. Carrie lay down and cried herself to sleep.

For the first time since her mother and Marianne had been killed, Carrie let herself cry. When Lydia died Carrie was too busy looking out for her father, who seemed to lose half of himself in the grief, and there simply hadn't been time for her to shed tears of her own. Carrie didn't know what to do for him, didn't know how to help him, no matter how she had tried. He sat and stared for days, neither eating nor sleeping.

Then one day he pulled himself to his feet and went back to work in the fields, chopping wood for winter, and over the next three years, Carrie hadn't seen him do much else. He rose before dawn and didn't come back inside till after dark. Carrie took food out to him at noon each day and left a plate for him on the table before she went to bed each night. Until the day he died she'd not heard him speak more than one or two words to her during the days. He nodded and muttered when she brought his meals to him, and that was as much of a conversation as they'd had in years.

The day before he died he showed Carrie the leather pouch he kept hidden in the bottom of the trunk, one of the few things not destroyed by the fire in Charleston that he actually kept. The pouch had over three thousand dollars in it, U.S. dollars at that, her father's entire life savings, and then he'd put it away and that was the whole of the conversation. The next morning, Charles got up, worked in the fields all day, then came in, ate and went to bed. He just didn't wake up again. Carrie wondered if her father had known he was going to die, wondered if he'd sensed his last day on Earth was upon him. She wondered about the money, but only for a moment. She was asleep.

Carrie dreamed of Charleston, dreamed of her sisters and mother, her father, all alive and well, laughing and talking over dinner in the big dining hall in the house where they all used to live. She dreamed of the long table covered with a linen cloth, china plates and cups, real silverware, and the crystal candelabra hanging from the high ceiling above them. She dreamed of the parties her parents hosted each Christmas Eve, the formal teas her mother held in the gardens every spring, with all the ladies dressed in their beautiful, new gowns with matching parasols. She dreamed of baking cookies in the kitchen with Liza, the old gray-haired cook. She dreamed of learning to bake, to make butter, and of licking chocolate frosting from the bowl. Life had been so good in Charleston.

Carrie sat up suddenly, looked around, startled and confused for a moment but then she realized where she was. They were gone, all of them, leaving Carrie to fend for herself and she didn't know how she'd be able to go on alone. She laid back down and curled herself into a tight ball with the quilt she and Marianne had made together pulled up over her head, and she wept until the tears soaked her pillow and she finally went back to sleep.

~ TWO ~

Noah Mosely crawled across the ground dragging his broken leg behind him as he tried desperately to find some shelter. Anything would work for tonight—a thicket, an outcropping, a cave. He didn't really care. He just needed to be somewhere, anywhere, except out in the open like he was now.

It was full dark, the creatures of the night would smell his blood and he only had a handful of bullets left, besides what was already in the pistol. He didn't have any powder or balls left for his rifle but he held onto it anyway. If nothing else he thought he could use it as a club if wolves or coyotes tried to get him. Or worse, another mountain lion.

Continuing his struggle across the rough ground with sticks and rocks digging into the soft flesh of his stomach and side, Noah gritted his teeth. He shoved the rifle ahead of him, and then pushed with his good leg as he pulled with both arms, cursing under his breath as a new spear of bright, hot pain shot through the broken leg.

With no choice but to continue on, he steeled himself against the pain, and crawled. He didn't know how long he struggled, and with no moon, he couldn't see where he was going either. Wolves howled in the distance, and nearer to him smaller, nocturnal animals scurried over the ground through the brush. Knowing what might be waiting for him, following the trail of blood he was leaving behind, Noah sighed in relief that he couldn't see them either.

Noah thought he'd never reach anything close to being a shelter, but some time during the night his hand reached out and caught a bush. Pulling himself up a little further, he felt around and grabbed the shrub at its base and pulled himself under it. He didn't know how well hidden he was, but he felt better anyway. Any shelter was better than none at all. Even thought he was exhausted and in pain, and his leg throbbed, Noah fell asleep almost immediately. He didn't sleep peacefully by any means. The nightmares came back to him, the nights of running for his life, fighting to get away to some place safe, any place where he wouldn't be found. His leg throbbed and even slight movement brought him wide awake and made for a very long night.

Awaking at sunrise, Noah shielded his eyes against the bright shaft of light filtering through the trees and looked around. If he hadn't been in so much pain, he might have laughed. He wasn't hidden under a thicket of brush as he'd thought, it was a single cedar sapling next to a tall pine and he wasn't hidden at all. He pushed himself to a sitting position, and held his broken leg in both hands.

Having swollen tight against the leg of his britches, the bone poked through both his skin and the material, and blood still oozed, though not as much as the day before. If he didn't find help soon the leg would probably be useless to him for the rest of his life, and that would mean he was as good as dead. That was if gangrene didn't set in. He leaned to one side, managed to get his good leg under him and got up on his knee, then held on to the trunk of the pine and pulled himself onto his one useful foot. Leaning against the tree, Noah shut his eyes. His leg throbbed and he felt as if he'd throw up.

Holding the tree for balance until the dizziness finally passed, he opened his eyes slowly. Blinking hard against the bright light, Noah wiped his face on his sleeve. Unsure if his eyes were playing tricks on him, he thought he could see smoke through the trees farther down the hill. He blinked against the sunlight again. There was definitely a thin line of smoke rising into the air, and Noah thought someone must be camping there, because no one lived so far out. He didn't want to get his hopes up, there was no telling who might be down there, but he had no choice. If he didn't get help soon, he would die.

15

Sitting down, he took a deep breath and rested against the tree, then looked around until he spotted a fallen branch he could use as a crutch. The going was slow and he had to stop every few feet to rest, but he made his way down that side of the mountain until a roof came into view down past the tree line looking out over the valley.

He stared in disbelief that anyone could be living here. He couldn't believe his good fortune though, and hoped whoever it was would offer him a place to rest until he could heal up. It was still quite a distance off, and he knew in his condition it would seem like the longest trip he'd ever taken, but it was definitely a homestead and that gave him hope. If he could just get to it.

Noah was in too much pain to continue for a long while and fell asleep as he rested against a tree. The sun climbed high in the sky when a sudden bolt of pain finally brought him awake once again. He continued the slow pace he'd been going, thinking the pain would take him under before he ever reached the cabin. He took a few deep breaths, closed his eyes briefly, then forced himself to go on.

When he finally reached the creek he laid down with his face in the cold water and drank long, deep gulps. Pulling himself back onto the bank, he immediately threw up. He laid down to rest, breathing heavily and waited for his stomach to quit revolting. When it did, he surveyed the area before him, trying to figure out how he was going to cross the babbling brook.

With two good legs it would be no problem, but with one busted one and water pouring over slippery rocks, he wasn't sure he could make it down the bank on his side and back up the other side without breaking his other leg as well. He dropped the branch he'd been holding onto and sat down with his back to the creek. Bracing his broken leg with one hand, he used the other one and his good leg to push himself into the water.

It wasn't easy but it was easier than trying to walk across with a busted leg and the possibility of falling and causing more damage to himself. He reached the opposite bank and leaned back to rest, then managed to get himself out of the water. Exquisite pain shot up his leg and he would have screamed but the distinct sound of a round being levered into the chamber of a rifle caused the sound to clot in his throat.

Raising his hands without looking back, Noah thought momentarily that the thought of being shot dead didn't sound half bad. The thought of the person holding the gun only wounding him made him reconsider. He had tossed his pistol and empty rifle across the creek before he'd tried to cross it himself and at the moment he didn't know if either was within reach.

"My gun is layin' over there and the rifle is empty," he said quietly, without turning around. "My leg is broke and I'm just trying to find a place to lay down a while so I can heal up. I don't mean no harm to nobody."

"Turn around," Carrie said. The sound of a woman's voice caused Noah's head to whip around to look at her. "Slow!" She shouted and motioned with the gun in her hand.

"I'm sorry," Noah said gently. "I wasn't expecting a woman to be out here. Where's your man?"

"You don't get to ask the questions," Carrie said, trying not to sound afraid.

"I'm not going to hurt you. Look at my leg. See?" He nodded his head to indicate the dark stain on his trouser leg and the hole in the material that revealed the jagged edge of broken bone.

"I've been up in these mountains a long time and yesterday a mountain lion spooked my horse. I got throwed to the ground and my leg snapped when I hit, then my horse ran off. I shot the cat before it could eat me, but I've got to get some place where I can set this leg and heal up. If it don't get set, it's gonna heal wrong and

17

I'll be crippled. And that's only if it don't get an infection that'll kill me. I just need some help, lady."

Carrie looked at his leg, the dark stain of wet blood, as she listened to him and then looked back to his face. He was a big man, probably taller than her father, and definitely broader, but this man didn't have a round belly like her father's. This man's stomach was flat, and the muscles in his arms and chest bulged. His thighs were muscled, and Carrie's eyes rested on his leg again, twisted at an odd angle, there was no doubt it was badly broken and the man was in a great deal of pain.

She raised her eyes back up to his and found him observing her coolly with eyes of liquid gold. His forehead was high, the bridge of his nose broad, and he had full, smooth lips. Carrie licked her lips unconsciously as she perused his face, trying to size him up, trying to decide if he posed a threat. She wished her father were alive.

"Can you walk?" She finally asked him.

"Barely. I've been using that branch there as a crutch, but it's slow and painful. I crawled last night."

"Can you get yourself to the barn? I can let you stay there while your leg heals, but I'll have to take your guns inside with me. Where's the rest of your ammunition?"

"I only have a few bullets for the pistol left, there's no powder or balls left for the rifle."

"Give them to me," she said.

Noah dug in his pocket, and winced as pain shot bright and hot up his leg when he leaned back.

"That's all there is," he said through gritted teeth, as he let the bullets drop into her open hand.

"The barn is over there." She indicated with her head, as she stepped around him and picked up his pistol and rifle. She waited until he was on his feet and cringed at the pain she knew he was experiencing with every slow, agonizing step. It took him thirty minutes to traverse the fifty yards to the barn. Carrie wanted to help him, but even if she wasn't being cautious, she knew she'd be of little help to the man. He was at least a foot taller than she was and more than twice her size.

When they were finally inside the barn, Carrie showed him to a stall that hadn't been used recently and had sweet, fresh hay covering the dirt floor. Noah held on to the stall crossbeams and lowered himself to the floor with a heavy sigh. He breathed heavily and laid his head back with his eyes closed to rest. Sweat ran down his face and soaked his shirt.

"You wouldn't happen to have a shot of whiskey handy, would you?"

Carrie looked at him, then turned and left the barn. When she returned, she no longer had a gun in her hands, and had left his inside as well. She handed him the bottle of whiskey, it wasn't quite full but he didn't seem to notice, or to care. He pulled the stopper out with his teeth and let it fall, then tilted the bottle back and took a long pull.

"Thank you," he said, wiping his mouth on his sleeve. "I need some help setting this leg. Do you know anything about it?" Carrie shook her head slightly. "I need you to get a pair of scissors, something I can use to brace my leg on either side, and some strips of cloth to hold it in place. A needle and some thread to sew it up once the bone is set, if you got it." Carrie nodded and left the barn. Noah took another shot of whiskey and rested until she returned.

Carrie came back with two long, thin, flat pieces of wood originally intended for use as fencing around the small garden behind the cabin to keep the rabbits out, but her father hadn't been able to finish it before he died. She knelt in the stall near the stranger, set the boards down beside him and looked at him.

"Use the scissors to cut up the length of my pant leg," he instructed, and she did as she was told. "Okay," he breathed and scooted himself more up-right. "I'm going to set the bone straight and I need your help to do that."

He looked at her and she nodded. "Good. Put your hands right here."

She hesitated as he reached for her hands, but she let him guide her. He placed her hands against his flesh and took a deep breath. "Now press firmly while I press against the other side."

He exhaled, then took another deep breath and quickly pushed against his leg. His jaw clenched and sweat beaded on his forehead and Carrie heard a growl deep in his chest, but the bone didn't set.

"Arrgh!" Noah growled and swore an oath. He breathed heavily, his eyes closed, he tipped back the bottle of whiskey and drank deeply. "You're gonna have to hold my ankle with both hands." He looked at Carrie, his teeth clenched. "When I tell you, I want you to pull just as hard as you can. All right?"

Carrie nodded and moved to his feet, held his ankle tightly in her grip, and as he braced himself, he shouted, "Now!"

She pulled hard and Noah screamed. She was stronger than she looked. The bone slid back inside his flesh, and the skin came together once again, though it had ragged edges.

Noah held his hands on the wound to brace the newly set bone. "Now you have to pour some of that whisky over the wound, then thread the needle and sew the skin together."

Carrie bit her bottom lip but picked up the bottle and poured whisky over the wound. She stopped suddenly when Noah shouted against the pain.

"I'm sorry."

Noah shook his head. "That's all right. The needle is going to hurt too but just get it over with quickly."

Nodding, Carrie quickly threaded the needle and stitched up his skin, tying a neat knot after each stitch.

Breathing in and out through clenched teeth, Noah waited for the pain to subside a little, and when it had, he looked at Carrie again.

"Now, hand me one of those boards." When she did, he laid it along the inside of his thigh and placed the other one on the outside. "I'll hold them in place and you cut that cloth into long, thin strips and wrap it around the boards tightly to keep them in place."

Carrie did as he said and soon the splint was tightly set. Noah took a deep pull off the whiskey bottle, swallowed and took another. He offered the bottle to Carrie but she moved away and shook her head. She picked up the scissors and left over cloth and walked back to the cabin.

She wondered about the man, wondered what he'd been doing so far up in the mountains, wondered why he was alone. Carrie didn't think he meant her any harm, and thought he had kind eyes and a kind demeanor. His voice was deep, yet he had spoken softly to her and she liked the sound of him. Even though his hands were big and calloused, they had been gentle when he'd guided hers to his leg. She'd never touched a man before, except for when she'd bandaged her father's knee once when he cut it on a piece of wire. This man's leg had little hair and his skin was soft. Carrie didn't know why, but it made her feel safe having a man around again. He was in no condition to do anything except lay there in the barn, but just knowing she wasn't all alone made her feel better.

Carrie put together a thick, vegetable stew, ladled some into a large bowl and set it on the cutting board to use as a carrying tray. Adding the rest of the loaf of bread and the butter, she poured a cup of hot coffee, then carried it care-fully out to the barn and set the meal beside the man. His eyes were closed and she thought he might be sleeping, but as she knelt, his eyes opened and he regarded her silently for a few moments.

21

"What's this?"

"Stew and bread. A cup of coffee," she answered quietly.

"That's very kind of you. Thank you," he said and picked up the bowl and spooned a big bite into his mouth.

He ate half of what was in the bowl, then ripped off a chunk of bread, swiped it over the butter and put it in his mouth. He tore off another hunk of bread and dipped it directly into the stew and ate it.

"This is good," he said through another bite of stew. "Did you make it?" Carrie nodded. Noah had never met a woman who talked so little. "My name's Noah," he said as he held out a hand to her.

She looked at his hand and then back at him. "I'm Carrie," she said, accepting his hand.

"Nice to meet you." He went back to shoveling up stew and tearing hunks of bread from the loaf.

"Would you like more stew?" Carrie asked when he took the last bite of carrot.

"No, thank you. That was delicious." He took another shot of whiskey and wiped his mouth. "I just need a little rest," he said closing his eyes. "Just a little..."

He was asleep. Carrie picked up his dishes, put everything back on the cutting board and carried them back to the cabin. She took a quilt and a pillow from her father's bed, as well as a pair of his pants and a clean shirt. Her father and Noah were nearly the same size, so she thought the clothes should fit. He was wet from crossing the creek and his pants were ruined. She thought about the splint and didn't know how he'd get the article on over it.

With the scissors she cut the trouser leg off altogether, and went back to the barn. She knelt quietly beside the man as he slept and laid the blanket gently over him, leaving the pillow near his head. She put the folded clothing on the hay near his hand and stood watching him for a long moment, then went back to the cabin.

Carrie had chores to tend and went about them as she had every day for the past three and a half years. Life was much different now than it had been in Charleston, she thought as she fed the chickens and picked vegetables from the garden. She would have to can the tomatoes, the green beans and peas. The corn, carrots, potatoes and onions would go into the small root cellar her father had dug.

Summer would be gone soon, and fall would pass quickly into winter here. In Charleston, Carrie had never had to worry about long, hard winters, she'd only had to worry about fashion and balls and which of her suitors would make the best husband. But the war had changed all that; the war had changed everything. She picked out one of the hens and wrung its neck quickly, then got it ready for the frying pan. In Charleston she had never had to pluck a chicken either.

She fried the chicken and some potatoes, boiled a couple of ears of corn, and baked biscuits. When the chicken was done, she made gravy from the grease and fixed a large plate for the man in the barn. She brought water for him to wash up with and set it down beside him. Sitting against the wall of the barn with the pillow behind him, she could see he had changed into the clean shirt she'd brought him, but he hadn't been able to manage the pants on his own. He'd used the thunder mug she'd left for him, which she took and emptied without a word.

When she returned, he stopped eating and looked up at her. "Thank you, Carrie. I don't know how to repay your kindness."

Carrie only nodded and remained standing where she was. Noah still looked at her with those luminous gold eyes and she could see pain and sadness in them that had nothing to do with his leg.

"Are you here alone?" He finally broke the silence between them. Carrie was afraid to tell him she was; yet she still felt he would do her no harm. She nodded again.

Noah wiped his hands on the cloth she'd brought with his supper. "Sit down, please," he said. "I'd like to talk to you." She hesitated, but then she sat with him. "Will you tell me how a young girl like yourself happens to be in a place like this alone?" He picked up a chicken leg and bit into it.

Carrie watched him. "My father died a few days ago, I have no one else," she told him simply.

Noah saw the pain in her eyes, heard it in her voice, though he somehow knew she wouldn't want sympathy. He knew what it was like to feel the pain of losing the ones you love. His mother had been dead for long years now, and he'd never had a father or brothers or sisters. He was twenty-four years old and had escaped to these mountains from Missis-sippi over eight years ago. Noah knew what it was to be alone.

"Have you no family anywhere? No one who could care for you?"

Carrie shook her head slightly. "My mother and older sister were killed in Charleston by Yankee soldiers. My younger sister died of an illness when my father first brought us here. There was no other family in Charleston."

"When this leg heals enough so I can get around again, I'll help you get ready for winter. Trying to get through the winter by yourself is going to be difficult for you. It's difficult for a man, but for a woman alone, it's next to impossible."

Carrie shrugged. "I'll manage somehow. My father taught me what to do, how to shoot and hunt. I have boots and a coat."

Noah finished a second piece of chicken and scooped up potatoes and gravy. Her cool, green eyes never left his and his fingers itched to touch her long, honey brown hair. "How old are you, Carrie?"

"Nineteen," she told him. "I'll be twenty come December."

He was five years older and had lived a very different life, one he doubted she could even comprehend. He'd been raised on hard work with a strap across his back, and he had the scars to prove it. Other than his mother, who'd died when he was barely ten years old, he'd never known love from another human being. He'd never known a soft or easy life, and except for the Indian tribe that had taken him in, he'd never known a family.

The Osage tribe had found him starved near to death, and half frozen that first winter in the mountains, and if they'd left him, he would have died where he lay. He was sixteen years old then and knew nothing about harsh winters, had never seen snow, but in the lodge of the tribe that took him in, he learned. The least he could do for her now would be to stay through the rest of the summer, into the fall and teach this little bit of a girl what the Indians had taught him.

~ THREE ~

Carrie spent the following days as she always did. Chores needed doing, chickens needed fed, the cow needed milked, and there was butter and cheese to be made. The horses needed fed and watered. The garden needed weeding. She cooked for Noah as well, and as the weeks passed and his leg began to knit back together, he felt restless.

With a hatchet and knife Noah fashioned a good branch into a crutch that fit under his arm and would allow him some movement. Carrie wrapped the crutch with some old cloths to make it more comfortable for him.

She helped him make his way down to the pool at the creek and left him with a bar of lye soap and another of her father's shirts to wear. She took his shirt and the one she'd given him when he first arrived so they could be washed. The laundry pot boiled over a fire downstream and she pushed the shirts into it with the long paddle, along with her own dresses and undergarments.

After the pot began to boil, she pushed the garments around with the laundry paddle, then used it to dip them out. When she finished washing all of the laundry, she hooked the paddle against the pot handle and used it to dump the dirty water onto the fire below to extinguish it. Then she took the clothing and dipped them in the creek to rinse them, wrung them out, and hung them on the line.

By the time she finished with the chore she thought Noah would also be finished and walked back to where she'd left him bathing.

He sat on a rock in the sun and watched her walk toward him. She was lovely and her young breasts were firm and high. He couldn't help but notice them, or her small waist and trim hips. The drab brown dress she wore couldn't distract from her beauty or hide her shapely figure. He felt his blood heat, felt a spear of desire curl through him, but he pushed it away. She wasn't for him and he knew it.

If they'd been back in South Carolina, or Mississippi, he'd be hanged for even thinking about her the way he was now. His father may have been a wealthy plantation owner, but his mother was a slave and so was he. Even now he knew he could never cross the line between them. It didn't matter there was white blood coursing through his veins, that he had light skin, or that his long, dark hair was soft and curly. To the whites, he was another nigger to be bought and sold, and to the other slaves, he was a white man's son. He'd never belonged in either world.

Noah didn't understand the kindness this young woman had shown him the past weeks. She didn't know he was a runaway slave, true, but it wasn't hard to see the African blood that ran in his veins either. He knew even though the Negroes thought of him as white, he still looked like his mother's people. Just because he had paler skin, softer hair and golden eyes, his African heritage was evident in the features of his face, the build of his body, and the strength in his limbs.

Besides, Carrie had been raised in Charleston, and although he didn't know for sure if her father had had slaves, Noah suspected he probably did. She dressed in plain brown now but he had no problem imagining her in fancy gowns dancing with fancy men at fancy balls. Yet she'd helped him, fed him, and clothed him. Other than the Indians he'd lived with, no other human being had ever showed him such kindness or respect.

They walked back to the barn together, slowly, but he was healing. She had brought the tick mattress off her father's bed from the cabin to the barn for him to sleep on, had managed to roll a good round of oak from the wood pile into the barn for him to sit on, and she'd brought a small table to the barn for him to eat his meals on. He'd never had more comfortable surroundings, but he knew better than to get too comfortable here because he'd have to leave in a few weeks. He wasn't looking forward to it.

Summer turned into fall and the leaves turned brilliant shades of gold and crimson. Noah gave up his crutch for a stick he could use as a cane instead. He was getting around much better now, even though the leg wasn't completely straight, and he'd probably walk with a limp the rest of his life, it was better than he'd been able to hope for left on his own.

He could help her some now, and picked pumpkins and squash from the garden, milked the cow, fed the chickens and gathered eggs. She never invited him inside the cabin, and he hadn't expected her to, but now she had moved the small kitchen table and two stools outside beneath the covered area in front of the cabin. The two of them ate their meals together there every day.

She still didn't talk very much, and most of the meals were eaten in silence. He watched her often and wished there was something he could say or do to erase the sadness in her eyes, but he knew there wasn't. She was too young to be alone like this, but he understood her desire not to go back to what was left behind. All he could hope for was maybe some other families would eventually move nearby and be company for her.

By the end of November Noah no longer used the cane and knew winter wasn't far off. He used the axe and chopped wood until his arms and back ached. He didn't want Carrie to be cold during the winter, and by the time he was finished, there was enough wood to last her far into spring. She'd returned his weapons to him and had given him powder and balls for the rifle. He hunted and when he brought back the huge buck he'd killed, he skinned and prepared it just like the Indians had taught him. She would have plenty of meat to last throughout the winter as well.

Later in the month Noah brought a wild turkey he'd killed and she prepared it and invited him inside the house to eat it with her. It was far too cold now to continue eating outside. She prepared mashed potatoes and gravy, biscuits, green beans and squash to go with the bird. For dessert, she baked a pumpkin pie, and whipped fresh cream with sugar to top the pie.

She told him she thought it was near Thanksgiving time, though she wasn't sure of the exact day. It didn't matter to him, Noah thought the meal was the best she'd served him yet, though he couldn't remember eating so well as he had since he'd arrived at her cabin. He looked at Carrie as he ate a second piece of pie topped with whipped cream.

"I'll be leaving tomorrow," he told her. She looked up at him, and though he thought he saw something flicker in her eyes, she only nodded. "I wouldn't be up and around like this if you hadn't been here to help me," he continued. "I appreciate it, Carrie. You've done more for me than anyone else ever would have. I'll always remember you."

He knew if she'd not helped him he would more than likely be dead right now. He'd been lucky the leg hadn't become infected as it was.

Carrie shrugged and nearly smiled. He had never seen a genuine smile cross her lovely face. He wished he had. He wished he'd known what her eyes looked like when they danced with joy, what her face looked like glowing with delight, what her voice sounded like laughing from her heart. He thought it had been a long time since she'd been truly happy.

"Where will you go?"

"Back to my tribe for a while, then," he shrugged, "I don't know." He smiled when she frowned, and said, "I'll be needin' some sleep now. I'll be gone early." He rose from the table and walked to the door.

Carrie walked with him to the barn. She gave him her father's horse and saddle, filled the saddlebags with stores of food, and told him to take the blanket and clothing she'd given him. Then she gave him her father's coat and gloves. They were well worn, but he was grateful nonetheless. She paused before she left him alone in the barn, and he thought she wanted to tell him something, but she just said goodnight and walked back to the cabin.

He was going to miss her, he thought as he lay down on the mattress. He would miss her quiet gentleness, her determination, and he would miss the sound of her voice, though he admitted he'd not heard it nearly as much as he'd like.

Noah rose while it was still dark, his breath freezing in the frigid morning air. He saddled the horse and looked around, felt regret gripping his heart. Regret for having to leave her, for not being able to stay with her, and for not being able to take her into his arms and hold her the way he had dreamed. And he felt sorrow, an ache deep in his heart he'd never before felt. The corner of his mouth curved slightly, he was in love with her, he thought, and he'd never loved another human being, besides his mother, in his entire life.

He mounted the horse in the yard outside the cabin and sat looking toward the window, thinking of her sleeping peacefully, all warm and snuggled beneath the blankets of her bed. How he longed to feel her warm body pressed against his while he held her sleeping next to him. How he longed to bury his face in her long, silky hair and inhale the soft scent of her. How he longed to feel her silken skin beneath his fingers as he touched her gently. How he longed for something he should never have allowed to enter his mind. He tapped his heels to the horse's side and rode slowly away.

Carrie rose at six the next morning and after she'd washed and dressed, she made coffee and started breakfast. She had a few left over biscuits and fried them in butter and sugar, then poured the glaze over them on a plate. She made cornmeal mush and put a big spoonful of butter on it and carried the plate of food out to the barn so Noah could eat before he left. She knew as soon as she entered the barn he was already gone.

She walked to the little table and set the food down and looked around. The pillow on the mattress still held the imprint of his head, and the pants she'd cut the leg off of for him were hanging on the stall. Carrie sat on the oak stump with the pillow in her hands. She raised it to her face and inhaled. His scent lingered there, the smell of lye soap, and a deeper, spicier scent all his own. Carrie had been alone before, but now, with Noah gone, she knew what it was to be truly lonely.

Picking up the food, Carrie went back inside. The cabin was warm now, but she didn't notice, and felt as if her world would never be warm again. She finished her inside chores without eating breakfast, then went outside to gather eggs and milk the cow. Snow had begun to fall before she was finished in the barn.

Winter had arrived and it would be months before she saw the sun again. Carrie looked across the land, cold and frozen, thought of her father and Lydia, also cold and frozen. She wiped a tear that slipped down her cheek. Unfortunately, her heart wasn't cold and frozen, and right now, she wished it were.

She had never asked Noah how he'd come to be so far up in the mountains alone, and he'd never told her. She could see he was a Negro, but she could see he was white as well. She'd seen many children of slaves who had the same look about them, and knew often white slave owners used the female slaves as bed partners. Whether they were willing or not.

31

She knew the children who came from those unions were treated as their mothers were and never claimed as the rightful son or daughter of the plantation owner. Carrie had never thought slavery was right, and even though her father had owned slaves, he'd never allowed them to be whipped, or to go hungry. And there had never been any blue- or green-eyed babies born to any of the females either.

When the war came, her father had given his slaves their freedom along with a hundred dollars each. Her father treated his slaves with more compassion than the Yankee soldiers had treated Carrie's mother and sister.

Carrie brought the eggs and bucket of milk inside. She cleaned the eggs and set the basket aside, then began straining the milk and separating the cream. When that was done, she churned the cream into butter. It was hard work, the churn paddle was heavy and caused her neck and arms to ache, but no matter how hard she worked, she couldn't get her mind off Noah. She covered the remaining milk and set it outside next to the front door in the covered box to keep it cold and safe from wild animals. When there were four gallons there she would make cheese.

Even one cow produced more milk than Carrie needed for drinking, making butter and cheese, and she poured much of it out, though she hated the waste. If she'd had pigs, she could use it in their feed, but her father had been opposed to pigs because of their smell. Also, there were enough wild pigs in the mountains he had hunted for food. Now, being alone here, Carrie had more than enough meat and other food to last her throughout the winter and far into spring.

Carrie sat on her bed that afternoon, the fire in the small fireplace was roaring and kept the cabin toasty and warm, cutting quilting squares from old clothing and other pieces of unused cloth and thought of Noah. She hoped he wasn't freezing out in the snow, and wondered where he was, and if she would ever see him again.

She wished she had spoken to him more, had asked questions of him, and learned more about him. These feelings she had for him were new and she didn't understand them. She knew she missed him and wished he hadn't left, but the ache he'd left in her heart was a new feeling for Carrie, and she didn't understand it at all.

In Charleston she would have never had the opportunity to be as close to him as she had been while he was staying in her barn. A slave could be hanged for even speaking to a white woman, and if not hanged, he'd surely be whipped at the post. But Noah wasn't like any of the slaves she'd known, he didn't speak like the same, and he knew how to read. A slave could be hanged for being able to read, and anyone caught teaching a slave would have been arrested as well. She didn't know how he'd learned, but she knew it wasn't from his owner.

The day she had seen him bathing at the creek, mesmerized by his body, she couldn't force herself to look away. His skin was a light, golden brown, not the deep chocolate brown color of the slaves she'd known before. It was smooth over his legs and buttocks and halfway up his back.

Across his upper back and shoulders scars marred the beautiful skin and she knew he'd been whipped on several occasions. That made her feel sick to her stomach, know- ing he'd been treated no better than an animal. No, he'd been treated worse than men treated their animals. Only the men she'd known of in Charleston could treat their animals better than they treated another human being, including their slaves and their wives.

Carrie knew her mother had been fortunate to have married for love. She'd grown up knowing her parents loved and respected one another, but she'd also known that was rare. Most of the young women Carrie knew had married whoever their fathers wanted them to in order to bring two wealthy families together, never considering how his daughter would be treated by the man who became her husband.

Carrie knew she would never have been forced to marry, but the men who came to call upon her sister, Marianne, as well as herself, were looking to marry the daughter of a wealthy plantation owner. They never cared for her or her sister, and she knew she would have been another piece of property, owned by them as surely as their slaves and plantations were also owned. She would have been a possession, expected to host lavish balls, run the household and produce sons. It wasn't a life Carrie aspired to. She wanted to be loved like her mother had been loved by her father, and she wanted to love a man the way her mother had loved her father. But it had never happened. And now, in this lonely country, in this little cabin, she suspected it never would.

She continued cutting the quilting squares until all the material had been used, then she began to piece them together to see if there was enough to start a new quilt. She kept her hands busy, but it didn't help quiet her mind. It didn't help take her thoughts away from Noah. And when she went to bed that night, with the fire burning low in the fireplace, she fell asleep and dreamed of him.

It was a gentle dream, walking beside him through a meadow of wild flowers, listening to him talk to her, laughing at something he'd said. She snuggled into the covers and sighed contentedly in her sleep.

~ FOUR ~

Noah made his way through the snow. He'd been riding for three days and the snow came down heavier the further north and east he went, and he knew it would be even deeper by the time he reached his destination. He was going back to the Indian tribe that had taken him in over eight years ago.

The Arkansas mountain ranges had been home to many Indian tribes, including the Osage, until the white man killed many of them, moved more of them to reservations in the west, and had robbed them all. Some of the more defiant ones, the stragglers that managed to escape and survive on their own, had also managed to regroup and reform. They remained high in the mountains, far away from white men, and those white men who might accidentally run across them didn't survive.

The Osage hunting party found Noah nearly buried in the snow the first winter after he'd escaped his owner in Mississippi. Hounds and white men with guns had chased him. He crossed swamps and rivers, had been bitten by insects, and attacked by wild dogs. There wasn't a part of his body that wasn't scratched, scraped, or cut by briars, limbs, and brush.

He'd had no shoes when he escaped and his feet were badly cut by rocks and sticks and the rough ground he'd run over. He kept running no matter how he hurt, no matter how he ached, no matter what he had to go through. And if they had caught him, they would have killed him. But Noah would rather have been dead than go back to the life he'd been born to.

No man should own another man and maybe that was why the Indians helped him. They knew what it was like to be hunted, killed, and enslaved by the white man. And they had to have recognized him as a slave, in spite of his light skin and eyes.

He was frozen in the snow when the Indian hunting party found him. They wrapped him in furs, fashioned a travois and took him to their village. He was battered, starving, and freezing, and they had taken care of him. When he recovered, they allowed him to remain with them, taught him about the mountains, and how to survive there.

They taught him how to hunt and fish, how to prepare and dry meat to last throughout the winter. They taught him how to track and hunt in the snow, how to stay warm and dry. He knew where they traveled in the winter, where they hunted in the summer, and how they avoided detection by the white man.

They didn't remain in Arkansas year round, but traveled through the mountains, crossing into Missouri, or into what was called the Indian Territory that would one day become Oklahoma, not caring the whites had drawn lines to divide the territory. It was their land and they would not give up on it.

Noah remained with them for many years and was accepted and adopted into the tribe. He knew their language and their ways. He was a member of the tribe, no longer a slave, but a free man. When he had grown into a man, and was no longer the boy who had been born into slavery, he ventured out on his own once again.

This time, however, he knew he would always be able to go home to the tribe whenever he wanted. They accepted him, he knew, but there was something inside of him that never allowed him to fully accept them as family. He cared for them, understood them, but he was not one of them. That was the problem in itself; there was no world Noah belonged to. He wasn't white, he wasn't Negro, he wasn't an Indian—he was a man without a place, or a people, to call his own.

Even though he'd convinced himself he could only rely on himself, and he didn't belong anywhere at all, he had recently discovered he had a heart, and right now it felt as if it was breaking in two. He couldn't get Carrie out of his mind, and he couldn't get her out of his dreams, either. He'd dreamed of her every night since he'd left her, and he could see her face before him every day as he rode.

In his mind he allowed himself the luxury of pre-tending life was different for both of them. He allowed himself to think what it would be like to be with her, really be with her. To be able to take her into his arms and kiss her gently. To be able to hold her warm, soft body firmly against his own. To be able to look into her eyes and tell her he loved her, and hear her whisper the words back to him. He longed to hear her laugh, to feel her hands on him, to have a life he had no right to.

He took a deep breath, forced himself out of the daydream. Too deep in thought to notice he wasn't alone, but it was too late by the time the body hit him full force, knocking him off his horse onto the ground. The air left his lungs in a *whoosh* on impact, and he was fighting for his life while still trying to breathe.

By the time he caught his breath he was on his stomach while someone sat on his back, pinning his arms behind him. Then suddenly, they released him and he heard a whoop of laughter. He rolled over quickly and looked up to see an Indian standing over him, grinning like a fool.

Noah grinned and shook his head as he saw four more Indians standing with the first. "Running Elk!"

The man leaned over and offered his hand. Noah took it and was pulled to his feet. "You are getting slow and weak," Running Elk said in his own language, still grinning at his friend. Noah's Indian name was Dark Horse, and that was the way everyone in the village addressed him.

Noah clapped him on the back. "Good to see you. I'm on my way to the winter village. How is everyone?"

Noah spoke their language nearly as well as they did, and greeted the other men with Running Elk. He knew them all and grinned happy to see them. They mounted their horses and began riding.

"You have been injured," Running Elk said. "You are walking crooked."

"Yeah," Noah nodded. "I broke my leg some months ago. A mountain lion spooked my horse and he ran off. My leg snapped when I hit the ground. Good horse too, I haven't seen him since."

"You are lucky to be able to walk now."

"I know. I wasn't sure for a while if I would, but I found some help and healed up."

Running Elk nodded and they rode on through the snow until the day was nearly gone. When they came around one final bend where the mountain seemed to suddenly end and dropped off steeply, Noah could see the quiet, snow-covered village deep in the gorge. They urged the horses down the steep trail and made their way slowly to the bottom, then crossed the distance to the village.

Some of the children came outside at the sound of the horses and ran along beside them until they dismounted. The tribal chief, White Bear, exited his lodge and greeted the men. White Bear had been called Little Bear when he was born, but before he was ever a grown man, his hair had begun changing and by his nineteenth year, the long, dark tresses had turned completely white. Now he looked at Noah, his face expressionless, and after a long while, he nodded and clapped his hand on Noah's shoulder.

White Bear held the flap that allowed entrance to the lodge open and ushered the men inside. Sitting comfortably around the fire, the men leaned back on furs that covered backrests made of limbs. They regaled Noah with tales of their travels during the summer, the hunts they'd been on, the white men they'd encountered. Noah took the pipe when it was passed to him, laughed and nodded at the stories. He was glad to be here, glad to see these men. He had missed them, had missed the company and the stories.

The women brought food in to the men, served them roasted venison on crude wooden plates, with thick stew made from wild roots they'd dug, and flatbread made from dried acorns pounded into a flour, mixed with water and cooked on hot stones. Noah ate and drank, laughed and nodded. And thought of Carrie.

When the other men had gone to their own lodges, White Bear indicated Noah should remain with him in the lodge. White Bear was the closest man to a father Noah had ever known, and he respected the older man greatly. White Bear had lost his wife and two sons to the white man and had barely escaped them himself. He knew the pain of loss and suffering much the way Noah did. He understood the boy they found all those years ago, and he knew the man well enough to see there was more to the story than the one Noah had told them earlier.

White Bear chewed on a piece of dried meat and looked thoughtfully at Noah. A patient man, he could wait until Noah was ready to talk. He had lived on the earth for nearly forty summers, as the Indians reckoned time, and he'd seen a lot of heartache and sorrow. He recognized it in Noah now, and knew it wasn't the same as what he'd seen when Noah first came to the tribe.

Then, Noah had been wild-eyed, terrified, angry, hurt and lost. It had taken a long time for the wounds on his body to heal, but it had taken much longer for the ones in his heart and soul to mend. And White Bear knew those wounds left much worse scars than the ones on Noah's body had. White Bear had a few of those himself, but he was no longer a young man and had learned not to let the scars encase his heart.

Noah observed White Bear for a long time, knew he had questions he hadn't asked, but his patience was greater than Noah's. "You have questions," Noah said.

"You may as well ask them or we'll never get any sleep tonight."

White Bear smiled, his even white teeth glinting in the firelight. "You still do not know patience."

"I'm just anxious to get some sleep, that's all old man." Noah's lip curved slightly.

"Tell me the rest of your story," White Bear said as he lay back comfortably on the warm furs.

"I told you the story. A big cat spooked my horse and I broke my leg when I hit the ground. I crawled until I found a place where I could get help. They helped me until I could walk again," Noah shrugged and looked into the fire.

"Where was this place you found?"

Noah took a breath and blew it out. "A cabin down the mountain in the valley, about three days south and west of here in the Indian Territory."

"Ah, the white man and his daughters?"

Noah looked at White Bear again. He hadn't realized anyone in the tribe knew of the place. "The youngest daughter and the man both died. The older daughter is alone there now."

White Bear nodded. "We saw them when they first settled there. We watched them, but we found no reason to fear them. The man was full of grief, and the daughters were young, without a mother. It will be too hard for the daughter alone now, she cannot survive on her own."

"She seems determined to. I stayed to help her prepare for the winter. It was all I could do to repay her for helping me."

White Bear nodded, though he remained silent for a long moment. Then, just when Noah thought he might be able to get some sleep, White Bear said, "She is on your heart." It was not a question, but a statement of fact.

Noah lay back on the furs and stared at the ceiling of the lodge. *Yes*, he thought, *but she is not just on my heart, she is in it completely.* She was seared into his soul.

"I will make sure she is okay through the winter, and I will make sure no others bother her. The word will go out she is to come to no harm."

He knew the rumors of a white woman living alone would travel fast—this tribe wasn't the only one that had survived the white man. There were bands of warriors who stalked and raided white settlers, then disappeared into the mountains like ghosts, but Noah would not have any harm come to Carrie. He would protect her and she would be safe.

"Be careful, Son," White Bear said. "The white man will kill you over one of their women. It is better for you to you take one of our women as your wife; you are safe here. Little Dove is still living in her father's lodge."

Noah grinned in the dim light. Little Dove had been only seven summers when Noah came to live with the tribe, so she would be fifteen or sixteen now. Taking to Noah immediately, Little Dove had sat with him while he recovered from his injuries. She brought him flowers she picked and helped him to learn their language. Noah thought she was a sweet child, the way he would have thought of a sister, if he'd had one.

Even now he knew she was too young for him, but aside from that, he could not think of her in a romantic way. In fact, he'd never thought of any woman in a romantic way until he met Carrie. He had never touched any of the women of the tribe in all the years he'd lived among them, and he wasn't planning to start now.

"She will meet a strong warrior one day and have many children," Noah said.

When White Bear had no reply, Noah turned to his side and shut his eyes. Carrie's face swam before him as he drifted off to sleep.

Noah woke early, movement from White Bear disturbing his dreams. He looked around, remembered where he was and smiled. When he was among the tribe he dressed in the buckskin tunics and leggings they wore, with fur lined boots wrapped snugly around his calves. He looked down at himself thinking of how he looked when he first came there. Freezing, half naked, and starving.

His head had been hairless, as the plantation owner had insisted all of the male slaves shave their heads. He hadn't known his hair was any different than the other slaves until he'd been with the tribe long enough that his hair actually began to grow out. It was soft and wavy, and now hung to his waist. He parted a section off on each side of his head, braided and tied it with strips of leather decorated with beads and bones. He stepped out of the lodge, and breathed deeply. It was good to be back with the People.

~ FIVE ~

Carrie stared outside at the heavy snowfall, heard the wind howling around and through the cabin, and wondered about Noah. She hoped he was warm and fed, and hoped he would return sometime soon. Turning from the glass, she put another log on the fire, then pulled the quilt more tightly around her shoulders and sat in front of the fireplace warming her toes. She kept the fire burning day and night now since it had been so cold, and the wind made it bitter out.

Carrie hated having to make the trip to the barn each morning, but the horses needed care, and the chickens had to be fed, even though they were no longer laying. She had to bring water in for cooking and bathing, but she tried to stay inside where it was warm as much as possible.

Though she tried not to think of her family gone, of her father and sister lying beneath the snow-covered ground, sometimes it was impossible not to think about them like that. She wrapped the quilt more tightly about her and cried deep, heart shattering sobs.

And she missed Noah. She had never really missed anyone before and certainly not anyone besides her family. Of course, she had never had a relationship with a man before, and she didn't think the few callers she'd had in Charleston counted. They certainly didn't seem to measure up to Noah as she thought about him now.

Noah was a big man, a powerful man, but he wore his strength lightly, as if he didn't realize he had the strength and size to crush a man in his arms. He spoke quietly, his voice deep, yet soft and resonant. And his hands, his hands were so gentle. Carrie felt the muscles in her stomach quiver and she smiled. She didn't understand the reaction she was having when she thought of Noah, the giddiness she felt when he filled her mind, but she liked the sensations.

They could ever be more than friends, being of different races, Carrie knew it just wasn't done. But she hoped he wanted to be her friend, hoped he'd come back one day. *Maybe in the spring*, she sighed. *Maybe when the weather is warmer*. Maybe...

Carrie started when she heard something bang against the cabin wall outside. She shrugged the quilt from her shoulders and quickly grabbed the Henry's lever action rifle her father left her and levered a round into the chamber. Peering out the window, she saw nothing. Waiting a moment, she heard nothing more. She opened the door carefully, peered out into the falling snow, then stepped outside and walked to the corner of the cabin and peeked cautiously around it. Just when she was about to go back inside, she heard the horses.

Carrie ran toward the barn and saw the small entrance door to the left of the big double doors flapping back and forth in the wind. She could hear the milk cow making a racket and hurried inside with the gun raised. Her eyes went wide with fear as they adjusted to the dim light, and she took a step backward, then another, and another, until she her back was against the doorway.

She raised the gun and squeezed the trigger, levered it again and fired another shot. The big bear stood on its hind legs, still advancing when the second shot pierced its flesh. It took another step, and then came down on all fours, and Carrie fired a third round that entered one of the animal's eyes. The bear faltered, shook its head, and rolled over on its side.

Staring at the large animal, Carrie was afraid to approach it until she was sure it was dead. She levered the Henry's, took a few steps toward the bear until she could reach the animal with the barrel of the rifle. She poked at the bear, it didn't move. Carrie looked around, not knowing what she would do now. The animal was far too large for her to move, and she didn't have any idea how to skin

44

a bear. She looked around the barn as if it would offer answers to her problem.

Suddenly, the barn doors flew open and she scream-ed when the Indian came in with his gun raised. She star-ed, frozen where she stood, too afraid to move. The Indian stared at her, then looked to the bear on the ground.

"Are you all right, Carrie?" It was Noah's voice, but Carrie hardly recognized him now. He lowered his rifle and looked down at the bear, then back at Carrie. "Carrie? Are you all right?" he asked her again.

"Y-y-yes," she finally managed. She stared at him for a long moment. "Noah?"

"I'm sorry I startled you," he said, and then he grinned. "I was coming to make sure you were all right and heard the shots. I got here as quickly as I could."

Carried nodded, still staring at him. Dressed like an Indian in buckskins and furs, with is long hair was flowing down his back, a braid on either side of his head, hanging over his chest. He looked so different than he had when she saw him last. She would have thought he was really an Indian, in fact, she didn't think she would have recognized him at all.

"I had to shoot the bear," she said as she looked at the animal. "I don't know what I was going to do. It's too big for me to move."

"I'll take care of it," Noah said.

He looked at her from head to foot. Even dressed in the bulky woolen overcoat, heavy boots, and her father's hat, she was a vision. Inhaling deeply, he blew the breath out slowly, trying to calm his racing heart. He'd been with his Indian brothers and when they had gotten within a mile of the cabin, he decided to visit Carrie.

It had been weeks since he'd left her that cold November morning, and he couldn't make himself pass so closely by without stopping to see her. When he had been no more than a quarter mile from the cabin, he heard the gunshots and dug his heels into his horse's flanks sending him into a high-speed gallop. He flew across the creek and his feet hit the ground before the animal had stopped running. All he could think of was that Carrie was in danger and he had to help her. He grinned now looking at her. He should've known she could take care of herself; she was the most capable woman he'd ever known.

Noah took care of the bear. He thought he would be able to take the hide back to the village with him and have one of the women prepare it and make a warm coat he'd bring back for Carrie. He carved the meat and buried it in a snow bank to freeze and take back to the tribe. The remainder of the carcass he hauled far away from the cabin for the scavengers to feed on.

When he returned to the cabin, he washed up in the icy creek, and then knocked on the cabin door. Carrie opened it immediately and brought him inside to stand near the fire to warm himself. She'd been cooking while he was taking care of the bear and the food was nearly ready to eat.

"Smells good," Noah commented as he stretched his hands toward the flames.

"It's some of the deer you killed in the fall," Carrie said and sat on the edge of her bed watching him.

She could see his back and the right side of his face glowing golden in the firelight. He was simply beautiful, she thought as she observed him quietly. His strong bone structure, his golden skin, and soft, black hair. Carrie sighed audibly and Noah turned to look at her. She blushed and looked at the floor.

Noah turned and sat on the edge of her father's bed across from her and Carrie could feel his liquid gold eyes studying her. "How have you been?" He finally said in a silky, deep voice that was both strong and gentle.

"I've been well, thank you," she said as if they were sitting in the parlor of a fine house in Charleston and he'd come to call on her. "And you?"

Noah's lips curved slightly. "I've been well, Carrie. I've been with my tribe up north."

Carrie nodded, then rose to check on the food. She finished frying the pieces of venison, and then mashed the potatoes, made gravy and pulled the cornbread from the oven. She set the food on the table and set plates and eating utensils alongside them. After pouring coffee for them both, Carrie sat down across from Noah. She filled his plate, then her own, and after she'd said grace, picked up her fork and began eating.

"Good food, Carrie. You sure can cook," he said and winked at her as he forked another bite into his mouth.

"Thank you." She blushed slightly and kept her eyes on her plate.

They finished the meal in silence and Noah helped her clean up, though she insisted he didn't need to. When the dishes were put away, they sat near the fire, both silent for a long while.

Then Carrie finally asked, "How long will you stay?"

Noah stared at the yellow and orange flames for a long while, then slowly raised his head and focused those gold eyes on her green ones. He smiled gently.

"A few days perhaps, until my people come back this way. Then I will join them on the ride back to the village." He paused for a moment. "If you don't mind, that is."

"Of course not," she said with a smile. "I don't mind the company."

Noah nodded. "Well, then, I'll go out to the barn for the night. It's getting late."

"Here," Carrie said as she rose and went to the trunk in the corner. "I made this for you as a Christmas present." She pulled out the quilt she'd made over the weeks since he had been gone and handed it to him.

Noah took it from her and stared at the gift for a long while, then looked up at Carrie. "It's the first Christmas present I've ever had," he told her. "And it means even more coming from you. Thank you for thinking of me, Carrie."

He didn't wait for her to reply, but picked up his rifle and went quickly out of the cabin to the barn.

Carrie stood looking at the closed door for a long time after he'd shut it behind him. It had never occurred to her that he had never had a Christmas present before and it seemed strange to her that a simple task could mean so much to him.

~ * ~

Noah piled hay on the floor of one of the empty stalls until it was deep and soft. He made a fire in the old cast iron stove Carrie's father had put in to keep the animals from freezing to death during the coldest part of winter, and settled onto the hay with the new quilt wrapped around him. Noah blew out the flame of the oil lamp and shut his eyes in the darkness with only the faint glow of the wood stove casting light.

Carrie's face swam before him and he sighed heavily. She had thought of him while he'd been away, had thought of him enough to make him a Christmas present. No one had ever given him a gift for Christmas in his whole life. Even when his mother was alive, the best she'd been able to manage was a piece of peppermint candy she'd pilfered from the master's house as she cleaned up after one of the lavish parties they'd thrown during the holidays.

Noah's mother had been born a slave on a plantation in Georgia. Her own mother had been brought from Africa on a slave ship, but she had been young and healthy and was sold for a good price to an elderly master who was kind to her. She had been his wife's personal maid and lived in the house with them.

48

The master's wife was older and frail, and she'd been sick for a long time. She loved Noah's grandmother and made her husband promise he'd never sell her, and would always care for her. She also taught the girl to read and write, to do sums, and taught her about Jesus. And made her promise she would never reveal to anyone that she could do any of those things.

When the man's wife died, he kept his promise to his wife and never sold Noah's grandmother, but he did visit her bed often. And when she'd given birth to a daughter, she taught her child to read and write as well. She named the baby girl Sarah, and when Sarah was twelve years old, the master sold her. He ignored her mother's anguished cries as the young girl was taken away from the plantation. Sarah never saw her mother again and never knew what happened to her.

Sarah's new master was not the kind man her first master had been. He was mean, loud, and rough. His slaves were whipped, starved and worked to death. He treated them like mules in the field and when one died, they were dragged off and buried without a word said over them or a rock to mark their grave.

The women who worked in the house were always young, and when they got too old, or became pregnant, he sent them back outside to live with the other slaves. The slave cabins were deplorable little huts with dirt floors and leaky roofs. They had no glass in the windows, only oiled cloths that were put up when it rained and taken down when it stopped. Sarah was young, she was half white, and he had beaten her the first time he took her because she resisted him. It was the only time she did. She hadn't even seen her fourteenth year when she'd given birth to her only child she named Noah.

Sarah didn't mind being in the slave quarters though; it meant she'd no longer be subject to ravishings by her owner. She tied her son to her back while she worked the fields and held him gently to her breast at night while she slept. As he grew stronger and bigger, she taught him to read, write, to do sums, just like her mother had taught her, reminding him each night to never tell anyone what he knew.

She read to him from Bible pages she had managed to steal from the main house and kept safely hidden in a secret place. At night she told him stories her mother had told her about Africa, and sang songs to him in the language of her mother, and she loved him. He knew his mother loved him, and when she died the year he turned ten, he cried all night long. After that, Noah only began thinking of getting away from the plantation, away from his master, away from any place where men owned other men.

His mother told him she prayed every night that he would know freedom, and she believed God would not allow slavery to continue forever. Noah remembered her words and began planning for the day when he would be a free man, but Noah didn't think he could wait until God ended slavery. He ran away the first time when he was twelve. The field master nearly beat him to death before leaving his bloody body lying unconscious on the ground. It had taken him several weeks to recover, but the whipping only made him more determined to leave than he was before.

At fourteen he ran away again and it was only by the grace of God he survived. He had broken ribs and other injuries besides the ones caused by the whip. His urine turned bloody, and food wouldn't stay in his stomach for a very long time. He wished he were dead night after painful night as he lay on the dirt floor of the little stone building where they'd locked him up. They tossed a slice of bread and a cup of water to him every evening, but it was a long time before they let him out again. And when they did, he was a skeleton with sallow skin stretched over it. Why God didn't have mercy on him and let him die, he didn't know.

Over the next two years something happened to him. His body began to grow, muscles began to develop, and by the time he was sixteen, he was the largest man on the plantation. The hard work made him lean and strong, and he had learned to control himself around the white men. He no longer defied them, no longer blatantly stared them down, no longer acted as if he would kill them if he had the chance. Then one night, feeling worn out and tired, he slipped from the slave hut into the woods, and into the swamp. And he ran like he had never run before because he knew if they caught him this time, there would be no going back to the plantation, no laying for weeks healing from the whipping--this time they would beat him to death and then hang him from the nearest tree, leaving his body for the scavengers to dispose of.

Noah took a deep breath and exhaled sharply. He gathered the quilt around him, and breathed in Carrie's scent. It clung to the material and shot straight through him to his loins. He felt a hot ball of desire curling through him, spreading heat throughout his body until he had to push the quilt back and allow the frigid night air to cool him.

Noah knew better than to start thinking of her that way, but no matter what he knew in his head, his heart seemed to have a mind of its own. He had spent the last several weeks thinking about *not* thinking about her, but it only served to make him think about her more and more. He'd driven himself crazy fantasizing about her, dreaming about her, wanting her. Needing her. He crossed his ankles as he lay on his back with his hands laced behind his head and stared into the darkness.

"God help me," he muttered. It was almost as if he could feel her, could sense her so near to him, wrapped warmly in her bed. He hadn't prayed in a very long time, but if he ever needed the Lord's strength, it was now. "God help me," he muttered again and closed his eyes.

~ SIX ~

Noah rose as soon as there was enough gray light to see by. He put on his boots and carefully folded the quilt, draping it over the stall. Outside, he looked at the heavily gray sky and the wind felt like knives slicing against his cheeks. It would snow again soon he knew, as he made his way to the creek to wash the sleep from his eyes. He could use a bath as well, but he wasn't ready to step wholly into the icy water just yet.

Back in the barn, Noah milked the cow, fed the chickens and other animals, then carried arms full of wood to the house to replenish what had been used. He didn't want Carrie to be out in the bitter cold any more than necessary, and had just stacked the last armful against the house when the cabin door opened and Carrie stood framed at the threshold.

"Good morning," Noah said with a broad smile, as he glanced up at her and placed the last of the wood on the stack. She always looked so beautiful, so soft and sweet. His heart thudded in his chest and the muscles in his stomach constricted. He took a deep breath and stood up straight.

"Good morning," she said and smiled at him. "Come in out of the cold." She ushered him inside and shut the door.

"Here." She handed him a cup of steaming hot coffee, and then went back to the task of preparing breakfast.

Noah stood with his back to the fire, cupping the coffee in both hands as he watched her. Her hair was in a single braid down her back and he noticed the way it brushed back and forth every time she moved. He watched her make dough for biscuits and hid a smile behind his coffee cup when he noticed the smudge of flour on her nose. He wanted to brush it off himself, to touch her soft skin with his fingers, but he stayed where he was and watched as she moved efficiently in the tiny space she used as her kitchen. When he finished his coffee, he stepped across the room and refilled the cup himself.

"It's good," he said and filled her cup as well.

"Thank you," Carrie said, and glanced up at him even as she patted out the biscuit dough.

His gold eyes always caught her off-guard. She had seen those eyes countless times when he'd been there before, and even more as she thought about him when he was gone, but still, every time she saw them they startled her. As if the unique golden color wasn't enough to cause her breath to catch, the way he looked at her with them...no, the way he looked *into* her with them, always caught her off-guard. It made her breath clot in her throat, made her stomach turn slow flips, and caused heat to spread throughout her body. She forced herself to look away, picked up the biscuit cutter and placed each round piece of dough in the cast iron skillet.

Noah sat on a stool at the table and watched her put the skillet into the oven and burned his lip on the hot coffee when she bent over. The room seemed to be getting much warmer now and Noah felt beads of sweat forming on his brow. He set the cup down and cleared his throat.

"I'm going to bring some wood in for the wood box," he told her as he opened the door and stepped out into the icy air.

The snow had begun falling again... big, heavy, wet flakes continued for three days. By the time it stopped, snow piled so high that if Noah hadn't rigged the rope between the cabin and the barn, he may not have been able to get out and feed the animals.

Carrie insisted he sleep in her father's bed now, and he helped her tack a blanket to the ceiling between the two beds for modesty, and propriety's sake, but being that close to her made for many sleepless nights for Noah. During the day, with so few chores to be done, there was a lot of empty time to be filled so Carrie and Noah played checkers, and she had an old deck of playing cards Noah used to teach her to play poker. Noah read to her from the Bible each evening after supper while Carrie sat on her bed knitting or crocheting, and Noah wound up with a new sweater and several pair of wool socks as a result.

They also spent time sitting, watching the fire, and talking. Noah told her of his mother and grandmother, of the plantation where he had lived, how he ran away and was found by the Indians in the mountains. Carrie wiped tears from her cheeks when he spoke of his mother, and he told her how he'd been whipped and beaten when he ran away the first two times. She had even reached out and touched his hand gently and Noah froze at the contact.

Her fingers on the back of his hand sent a shiver up his arm, made goose flesh rise and then he looked up and their eyes held for a very long time. It seemed to Noah time stopped right then, that they were the only two people in the world, and there were no rules that prevented him from telling her how he felt about her, no rules preventing him from reaching for her and brushing his lips against hers.

In those moments when time stood still, Noah could see it all so clearly in his mind. Could feel it even. He knew how she would feel against him, how soft and warm and willing. She wanted him, he could see it in the way her heart thumped in rhythm with his, could see her breasts rise and fall with each heated breath she took. He watched as she swallowed hard and looked at him. Her tongue flicked out, just the tip wetting her lips, and Noah felt a hard fist of desire squeeze deep inside of him.

He took a deep breath and looked away. Another few seconds and he would have pulled her to him, would have kissed the breath from her lungs, and told her he loved her before he could care what the aftermath would bring.

He inhaled slowly, deeply, carefully, and then let it out. He wiped his arm across his forehead, picked up the deck of cards and saw his hands were shaking. He shuffled the deck a few times and then forced himself to look at her again. She played with her fingers in her lap, still watching him with her bottom lip between her teeth. Noah smiled at her and shuffled the deck again. Carried stood and smoothed her dress.

"How about some dessert? It'll only take a few minutes," she said as she turned her back and poured milk into a pot.

She added a few simple ingredients and took the mixture to the fire and sat stirring until it was bubbling and thick. She took it back to the table, added a dollop of butter and a little vanilla, and then spooned it into two bowls. She set the bowls outside on top of the milk box and allowed them both to cool before bringing them back inside and handing one to Noah.

"Thank you," Noah said and took the bowl from her. They sat in silence eating the pudding, and when they were done Carrie washed the dishes, and then blew out the lamps. Noah banked the fire and tacked the end of the blanket back up, separating them once again.

Carrie stood on her side and Noah stood on his side, but neither said any of the things they really wanted to. Carrie took a deep breath and sat on her bed, took off her dress and put on her nightgown, then climbed into bed.

"Good night, Noah," she whispered.

"Good night, Carrie," Noah said softly. He lay down and closed his eyes.

~ * ~

Running Elk made his way through the snow, through the black of night. It was freezing, but he was grateful for the dark that concealed him. He knew where Noah had gone and all he had to do was get to him. He was hurt, blood dripped from the bullet wound in his shoulder, but the one in his side wasn't bleeding. It was puffed up, purple and black, but no blood oozed from the hole the bullet made where it entered his body. Running Elk knew that was not a good sign.

He was in so much pain he could barely walk, and now his feet had lost all feeling, his hands and fingers as well. He didn't know if he would make it to the white woman's cabin alive, but sheer determination and will power kept him putting one frozen foot in front of the other. His lungs burned from breathing the frigid air, and he moved slower and slower with each step. Running Elk leaned against a tree and rested, then caught the scent of wood smoke on the air. It had to be the woman's cabin, he thought, and set off again in the direction of the welcome scent.

~ * ~

Noah listened to Carrie's slow, gentle breathing and knew she slept peacefully. He was glad at least one of them was. He tossed and turned for a long while, trying to will himself into sleep, but only succeeded in being more wide awake thinking of that moment earlier when time stood still. He nearly moaned aloud thinking about holding Carrie close to him, thinking about kissing her. Thinking about why he hadn't done any of that and let the moment pass. Wishing he hadn't.

He threw the quilt back, sat up and quietly put on his boots. He stood and went to the door, paused for a moment to look at Carrie sleeping, barely enough glow from the fireplace for him to make out the soft features of her face. He had nearly convinced himself to brush a finger over her cheek when he heard a noise that brought him back to reality, and instead, he quietly picked up the lever-action Henry's Carrie kept next to the door.

Opening the door quietly, with just enough to room to slip his body through and shut it behind him, Noah listened and heard the sound again. Although familiar, he shouldn't be hearing it now. *Here.* He walked around the side of the cabin, his back to the wall, and on silent feet went toward the sound. He knew it well. He and Running Elk had come up with it years ago when they went hunting together to keep track of each other in the woods. It had also come in handy as a warning when white men had gotten too near and it had been necessary to hide. What Noah couldn't figure out was why Running Elk was using it now; he wasn't supposed to be anywhere near here for at least another week.

Noah crossed the creek on frozen rocks, went slowly through the deep snow, thankful for the darkness and the thick clouds that blocked the moon's light. He went up the bank and heard the sound again, closer this time, within reach, and found Running Elk slumped against a tree, barely able to keep himself upright. Noah reached for him and Running Elk collapsed into his arms.

Noah shouldered him over his back and held his legs, then made his way back across the creek and through the snow to the cabin. When he reached the door, he shoved it open and called Carrie's name to waken her, then took Running Elk to the bed he'd been using and laid him down. Noah lit an oil lamp, and then stoked the fire to a brilliant blaze.

"What happened?" Carrie asked, pulling a quilt around her shoulders.

"I don't know," Noah said. "He's hurt bad. I haven't had a chance to look at him yet, but he's bleeding."

"I'll get some bandages," she said and went to the trunk, taking out clean cloths and scissors.

Noah knelt beside Running Elk, then turned to Carrie and took the scissors from her. He cut the deerskin tunic off him and examined his shoulder and side. The wound in his shoulder went all the way through, it was clean and the bleeding had stopped. The wound in Running Elk's belly worried Noah. It was an ugly shade of blackish-purple and his belly was swollen and distended. Running Elk's brow burned with fever and Noah didn't think there was much hope for survival.

Noah handed Carrie his own hunting knife, it was the sharpest one in the cabin, and told her to hold it in the flames. He pressed his fingers gently to the wound on his friend's stomach, then poured a little of the whiskey over it. There wasn't much left in the bottle since it was the same bottle Carrie had given him when he first came to her with his broken leg. He knew the bullet was still inside Running Elk's body and had to be removed. He just hoped it wasn't deep or lodged in one of his vital organs.

He took the knife from Carrie and waited a few minutes to allow it to cool, then made the first cut. Blood spurted onto the blade of the knife and ran over Noah's hand. Carrie gasped but Noah's hand didn't waver. He made another cut, wiped the blood with a cloth, and then put a finger inside Running Elk's body through the hole. He felt around cautiously, trying not to cause any further damage than what the bullet had, but he didn't feel the slug anywhere. He pulled his finger out, pressed on the outside of the man's body, and then he found what he was looking for.

Somehow the bullet had entered Running Elk at an angle and lodged between two ribs. Noah made another cut into the bruised flesh and dislodged the bullet with the tip of his knife and pulled it out. Noah wiped the area with the cloth, and then pressed against Running Elk's stomach again, watching as dark, clotted blood oozed out of the hole. When Noah was sure all of the blood was expelled, he turned to Carrie and asked for a needle and thread.

She put her hand on Noah's shoulder. "I'll do it," she said quietly.

Noah looked at her for a moment, then stood and moved out of her way. She knelt beside the bed and Noah handed her a wet cloth. She washed the blood from

Running Elk's skin, and then sewed up the ragged wound with neat little stitches. Then she sewed up the cuts Noah had made, wiping them off again. She stood and turned to Noah. He had heated water for her to wash up with, and while she did, he cleaned up the bloodied cloths.

"Go to bed, Carrie. I'll watch over him tonight."

When Carrie awoke the next morning, Noah sat on the floor next to the bed, his head nodding forward. She shook him lightly and he jerked awake.

"You sleep now," she said. "I'll watch over him."

"I can't ask you to do that."

"Noah, you're exhausted and Running Elk is asleep. If he wakes, I'll call you."

While Noah slept, she bathed Running Elk in cool water and sat with him throughout the morning until late afternoon.

Noah woke and took over the vigil of watching his friend, while Carrie fixed them both something to eat. Run-ning Elk had not made a sound the entire day, but he was still breathing, though it was shallow, and his heart was beating, though it was difficult to tell at first. He was alive and that was all that mattered to Noah. If Running Elk could stay alive for the next few days, Noah knew his chances of surviving would be increased greatly with each passing day.

Carrie made a clear broth from a piece of chicken, and then fried the rest of the chicken for Noah and herself. Running Elk had still not woken up, but it had been three days since he'd shown up at the cabin and he was still alive. Noah knew his patient had to eat and carefully spooned a few drops of the cooled broth into Running Elk's mouth, which he reflexively swallowed. That was a good sign, Noah had told Carrie. He was beginning to think Running Elk would survive, but he wasn't sure how long it would last if the man didn't wake up and begin eating and drinking a little water.

The snow outside was still deep and although it hadn't snowed in several days, the temperature had dropped and the snow turned to ice. Noah wished he could take Running Elk to the tribe. They had big medicine there, had roots and herbs they could use to help Running Elk. Noah didn't want to take Running Elk home for burial.

The days passed slowly and Noah and Carrie took turns sitting with Running Elk. Noah made his way to the barn each day to feed the animals, and to keep the fire burning in the wood stove so the animals didn't freeze as well. Noah didn't remember ever seeing the temperatures this cold since he'd been in the mountains. It seemed as if the world would never thaw.

Noah and Carrie sat at the table talking quietly, drinking coffee together. Noah told her that when he was first brought to the Indian village Running Elk was a young brave, just a year older than Noah, but Running Elk didn't like Noah at all. Noah didn't know why, maybe it was a young man's jealousy of the newcomer, maybe it was because the tribe so readily accepted him, or maybe it was because Noah was so angry and ready to fight at the slightest glance from someone else.

He shrugged and smiled at the memory of the two young boys he and Running Elk had once been. He told her about the fights they'd gotten into, the ways they'd tried to kill each other, and he laughed when he told the stories. Running Elk was the brother he'd never had, and the thought of him dying was something Noah wouldn't allow. Even if he had to breathe for him, even if he had to squeeze Running Elk's heart with his own hands he would. But he would not let him die.

Rising suddenly, Noah went to the bed where Running Elk lay silently and stood watching him. He felt his breath stop when Carrie's arm slipped around his waist. Standing still, afraid to move, and afraid if he did she would move away. He kept his eyes focused on his Indian brother and slowly slipped an arm around Carrie's shoulders.

She moved against him, wrapped her other arm around his stomach so she her arms encased him, with her cheek resting against his rib cage. Noah took a deep breath and looked down at her. She was all warmth and innocence, holding him because she knew how worried he was about Running Elk. Noah felt his heart squeeze inside his chest.

He reached for her, allowing a finger to graze over her cheek. It was even softer than he'd thought it would be. And he found himself leaning into her, over her, inches separated his lips from hers, and she didn't move away from him. Her eyes held his, and he was lost in them.

Then he move, turned to face her, wrapped his arms around her and drew her to him. Her arms went around his neck as he laid his cheek against her hair and inhaled deeply, the scent of her causing his heart to race, his breath to catch. Her fingers moved into his hair and he felt as if he'd never been touched by a woman before.

He lifted his face, looked into her eyes and lowered his mouth to hers. Her tongue darted out, moistening her lips, just before his touched hers. He brushed her mouth softly, slowly, pulling her more tightly against him, and felt her body heat searing against his.

Her mouth opened to him and his tongue touched hers. She melted against him, her knees buckled and he held her up, held her suspended in time with only that kiss. It seemed to go on and on. Then he heard a soft moan escape her chest and slide inside of him. He breathed the breath from her lungs and she clung to him as his hands moved slowly over her back.

Noah felt like he was under water, drowning, and enjoying every second of it. Relishing the feel her beneath his hands, beneath his mouth, her tongue mating with his, her fingers in his hair. Her body hot next to his, burning him at each point of contact, as the kiss went on and on.

Noah had never kissed like this before, had never *been* kissed like this before. Had never felt such waves of emotion crash over him. He didn't know if this was the only kiss they'd ever share, or if it was just the first of many to come, but right then, all he knew was he felt his every dream coming true.

Carrie felt her stomach flip and heard her own heart thud against her chest. Noah's mouth was on hers, soft and gentle, sweet and slow. Then his tongue was against hers and she had never felt such liquid heat racing through her bloodstream before.

Noah felt warm, so very warm, and every place his fingers touched her left a trail of fire she felt right through her clothing. She'd never kissed a man before, not a kiss filled with passion. She'd had her hand kissed, her cheek pecked by suitors back home in Charleston, but never had she felt a man's warm lips on her own like this.

He tasted of spice and wood and something she couldn't quite identify, and it seeped into her blood-stream. His scent was wild, untamed, dangerous, and so very male. There was a fire burning inside of her and as he continued to kiss her, the fire burned brighter and hotter until Carrie was sure it would consume her and she'd float away like ash on the wind.

She felt a pull from somewhere so deep and dark and secret she didn't know it even existed inside of her until now. And although she didn't know exactly what it was she needed, she knew she needed it from him.

Noah caressed her cheek, pulled the kiss back and was going to pick her up and lay her on the other bed, but he suddenly heard a soft whisper. He felt Carrie still in his arms, and then he looked down at the bed beside them. Running Elk looked up at them, grinning like a fool. Noah grinned, then looked at Carrie. Noah could see her cheeks heat and knew she was embarrassed.

"I'll get him some broth," she murmured, as she quickly turned and moved toward the kitchen.

Noah knelt beside the bed and in the Indian language he spoke with his brother said, "You picked a fine time not to die."

"I waited as long as I could," Running Elk said weakly. "But I need to pee."

Noah nodded. "I'll get the thunder mug."

Carrie kept her back turned while Noah helped Running Elk take care of his personal needs. It was all the strength Running Elk had.

Noah spooned broth into Running Elk's mouth, and forced him to take another bite each time Running Elk shook his head to refuse the nourishment.

"You've gone without eating for too long," Noah insisted. "You've been here for six days without waking up, I thought you were going to die on me."

Running Elk managed a crooked smile and whispered, "I can't leave this world with you in it. Who would protect everyone?"

Noah laughed and shook his head. "And to think I spent all those nights keeping you alive."

Running Elk fell asleep again and Noah had experienced too much emotion in a matter of a very few minutes.

"I'll be back," he said to Carrie and walked outside. He took a deep breath of very cold air, and walked toward the barn, roughly wiping a tear from his face.

~ SEVEN ~

The sun came out for the first time since before Thanksgiving and Noah thought it must be the end of January, or maybe the beginning of February. It wasn't warm sunshine, but it was bright against the frozen snow and he watched Carrie standing with her eyes closed, her face tipped skyward with her lips turned up slightly in a contented smile.

Noah smiled while helping Running Elk outside. It had been weeks since he'd been shot and although he was feeling better, he was still weak and moved slowly. He had wanted to get out of bed for several days now, but neither Noah nor Carrie would allow him to do more than sit propped up on the bed to eat his meals. Now he leaned against Noah, still too weak to stand alone, but the desire to be outside, to breathe fresh air went far in improving his health, although it didn't take more than ten minutes before Running Elk was grateful to be lying down again.

Noah sat on a stool beside the bed. He had left the cabin door open and looked out at Carrie as she stood basking in the sunshine.

"Running Elk, you have to tell me what happened to you now, what happened to everyone else. White Bear will be worried about all of you, and as soon as you are able, I will take you back to the tribe."

Running Elk closed his eyes and took a breath that caused him to flinch when his ribs pulled. "We were near the river when the first shot rang out," he began. "I never saw anyone. I saw Spotted Pony die just before I was shot in the shoulder. My horse spooked and ran, but not fast enough to keep me from being shot the second time. I hit the ground hard and rolled under some brush out of sight. I lay there for a long time and heard the other men shouting, heard the white men coming. They had guns like that one." He nodded toward the Henry's.

"Our guns could not be loaded fast enough to keep up with them and I had lost blood. When I woke up and it was dark and everything was quiet. I knew I would die if I didn't get help. You were the only one I could get to. The village was too far."

Noah sighed heavily as he thought of his Indian brothers dead. "Where were you? Near a town or settlement?"

"No." Running Elk shook his head. "These men were out hunting. For food or Indians, I don't know. But we don't go near the white man, you know that. We are so few now, and the last to escape the reservations and the white man's lies. We stay away from them."

"I know," Noah nodded. "Get some rest now."

Noah sat with Running Elk for a few moments as he closed his eyes and sank into sleep, and then went outside to find Carrie. She was in the barn mucking out the stalls, taking care of the animals.

"You don't have to do that," he said as he walked up behind her. "I'll take care of it."

"I know, but it feels as if it has been forever since I've been out here doing anything useful. It feels good to stretch my muscles." She smiled and leaned on the handle of the hayfork she'd used to clean the stalls.

"You don't think you've been useful?" Noah eyed her with a slight curve on his lips. "If not for you, I probably would have died, or been crippled so badly it would have been the same as death for me. And without you, Running Elk would not be alive today."

Carrie looked away from him and shrugged. "It was because of you he came here. And anyone would've helped you with your leg."

Noah took two slow steps toward her, put one hand on the handle of the hayfork and closed his other hand over hers.

"No Carrie, not just anyone would have helped me. Shot me and put me out of my misery maybe, but that's the only help they would've given me."

He took another step and there was no more space between them. He lifted her hand from the handle of the tool she still held and moved to lean it against the stall. He hadn't touched her since the day Running Elk had woken from his coma. Even though he wanted to so badly but with Running Elk right there, he had to be in control of himself. He had lain on a pallet in the floor before the fireplace each night with Running Elk sleeping in one bed and Carrie sleeping in the other, driving himself crazy remembering the kiss he and Carrie shared.

Now he gently grazed her cheek with the back of his fingers, caught her chin and tipped her face up so their eyes met. He could see the war between propriety and desire flash in the cool, green depths. Her lips parted as she sucked a breath into her lungs and he felt her pulse skittering in her wrist as he held her small, soft hand in his large, rough one. He leaned into her, slowly lowering his mouth to hers, giving her time to say no, time to stop him. Hoping she wouldn't.

His lips touched hers and he felt the jolt of electricity go through him like being struck by lightning. He slid his hand from hers, up her arm to her shoulder and cupped her face in both hands, then sealed his mouth over hers. He felt her body melt into his, felt her breath escape her lungs into his, and then there was nothing else except the two of them. Sensation crashed over him, filled his heart, filled his body, seeped into his blood, and exploded in his soul. He kissed her slow and deep, savoring the flavor of her mouth, as the scent of her body filled him, overpowered him, and thrilled him like no other woman ever had.

Carrie clung to him, fisted her hands in his long, silky hair. Her body molded to his and her nipples puckered, crushed against his chest. She let herself go, let herself feel only him, breathe only him. She could feel the slow, languid way his tongue moved in her mouth to the bottom of her feet.

Every fiber of her being felt as if it were on fire; every part of her mind attuned only to him. Her heart beat so fast and hard, or maybe it wasn't beating at all. She couldn't tell. All she could do was feel wave after wave of warmth and desire crash over her body, washing up on the shore of her soul. She didn't care anymore that the world around them said this was wrong, that race dictated who she could, or could not love. She loved Noah and if the world didn't like it, she decided, and then the world could stay away from them.

The world slid away for Noah as he took the kiss deeper, and deeper still. He could stand there kissing her like this forever, the fleeting thought went quickly through his mind as his hands moved from her face. He wrapped her long, single braid around his hand as the other one moved beneath her overcoat to her back.

He pulled her in closer until the feel of clothing between them was a barrier of frustration. He wanted her soft, silky skin next to his, and wanted to be flesh-to-flesh, heartbeat-to-heartbeat with her. He wanted it to not matter that she was white, or that he was born a slave. And it was that thought that broke the kiss and brought him back to reality. He was a slave. He was the child of a slave, and no matter that he had white blood in his veins, the white world would never accept him.

Noah could never hurt her, he loved her too much, and if anyone ever found out she had even kissed him, she would be marked for the rest of her life. If anyone ever found out he had kissed her, they would see him hanged, or worse. He couldn't risk it, couldn't risk her because of his want and need of her.

They could never marry, could never have the life she deserved, could never have the life he wanted to give her. He held her shoulders as he broke the kiss and set her away from him. Her lips swollen and shiny from the kiss, her eyes dark green with passion, her chest heaved and her cheeks flushed. She looked up at him, her hands flat against his chest. He covered her hands with his own and smiled gently.

"I shouldn't have done that," he said, his voice barely above a strained whisper.

"Why?" She looked at him, her brow crinkled with question.

Noah took a deep breath and exhaled slowly. He stepped away from her, though he continued to hold her hands in his, unready to lose the warmth of contact just yet.

"I want you Carrie. I want you more than I've ever wanted in my life. More than I wanted my freedom when I left Mississippi. But I know it can never be, and if anyone ever found out, you'd be ruined. I can't give you what you deserve, Carrie. I can't marry you, I can't have children with you, and I can't love you."

Carrie searched his face, saw the desire, felt the sorrow. But she didn't understand. "I want you too, Noah. I do love you."

At that moment, Noah heard a sound he'd never heard before—the sound of his own heart breaking in his chest. He drew a ragged breath and shook his head slowly.

"You shouldn't love me, Carrie. There is too much that can hurt you by loving me. If anyone ever knew we had kissed, they would call you horrible names, ostracize you, and maybe even arrest you. And me, they'd hang. The world we live in isn't ready for people like us to live among them. Maybe it never will be."

"I don't care what the world thinks, Noah. I don't care what anyone would say." Carrie released his hand and walked away from him. She stopped near the woodstove and turned around to face him. "What is more important to you, Noah? What the world thinks or that we love each other?"

"Your safety, Carrie. That's what's most important to me. And even living out here like this, someone would eventually find out and there would be trouble. I can't risk it with you. I've known it all along and I shouldn't have let it go as far as it did. I should have..." He trailed off and scrubbed his hands over his face before he continued.

"As soon as Running Elk is able to travel, I will take him back to the tribe. I don't know what White Bear will want to do, but it may be a while before I can come back. But you will be safe from any Indians that may come across the cabin. I have made sure everyone knows they are to never harm you."

Carrie walked back to where Noah stood and stopped in front of him. "Noah, I love you. And if you loved me too, you wouldn't let stupid ideas by stupid people stand in our way." She crossed her arms over her chest and walked back to the cabin.

Noah stood where he was, though every fiber of his being wanted to reach out to her, wanted to call her back to him, wanted to hold her close to him. But he didn't. Instead, he reached for the hayfork and went to work mucking out the rest of the stalls.

~ * ~

Carrie spent the next few weeks caring for Running Elk and cooking for all three of them. Noah spent much of his time in the barn taking care of the animals or chopping wood that didn't need chopped. The mild weather held for two more weeks, then another blizzard blew in. The snow was deep and the wind had blown it into huge drifts against the cabin until the cabin door wouldn't open. When they finally got it to move enough that Noah could slide his body through the opening, he had to dig his way through the snow until he found the rope tied between the cabin and the barn. The snow was still deeper than Noah was tall and it took a long time for him to dig through it to reach the barn.

Noah found a few chickens had frozen to death, but the cow and horses were doing all right, other than being hungry and in need of water. He built a fire in the woodstove, melted snow in a bucket and watered the animals. After they'd been fed, Noah melted more snow in the bucket, brought the water to a boil and dunked the frozen chickens in it. He plucked and cleaned them, then took them back to the cabin.

"I guess we're having chicken for a few days," he said with a grin when he walked back into the cabin.

Carrie took the birds from him and carried them to the cutting board. "We only lost three birds?"

Noah nodded. "The rest are doing all right and the cow and horses were thirsty and hungry."

Carrie spitted one of the birds over the flames in the fireplace, put one in a skillet to fry, and set one to boiling.

"I hope everyone likes chicken for breakfast, dinner and supper the next few days."

She wound up serving the roasted chicken for supper that night, served fried chicken, gravy and mashed potatoes for dinner the next day, and made a chicken pie with vege-tables for supper. They ate leftovers for two more days, and all three agreed that while the chicken meals were tasty, they wanted something different for a change of pace.

~ * ~

The weather improved gradually. Snow clouds turned into rain clouds and water came down in torrents washing away the snow that piled up over the winter months. Spring came so slowly Carrie wondered if it would come at all, and summer came more slowly than that.

Running Elk was able to move around almost normally by the time the rains came and was able to spend most of the day out of bed without tiring. The wounds on his body had healed, at least on the outside, leaving ugly scars, but Noah wasn't sure if Running Elk would ever recover completely or feel like he did prior to being shot. He'd lost a great deal of weight during his convalescence, but was now starting to gain some of it back.

Even so, Noah thought he still looked much too pale, and there were dark circles beneath his eyes. His cheeks were too hollow, and Noah didn't want him traveling but Running Elk became restless and wanted to go back to the tribe. Noah also knew Running Elk wanted revenge for those who had been killed.

When the rains finally let up and the sun began to shine once again, Carrie knew it wouldn't be long until Noah and Running Elk would leave. She knew she may not see Noah again for months, maybe years, or maybe never again, and her heart broke.

She had not been alone with him since the day in the barn, and he had not attempted to kiss her again either. Carrie was not willing to let him go away with the chance she'd never see him again without at least one more kiss between them.

Seducing a man wasn't something Carrie knew much about, but she remembered the way Noah looked at her, remembered the way his hands felt against her back, on her arms, and on her face. And she planned on having them there again—one way or the other.

The sun shone warmly and the weather became quite pleasant. Noah walked with Running Elk every day now, helping him to build his strength back up so he could endure the trip to the village without having to stop except when absolutely necessary. When the two men were out of sight of the cabin, Carrie brought the tub inside, cleaned it out, and filled it with water she had been heating on both the stove and over the fireplace.

During the summer the pool at the creek was fine for bathing, but this early in the year the water was still like ice. They had all used the tub from time to time over the winter months, but they had been quick baths and now Carrie had the luxury of time since she was now alone in the cabin.

Adding dried flowers she'd picked last spring to the hot water, Carrie sank into the fragrant, steaming bath as deeply as she could. The tub wasn't big enough to stretch out, but the scented water lapping over her skin made her feel beautiful and elegant, and reminded her of the luxurious baths she used to have in Charleston.

She washed until the water began to cool, and then used a pitcher to dip water and pour over her long hair. She washed her hair, rinsed it, and then dried it with a cloth. She brushed it out in front of the fire until it was nearly dry.

Carrie opened the trunk and pulled out a quilt, some material she hadn't used yet, a painting of her parents that had once hung above the mantel in Charleston, and another smaller painting of her parents with their three daughters commissioned a year before the war. Her father had never allowed the pictures to be hung in the cabin, but they, and the trunk they were in, were the only things that hadn't burned when the Yankees came to Charleston and destroyed their home.

Carrie thought it strange the only things she had wanted to save from the fire was the very things that hadn't burned. She rolled the canvases back up and wiped the tears from her face, now was not the time for crying. At the bottom of the trunk she found the item she was looking for, a beautiful dress Mrs. Ellis had given her while she and Lydia waited for their father to return.

She had worn it only once at the Ellis's. And now she smoothed it out on the bed, put on clean bloomers and a camisole, then slipped the dress over her head. She didn't have hoops for it now but she thought it still looked beautiful. It was a deep wine colored satin dress with cream-colored lace edging that laid across her cleavage.

The bodice scooped deeply, almost to an immodest depth, but the lace kept it from being completely im proper. The neckline fell off her shoulders into short puffy sleeves. The dress accentuated her small waist and flared with her hips, then fell to the floor. Without hoops, it was a little longer on her than it would've been with them, but since she no longer had dancing slippers to wear with it, she didn't mind that it covered her bare feet completely.

She propped the hand mirror against the wall in the kitchen area and brushed her hair until it was shiny and fell through her fingers like silk off a spool. She wished for a real mirror, one she could hang on the wall like she'd had in Charleston so she could see how she looked in the dress, but as she looked down at herself and smoothed her hands over the garment, she hoped it would serve her purpose.

After cleaning up the bath and replacing the tub on the hook on the wall outside the cabin, she tidied up everything inside, built up the fire as well, and made a pitcher of fresh, sweet tea. She looked around and sighed, and then she heard Noah's voice and felt her heart begin to race in her chest. She set three cups out and began pouring the tea just as the cabin door opened.

Running Elk entered first with a smile on his face but as soon as he saw her, she knew he knew exactly what she planned. He said nothing as Noah followed him inside. Noah's eyes lit up when he saw Carrie standing there and he couldn't help it as his eyes raked over her body in a slow, heated gaze. When he reached the bottom he went back up her body, pausing for a moment as her breasts rose and fell with each breath she took.

Carrie blushed until her cheeks were as deeply colored as her dress. The look Noah gave her made the muscles in her belly quiver, made her heart race, and her breath came in shallow hitches.

She looked away from him then and said, "I made sweet tea if you're thirsty."

Noah nodded. His mouth had suddenly gone so dry he couldn't pry his tongue from the roof of his mouth. He took the cup from her, noticing her hand shook slightly, and she handed one to Running Elk as well. They sat in silence and drank the tea, and then Running Elk set his cup down and said something to Noah. Noah nodded and Running Elk nodded to Carrie and left the cabin. Carrie looked at Noah.

"He said he was going to check on the animals," Noah translated for her, but he knew Running Elk was giving them time alone.

He had asked Running Elk for a few minutes alone with Carrie while they'd been outside, because he wanted to be alone with her when he told her they were leaving the next morning to return to the tribe. As he looked at her now, he knew Running Elk would have left them alone even if he had not asked.

Noah set his cup of tea down and looked at Carrie. She sat on the edge of her bed with her back straight, the dress spread out around her, holding her cup of tea as if she were in a fancy parlor drinking from china instead of tin.

She was beautiful, he thought. A vision in the dress, a dream he had no right to dream, but he was leaving her in the morning, maybe never to return, and, he decided, he was going to leave with the taste of her lips on his. He took a deep breath and as he started to speak she rose suddenly, set her cup on the table and came to stand before him. She reached for his hand and the words he'd intended to say stuck somewhere inside his chest.

He took her hand and came to his feet. She placed a hand on his chest and looked into his eyes. He could see emotion playing there, could see desire turning her eyes a deeper shade of green, and when he heard that little voice in his head warning him this time he might not be able to control where they were going, he ignored it.

Carrie's hand moved slowly over his chest, moved upward until he felt her cool fingers on the skin of his throat, then on his cheek. She caressed his cheek, traced a finger over the outline of his lips, over the bridge of his nose, over each eye, across his brow. His heart was thudding in his chest, his blood humming like honeybees through his veins, desire coiling into a ball of white heat moving deeply into his body. He knew she was he was seducing him. He also knew he should stop her, but for the life of him, he couldn't remember why.

Noah's hands moved over Carrie's arms, moved up her satiny skin to the satiny fabric of her dress. He moved slowly, touched the skin of her shoulder, up the column of her throat and over her cheek. His fingers slipped around her head, fisted in her thick, soft hair. He pulled her to him then, rested his cheek on top of her head, and inhaled the scent of her hair. She smelled like wildflowers, he thought. Wild-flowers and something more mysterious, more potent than anything he'd ever known before.

She pushed against him slightly, slid her arms around his neck and pulled him to her. His mouth came down on hers and she flicked her tongue over his lips, her eyes open, looking into his.

She'd never been so bold in her life, Carrie thought, as Noah's liquid gold eyes watched her deep green ones. She felt a little shiver of excitement shooting through her as she fisted her fingers in his hair and flicked her tongue across his full lips.

She nipped his bottom lip with her teeth, and then sucked it into her mouth. How she knew to do such things was beyond her, but she didn't care. All she cared about was Noah, how he felt against her, how she felt now with his lip in her mouth.

His hands fisted and un-fisted in her hair, moving over her back, against the bare flesh of her shoulders. She moved her hands over Noah's deerskin tunic, and then released his lip. She took a small backward step to give herself room to maneuver, and then slid both hands beneath the tunic. She felt Noah's muscles quiver at the contact, felt goose flesh raise on his skin, on her own skin as well. She moved the tunic up further, looking into his eyes, hoping he wouldn't try to stop her.

"Carrie, we can't do this."
"Why?"
"You must be a virgin for your wedding night for one thing, and you know according to the Bible, it's a sin for us to do this. I don't want you to be sorry tomorrow."

Carried gazed into his eyes. "Isn't God everywhere? Can't He see us and hear us right now?"

"Yes," Noah agreed and kissed the top of her head.

"I, Carrie Robertson, take you, Noah Mosely, as my husband. I promise to honor you, cherish and love you, all the days of my life," she whispered.

"I, Noah Mosely, take you Carrie Robertson, as my wife. I promise to honor you, cherish and love you. I promise to do everything in my power to keep you safe, now and forever."

Much later, as they lay wrapped in one another's arms, Carrie whispered, "I love you."

Noah held her close, and whispered, "I love you too, Carrie." He held her for a few more minutes, and then kissed her softly. "Carrie, I still have to leave tomorrow."

She was silent for a long moment, and then she nodded. "I know."

~ EIGHT ~

Carrie didn't cry when Noah and Running Elk left her cabin. She had packed food for them, and hugged an embarrassed Running Elk as he climbed onto the horse she'd given him. Noah stood looking at her, she could see the emotions from his heart overflowing into his eyes, and she wanted more than anything to beg him to stay. In the end he had simply kissed her softly and held her close to him. Then he had ridden away with Running Elk just ahead of him.

The night before, Carrie had fixed supper for them all, and afterwards, Running Elk insisted on sleeping outside. He said he'd spent too much time on the white man's soft bed and was afraid it had made him lazy. She and Noah both knew he was giving them one last night together.

That was over two months ago and Carrie could feel summer trying to break free of the hold spring had on the mountain. Carrie had a lot of work to do; animals to care for and she had been planting the garden that would provide vegetables throughout the summer and long into winter for her.

The chickens had begun laying again and Carrie was grateful for the first bite of fresh eggs she'd had since last December. She was twenty years old now and laughed that she hadn't even remembered. The randy old rooster was randy once again and Carrie left many of the eggs to hatch and replenish the supply of birds she'd need for meat.

Carrie rose early to milk the cow, feed the animals, and get started on the garden again. It was slow, backbreaking work, but necessary for survival if she planned on staying in the cabin. And she knew she did. She was waiting for Noah to come back, and she knew she would wait for him if she had to wait for the rest of her life. Carrie went to the hen house and tossed feed into the yard, then went inside to collect the eggs.

She ran outside again, leaned over and threw up. It was the second time in as many days she had been sick but it seemed only to happen in the morning, the rest of the day she felt fine.

She leaned against the henhouse wall with her eyes closed and waited for the nausea to pass, and when it had, she went inside and washed her face. After making a cup of tea, she sat down to rest.

Carrie thought about Noah and wondered how much longer till he returned. She took a sip of her tea, and then it dawned on her she hadn't had her monthly since before she had been with Noah. And he'd been gone just over two months now. Carrie gasped aloud. She stood, pulled up her dress and looked down at her stomach. She pressed one hand to her flat abdomen.

Could she be pregnant? Had Noah left her with his child growing inside of her? Carrie dropped her dress and sat down because she suddenly felt dizzy and her heart raced.

Something very close to panic rose inside of her. She took a few slow, deep breaths and pressed her hands to her face, and didn't know whether to laugh or cry. Or what she was going to do all by herself. She'd never been present at a birth, hadn't the slightest idea what happened during one, and didn't know how she'd deliver her own child.

She just hoped Noah returned soon so she could tell him. Then she hoped he would know what to do. There wasn't a homestead closer than three or four days ride from the cabin as far as Carrie knew, and she also knew she wouldn't be able to travel that far from her home when the time came. The Indian tribe Noah lived with was about three days ride northeast, but she also knew they moved during the summer months, and she had no idea where they might already be.

The only thing Carrie did know to do was plant the garden, take care of the animals, and get ready for the next winter. She counted, tried to figure when the baby would be born but she wasn't really sure what month it was now. She thought maybe it was May, and if she was right, the baby would be born in January. Right in the middle of winter.

Carrie knew the baby would need clothing and blankets, diapers, and had to be kept warm. She finished her tea and went back to the henhouse. Smiling now, she had a long summer and fall ahead of her, but she had a wonderful surprise for Noah when he returned. And she refused to believe he wouldn't.

~ * ~

Noah missed Carrie liked he'd never missed anyone in his life. He thought of her every moment he was awake, and he dreamed of her every night.

He had gotten Running Elk home to their tribe and had wound up staying for over a month while Running Elk regained his strength. The trip had cost him, and by the time they reached the tribe, Running Elk was weak and running a fever again.

While in White Bear's lodge, he recounted Running Elk's story, but he didn't have any of the details White Bear needed and they both had to wait until Running Elk was able to sit up and speak again. Then they'd spent another month hashing and re-hashing whether a raid on the whites was the best way to go.

Noah had known the braves of the tribe would want to retaliate, to seek revenge for those who had been killed, but he hadn't mentioned that to Carrie. He hadn't made her any promises, even though he wanted to. He wanted to tell Running Elk to go back without him; he wanted to tell White Bear he wouldn't go with them if they planned a raid against the white settlers.

The urge to ride back to the little cabin and wrap his arms around Carrie and promise to love her till death parted them, nearly overwhelmed him. He no longer cared what the consequences would be if anyone discovered them living together. He knew he couldn't marry her in a church; no white preacher would marry them. He also knew no Negro preacher would marry them either.

The Shaman of the tribe will marry us for real! he thought suddenly. And he didn't know why he hadn't thought of it before. He could bring Carrie to the tribe and marry her in an Indian wedding ceremony. It wasn't legal as far as white men were concerned, but Noah considered the Shaman a holy man, just as holy as any white preacher, and Noah didn't much care about the laws of the white man anyway.

When this was over, he would come back with Carrie and introduce her to the tribe and marry her, he decided.

There was no way the Indians could successfully fight the white men with cap and ball rifles when the white men were using repeaters. Noah had argued the point to the tribal council and told them it would be a suicide mission. Noah wanted to handle things differently, but no one listened. They had revenge in their hearts and nothing Noah said could change their minds.

Noah knew he would go with them though, he couldn't walk away knowing these men were putting themselves in danger. In the end, they raided settlements farther south, stealing repeater rifles and ammunition, but no lives were taken. It took time, but they finally acquired enough weapons for everyone, enough ammunition to get them through a firefight if it came to that. Noah hoped it wouldn't.

By the end of the second month, Running Elk's health was completely restored, and he was able to ride and hunt, wrestle and shoot. Noah tested him time and again; had ambushed him, tackled him, wrestled him to the ground, and chased him through the woods.

Noah wasn't taking any chances that the only man he considered close enough to be his brother wasn't physically able to withstand the hard ride ahead, the intense battle that might come, or the harder ride back home.

They left early one morning before daylight, ready to wage war on the whites near the Arkansas River. The plan was for them to ride in, kill the men, ride out without being followed, and hopefully not encounter the Calvary.

Noah knew some of the more violent tribes in Texas and Arizona were raiding settlers, riding into confrontations with the Army, and winning many of the battles. He also knew that it wouldn't go on forever.

The white man had always taken what they wanted by force, would continue to force their way of life, thoughts, and religions, on all the people of this country, no matter how anyone else felt about it. They had proven it time and again, not just in America but all over the world. And those who refused to accept the white man's ways were simply killed, or, in the case of Indians, the survivors were forced onto reservations.

The fact that white blood ran in Noah's veins, or that the woman he loved was white, made no difference to his way of thinking. The white man would still see him as a slave, no matter that the war was over and slavery had been abolished. And the white man would also shun Carrie for having been with him.

The thought of what they would do to her, the names they would call her, the way they would savage her, thinking she was there for the taking simply because she'd been with him, because of who he was, enraged him. They'd treat her like a common whore and Noah clenched his jaw, trying to shove the thoughts from his mind.

Noah held no sympathy for the white man, felt no guilt that the men who'd murdered of the braves from the tribe would be killed, but he still didn't want to see innocent people die. Since they really had no way of knowing who had committed the murders, Noah knew the chance of innocent people dying was great. The only survivor, as far as they knew, was Running Elk, and he hadn't seen who had ambushed him and the other braves.

Noah killed a buck while he was with the tribe waiting for Running Elk to recuperate. He dried the meat and had the women make Carrie a tunic and leggings like the ones they wore from the animal's hide, as well as a pair of soft boots.

He wanted to see her, wanted to hold her, but he knew if he saw her, he wouldn't be able to leave her again. He hated doing it, but he would leave the meat and clothing for her at night when he knew she'd be sleeping. He couldn't risk seeing her; he knew if she asked him to stay, he would.

When he broke off from the other braves, Running Elk nodded and said they'd be waiting for him to re-join them. Noah knew Running Elk wondered if he would come back or not. Running Elk knew how he felt about Carrie, and he knew Noah's heart was with her and not in this raid. Running Elk smiled as Noah waved and rode off.

Noah took the meat to the cabin, walking on silent feet, and hung it on a hook from the overhang in front of the cabin. He started to leave the tunic and other items on top of the milk box by the door, but being separated from Carrie by only the door in front of him was more temptation than he could take.

He opened the door carefully, silently, and slipped inside the cabin. The glow from the banked fire allowed enough light for him to see and he moved to stand beside her bed.

So beautiful, he thought as he looked down at her. She slept deeply, peacefully; a slight smile curving her lips. He hoped she was dreaming of him.

Kneeling beside her, inches from her face, Noah dared to touch a lock of hair that had fallen across her cheek. He inhaled deeply, letting her scent seep into him. He shouldn't have, he knew it immediately.

His blood thrummed through his veins, the thought of waking her and taking her into his arms was nearly more than he could resist. He leaned down and kissed her softly on the cheek, then had to force himself to leave quickly before she woke.

He shut the door softly behind him, and hurried down to the creek where he'd left his horse and rode quickly away to join his Indian brothers.

Carrie's eyes fluttered open, Noah's name on her lips. She sat up in the bed and looked around. She could smell him; his scent lingered on the air. A spicy, musky, wild scent that was all Noah.

Carrie jumped out of bed and saw the deerskin tunic and leggings on the table with the soft boots next to them. She ran outside calling Noah's name, but he was already gone. Back inside, she fingered the items he'd left on the table, then climbed back into bed and cried herself back to sleep.

~ * ~

Noah rode hard until he was with his Indian brothers again. It was late and they had stopped for the night, after a couple of hour's sleep they'd be on their way once again. Noah lay down on the fur he carried with him.

Riding bareback like the others, he carried no food or water, only weapons. He had two repeater rifles, a quiver of arrows, a bow, one large knife in his boot and another on his hip, and plenty of ammunition.

Noah stared up at the sky above the trees that surrounded them, the stars winking at him, and he thought of Carrie. He thought of what would happen once they reached the river, and he hoped they would find enough answers there to satisfy the men.

He didn't want to go to war, he'd had his fight against the white man in Mississippi, and as far as he was concerned, he'd won. And now that he'd met Carrie, his thoughts had turned toward a future he never dreamed of having before. All he wanted was to go back to the little cabin and hold his woman in his arms, and he'd worry later about what would happen if anyone found out.

~ * ~

They reached the Arkansas River and found the place where Running Elk had been shot. There was no sign of any of the other braves, dead or alive. The white men would not have taken the time to bury an Indian, they would've left them where they died.

The winter had been cold enough that the bodies would have frozen and there would still be evidence of the remains even this late in the year. Even if predatory animals had gotten to the bodies, there would have been some evidence. The lack of evidence meant only one thing, the men had been taken captive and likely killed elsewhere.

Gray Wolf moved ahead of the other men. He could track a fish through water, and he could track his own people no matter how long it had been since they'd been there. He walked slowly over the area, not speaking, only looking and occasionally picking up a twig or turning over a rock. Then he motioned to the men to mount up and took the lead. They followed him to White Mountain and further still, riding steadily, slowly, watching for any signs of the men. They came to the top of Bald Point and dismounted once again.

Gray Wolf picked up a piece of deerskin leather he recognized as being unique to their tribe. He walked slowly to the only trees on Bald Point, a few pines leaned precariously to one side, having been battered year after year by high winds.

Inside the small copse of pines they found the remains of two bodies. The deerskin tunics and leggings had held up to the weather, the bodies had not. There were also signs of scavengers having eaten much of the

84

remains. The men gathered up the bones, wrapped them in a large piece of leather and tied it securely. They'd take them home for burial.

The remains, and Running Elk, accounted for three of the men that had been out that day, and that left Little Hawk and Jumping Pony unaccounted for.

They rode slowly down the southeast side of Bald Point, following what Gray Wolf insisted was the path the white men took. The going was slow and the trail growing cold they all knew, but no one was willing to give up either.

If there were even a slight chance they'd find the men alive, they'd take it. Even if they weren't alive, they wanted to collect the remains and take them back to their own people where they belonged.

~ NINE ~

Carrie rose early as usual, dressed, and ate breakfast. For weeks she had worn the deerskin tunic and leggings Noah left for her, but now her stomach had gotten so large she was back to wearing the only two dresses she had that fit. They were old, but they were loose from the bodice down and she hoped they would continue to fit until the baby was born.

Four months had passed since Noah's late night visit, and she had three months left until the baby would arrive. Summer came in hotter than she ever remembered one being and the heat added a lot of work for her.

She had to water the garden more often, and she'd moved the chickens into the barn where it was cooler. Some of the chicks were lost to the heat already and didn't want to lose any more. Now it was October, the time of year when the heat usually began to give way to cooler fall temperatures, but still, there was no sign of relief.

Carrie took care of the chores, and then went to the pool at the creek. The water was so low that after she'd stripped and waded into it, it barely came to her waist. She dipped her body beneath the surface, dunked her head under and appreciated the relief it brought.

Rubbing her belly, Carrie felt the baby move beneath her hands and smiled. She hoped for a boy, a son who would look just like his father. She'd already started calling him Noah, as she planned on naming him after his father. Imagining the child to have golden skin and golden eyes, with long, dark, curly hair, she imagined holding him, nursing him at her breast, having a part of Noah with her always. It brought comfort, yet it also brought pain she was sure would break her heart in two.

After a while she walked back onto the bank, wrung the water from her hair and picked up her dress. She no longer wore drawers or a camisole since they wouldn't accommodate her increased size. It didn't matter though, as hot as it had been she wore as little as possible now. The baby stretched lazily inside of her and Carrie wiped a tear from her eye as she thought of what Noah's reaction to feeling their child move within her might be.

Carrie went inside and poured a cup of sweet tea and looked around the cabin. She opened her trunk and looked inside. She'd used all of the yarn she had saved to make a blanket for the baby, had used all the extra material to make baby clothes, but she knew it wasn't enough and the baby would grow quickly and need more clothing. She was also running out of flour, sugar, coffee, and ammunition for the Henry's.

Although she needed to go into town, she didn't want to make the trip alone. It was at least three days there and three days back, and that meant she'd have to leave the animals alone for an entire week.

She wished Noah were there, and wished she wasn't so alone now. Having a baby alone was bad enough, but having to go into town alone and pregnant was not something Carrie looked forward to.

Thinking of her mother's wedding ring Mr. Ellis had given to Carrie's father when he returned, Carrie went to the trunk to find it. Wearing a wedding band might keep embarrassing questions from the town folks at bay. It wasn't as if she was lying, she was married to Noah, even if a minister wasn't present.

The trip into town had become necessary, even though Carrie didn't want to go. It had been five years since she had last been to town when her father brought her and Lydia to the mountains. Her father went into town on a couple of occasions, leaving Carrie and Lydia at the cabin until he returned. The last time he'd gone was a few weeks before he died, and Carrie remembered him com-plaining about the high prices of goods when he'd re-turned.

She didn't know how much things would cost now, but she remembered her father saying it had cost nearly fifty-dollars the last time. Perhaps seventy-five dollars would be enough now, at least she hoped so. Removing the leather pouch her father kept his money in from the trunk, Carrie counted out the bills. He left her with plenty of money if she was careful with it. She hid the pouch in the bottom of the trunk beneath all the other items, shut the lid and latched it.

Carrie went back out to the barn and looked the buckboard wagon over, it seemed sturdy enough, but she only had one horse left now. She'd given her father's horse to Noah, and hers had gone to Running Elk. The mare she had left had been Lydia's.

Nellie was gentle and she was strong, but Carrie didn't know if the old girl was capable of pulling the wagon loaded with supplies all the way back from town. And besides that, there was always the risk of an axle or wheel breaking along the way. If that happened, Carrie would have no way of fixing it on her own.

She took a deep breath and blew it out. Supplies were needed, so she really had no choice and would just have to hope that nothing went wrong.

Deciding to leave the next morning, Carrie spent the rest of the afternoon hauling water up for the chickens and left plenty of feed for them as well. She left the eggs to hatch, hoping to replace the chicks that died from the heat.

She put hay out for the cow who was now wandering on her own to graze at the creek bank where grass still grew sweet and green. She milked the cow that evening, and would milk her again in the morning before she left. Carrie didn't know if going a week without being milked would hurt the cow or not, but she had no choice. She couldn't take the cow with her.

After eating supper that night, she packed food for the trip, along with the remaining ammunition for the Henry's, and went to bed.

Early the next morning Carrie finished milking the cow, hauled water up for the garden again and hoped it wouldn't die from the intense sun while she was gone. This was the second garden this year and she considered herself lucky to have been able to plant twice since the weather had held for so long. She left it very wet and hoped that would be enough to get it through the next week.

Nellie was found grazing down by the creek, feeding on the last sweet shoots of green grass growing near the water. Carrie led her to the barn where she harnessed the animal to the wagon. She led the horse and wagon to the yard, put the food, a quilt, a pillow and the Henry's in the wagon and climbed into the seat and picked up the reins. By the time the first rays of sun lit the tops of the pines, Carrie was half way down the hill.

She had never been jarred and rattled about so much in her life. Every bump, rut, and rock was intensified tenfold by the wagon, and the fact that she already had to pee every ten minutes wasn't helped by the rocking wagon.

The wooden seat of the wagon was hard and uncomfortable and Carrie had to put her pillow beneath her bottom to be able to sit. She had never been more uncomfortable, or more aware of her size than she was now.

By the time the sun set that evening Carrie had reached the valley below and the path became much smoother. She found a large oak near a creek and pulled Nellie to a stop. Carrie's back and bottom ached as she climbed down from the wagon and unhitched the horse.

She hobbled Nellie so she wouldn't wander too far away during the night, and then went to the creek and washed her hands, and splashed water over her heated face. Sitting under a tree, Carrie ate a dinner of venison, bread and butter. She climbed into the back of the wagon and laid down on the quilt, her eyes shut, but her body ached and sleep was a long time coming.

Early the next morning, she hitched Nellie to the wagon and started off again. The ache in her back started almost immediately and by the time she stopped that evening, her hands and feet were both swollen. She thought her fingers and toes looked like pork sausages, and if she hadn't been in so much pain, she might have thought it funny.

She slept on the ground that night, thinking it had to be softer than the bed of the wagon. It wasn't any more comfortable and she spent a fitful night trying to find a position that would relieve the aches throughout her body. Late in the afternoon of the third day Carrie spotted the outline of the town on the horizon and an hour later she arrived.

Carrie hadn't seen civilization in five years and felt giddy at being back in town. She saw the sign for the livery stable and headed Nellie in that direction. The stable master assisted her to the ground and she took the Henry's, her quilt and pillow and walked across the street and down the wooden sidewalk to the hotel.

Thinking she must look a mess, dusty and unkempt from the long trip, Carrie didn't care, she just wanted a soft bed and some sleep. She ordered a bath and dinner to be sent up to her room, and her legs felt like lead as she climbed the wooden stairs to the second floor.

Finding her room, she fitted the key in the lock, opened the door, and nearly wept with relief when she saw the huge bed with a feather mattress. She fell back onto it and closed her eyes. Had anything ever felt so wonderful?

It wasn't long before she was forced to get up to answer the knock at the door. Two men carried the long, metal tub into her room and two maids spent the next thirty minutes hauling hot water up the stairs to fill it.

Carrie couldn't wait until she could sink into the steaming water and soak until her stiff muscles relaxed, but dinner arrived while the maids' hauled water, so Carrie ate while she waited till they were finished.

When they were finally done, she thanked them and locked the door as they left, then stripped out of her dress and stuck a foot into the water.

It was hot and steaming and took a little bit for Carrie to adjust to the temperature, but soon she was sinking in up to her neck and inhaling the lovely scent of roses the maids had added for her. The soap was scented with roses as well, and Carrie took a long time rubbing it over her skin, washing the trail dust from her body.

Slipping beneath the water, then used the fragrant soap to wash her hair as well. Remaining in the tub until the water was cool, she smiled when she saw her fingers and toes were wrinkled as prunes. After allowing the water to sluice off her skin, she dried with the rough towel, and then wrapped it around her hair.

Dressing in a simple gown, she dunked her dusty dress and undergarments into the tub, then scrubbed the items with the cake of soap she'd washed with. After rinsing the clothing, she wrung them out, then hung them to dry overnight.

Carrie sat on the edge of the bed and blew out the oil lamp on the bedside table and slid under the cool sheet, sinking into the soft mattress. She closed her eyes and was asleep almost instantly. Sleeping a dreamless, restful sleep, she didn't wake until the maid knocked on the door the next morning when she brought breakfast.

Carrie called through the door to have the maid leave the tray on the floor, and when she heard the woman's footfalls fade, she opened the door and peeked out. Seeing no one about, she held the sheet around her breasts with one hand and pulled the tray inside with the other. Sitting on the bed, she ate the steaming mush, eggs, hotcakes and fried meat. After pouring a little of the milk into the coffee, she drank the rest, then sipped the coffee while she washed up, brushed her hair, and braided it into one long strand down her back.

When she was finished, she pulled the dress over her head, it had dried a little stiff, but it was clean. Then she gathered up her belongings and checked out of the hotel.

Following the directions to the mercantile the desk clerk had given her, Carrie walked down the street, looking into the other shops as she went. When she entered the store, the proprietor, Mr. Hopkins, greeted her and introduced himself.

"What can I do for you today, ma'am?" He smiled at her.

Carrie smiled too and handed him the list of supplies she needed. "If you can fill this order for me, I would appreciate it," she told him.

Mr. Hopkins looked it over, then said, "I think we can handle that." He winked at her and went into the back to get the flour, sugar and coffee.

While he was gone, Carrie went to look at the bolts of fabric and found some nice, soft flannel she could make nightgowns from for the baby. She let her fingers trace over a bolt of gingham with tiny pink flowers on it, and found a plaid flannel she thought she would like to use to make a shirt for Noah.

She also saw a beautiful pair of new leather shoes she wanted, it had been so long since she'd had new shoes. Mr. Hopkins returned to the counter and was writing on his pad of paper.

"How much does it come to?" Carrie inquired as she approached the counter once more.

"Just one second," he said and continued to figure. Then he looked up at her and smiled. "It's thirty-two dollars and fifty cents."

Carrie smiled brightly. "I'm going to be needing some of this material as well, and some knitting yarn, thread, and I was hoping to buy a pair of shoes on the shelf over there if you have them in my size."

"If you'll sit over here, I can measure your foot and then I'll check the sizes," Mr. Hopkins said, gesturing toward a chair. Carrie sat down and slipped the worn shoe off so he could measure her foot. "I think we do carry your size, ma'am."

He smiled at her and she waited while he got the shoes and brought them for her to try on.

Carrie walked up and down the aisle and smiled. "I'll take them."

She pointed out bolts of fabric she wanted, picked out several skeins of yarn, different colors of thread, a new package of sewing needles, and when she saw the rack with leather belts, she picked one out for Noah.

When Mr. Hopkins had brought everything to the counter, he looked at her again. "Is your husband joining you, ma'am?"

Carrie looked up, took a deep breath, and thought quickly as to the lie she was about to tell. She smiled brightly. "He was supposed come instead of me, but business took him away at the last minute and I was forced to come alone."

Mr. Hopkins smiled slightly, glancing at her left hand. When he saw the ring he smiled again, and she could tell he'd bought her lie and was now satisfied she was indeed a married woman.

"Is that everything for you now?"

"I think so," Carrie said. "Oh, wait a moment. Do you have whiskey here? My husband was going to pick up a bottle when he planned on coming in for supplies, but I can't go into the saloon myself to get it."

"Of course you couldn't! I'll be happy to get it for you," he said, as he finished writing on his pad once again and added it all together. "Did I tell you about the new ready-made diapers we just got in?"

"No," Carrie said and shook her head.

Mr. Hopkins walked around the end of the counter to a shelf. "Yes, these just came in last week from St. Louis. See, they even come with pins to hold them in place." He laid the package on the counter and showed them to Carrie.

"How much are they?"

"Ten cents apiece, or a dozen for a dollar."

"And how much does my order come to?"

"Fifty-seven dollars and fifty cents, plus the whiskey, which will be two more dollars, so altogether it comes to fifty-nine dollars and fifty cents."

"Fine," Carrie said. "I'll take the diapers as well."

She owed the livery stable a dollar and a half, and after the five dollars she'd paid at the hotel, she still had enough to buy everything she wanted. It had been so long since she'd been shopping, Carrie felt like a new woman.

"I'm going to go get the wagon over at the livery stable and I'll be right back for the supplies."

"That's fine then. I'll fetch the whiskey over at the saloon while you're gone."

Carrie walked down the sidewalk, nodding and smiling at people who were out strolling before the heat became too intense. Carrie found the stable master talking to two men, and waited until he noticed her. She paid him and he hitched Nellie up to the wagon, led her outside, and then handed Carrie up onto the seat.

"Thank you, ma'am," he said and tipped his hat.

"Thank you, sir, for taking such good care of Nellie." Carrie waved as she turned Nellie down the street toward the mercantile.

"They'll be hanging them." She heard one of the men at the livery say from behind her.

"Oughta just hang 'em all, not even worry about puttin' 'em on the rez," another man said.

That was all Carrie heard but it caused a flutter of panic in her stomach. They couldn't be talking about Running Elk or Noah, could they? Carrie shook her head. She was just worrying unnecessarily she knew. She pulled Nellie to a stop in front of the mercantile and hoped it really was unnecessary worry.

Mr. Hopkins hauled a hundred pound bag of flour to the wagon, a fifty-pound bag of sugar, fifty pounds of coffee, fifty pounds of cornmeal, twenty-five pounds of beans, and all the other items she'd purchased. The wagon was loaded and he set the ammunition and whiskey in a place between other items so they wouldn't bounce around.

"Thank you, ma'am," he said. "I look forward to meeting your husband next time."

"Thank you, Mister Hopkins. I will tell him," Carrie said with a smile, as she clucked her tongue and lightly smacked the reins against Nellie's flanks.

~ TEN ~

Noah had no choice now but to kill or be killed. His horse had been shot out from under him and through the smoke and dust he hadn't been able to tell where Running Elk had gotten to, or if the other men were dead or alive.

He fired and shot one of the men that ambushed them off his horse. The man didn't move once he was on the ground.

Noah scrambled over the embankment and hid in the cleft between two boulders. He reloaded the rifle and rested it on top of one of the rocks and waited.

Listening to men shouting and the sound of horse's hooves getting closer to the edge of the embankment, when Noah could finally see the man on the horse, he fired again, making the shot count. The man's head exploded and his body shot forward to the ground. The horse reared and took off at a dead run. There were other shots and shouting as the smell of gunpowder and blood filled the air.

Noah lay back in the boulders and waited, but the hoof beats began to grow fainter and then disappeared altogether. Noah stayed where he was, his rifle ready. He didn't trust them, and he wasn't going to show himself until he was sure they were gone.

He didn't know how much time actually passed, at least an hour, maybe more, when he heard a faint sound and leaned forward listening intently. The wind picked up and was interfering with his hearing the sound clearly but it sounded like his name, and he moved slowly from the cover of the boulders on silent feet.

Climbing the embankment on his belly, just as he reached the top, he rolled onto his back and listened again. He heard nothing now, and after a few more minutes, climbed over the top of the embankment, crouched, wary, and ready to fight.

He saw Running Elk lying on the ground about fifty yards away and covered the distance quickly. He was already dead as Noah held him in his arms and stared into his dead, open eyes.

Noah knew he couldn't stay there, but he didn't want to leave Running Elk there on unfamiliar ground without a proper burial. He put his hands on Running Elk's face and closed his eyes, whispered good-bye in a hoarse voice and got to his feet.

Gray Wolf was also dead, and two of the other men beside him. He looked around, but didn't see Great Wind anywhere. He hoped that meant he'd escaped and not been taken captive.

Noah began running down the side of the hill when he spotted two horses grazing in the valley below. He caught Gray Wolf's mount and straddled him quickly, then led Running Elk's horse, the one Carrie had given him, behind him.

Noah's heart filled with grief and sorrow, and with longing to be back at the cabin wrapped around Carrie. As darkness fell, Noah felt safer in the black of night and rode until dawn.

When he finally stopped he found a safe place to let the horses graze and went to sleep on the ground. Sleeping until late afternoon, Noah rode Carrie's horse and led the other one. He hoped to make it back to the mountains to tell White Bear what happened, and he would no longer be going out with the tribe; he was going to build a life with Carrie and stay right there in the cabin with her. He wanted no more battles, no more war. He was through.

That was until he ran into the U.S. Calvary. He knew he couldn't outrun them and he couldn't fight them. The only thing he could do was wait and see what happened. He stood his ground, and watched them with wary eyes.

The troop halted and sent four men to meet him; one was an Indian scout. They thought Noah was an Indian and the scout spoke to him in an unfamiliar dialect, but

Noah said nothing, so the scout tried another dialect and Noah finally answered him.

"I am on my way home," Noah told him. "I want no problems with anyone here. White men killed the men I was with in an ambush. I am just going home."

The scout gazed at him levelly, sizing him up. "You are not one of the People."

"No, they took me in. I would have died without them."

"Slave?"

Noah looked at him, and then nodded slightly. "I was."

The scout turned to the captain who accompanied him, and had been listening intently to the conversation, but didn't understand the language. He explained the situation to the captain and Noah had an uneasy feeling. He wanted to run, but he knew it would do no good. When finally the captain nodded, he said something to another man on his right and sent the man riding back to the troops. After a few minutes the man returned with a different man following behind.

"I am Captain Benjamin Carver," the captain said as he urged his mount closer to Noah's. "I understand you were a slave." Noah nodded. "This," the captain glanced back to the man who'd just arrived, "is Major Elijah Johnson. He's with us temporarily, as his normal post is St. Louis. He recruits for a special unit of men called Buffalo Soldiers.

"It's made up of Negro men who used to be slaves and ran away, or were freed by their owners. He's been looking for a Negro who speaks and understands the Indian language. He'd like to speak with you."

Noah nodded and introduced himself as he shook hands with Major Johnson. "Noah, I'd like you to ride with us and listen to what I have to say before you turn me down," the Major said with a broad, friendly grin.

Noah nodded and the Calvary began moving again.

"I was a slave just like you," the Major began. "When the war came, I left the plantation, and not because the owner said I could go. I ran away and made it into Tennessee where I met a man who told me about the Buffalo Soldiers. I made it to Memphis and joined up. They gave me clothes and food and a rifle. It's the best life I've ever known.

"I didn't mind fighting against those who wanted slavery to continue, but I had a hard time justifying the killing of Indians. I understood why they didn't want to go to the reservations, and I understood why they fought the white settlers and the Calvary, too. They didn't want to be slaves. I could understand that all too well. So what my men and I have been trying to do is bring the Chiefs of the tribes together, make them understand fighting the white man will mean only death for their people.

"One of our biggest problems is that we don't have the people we need to communicate with the tribes hiding in the mountains here, and those over in Indian Territory and beyond. We are trying to keep things here from getting to the point like they are down in Texas and over in Arizona. That's where you could be a big help if you would join us."

Noah looked at Major Johnson and considered his words. Noah understood all of those same things, probably better than the Major realized. He also understood fighting the white government would only lead to death, no matter if it were Indians or Negroes. Noah knew survival meant adapting to change whether or not one agreed with those changes.

Some changes were good since some of those changes had abolished slavery. On the other hand, Negroes were still second-class citizens who knew no other life than the one they'd been born into. Maybe the future would bring more changes, maybe not in Noah's lifetime, but maybe sometime in the future people wouldn't be so narrow-minded. Maybe both the Negroes and the Indians would find a place in the world if everyone worked together in that direction.

Noah knew not everyone would accept such changes, there would always be prejudice, there would always be inequality, but maybe in his own small way, working with the Army to bring peace between the government and the tribes, Noah could help change the way things were right now.

"I won't wear a uniform. I have my own rifle but I'll expect the Army to provide me with ammunition. I will answer to you alone, and I won't sign any contract with this government. If you need some time to get approval, I'll stay until you get an answer."

Major Johnson looked at Noah and grinned. "I don't need to get an answer, you have a deal." He extended his gloved hand and Noah shook it.

Noah nodded and they rode in silence for the rest of the day. That evening when they made camp, Noah refused the Major's offer to share his tent. He slept beneath the stars at the edge of camp and thought of Carrie.

It had been seven long months since he'd left her and looked like it would be even longer before he got back to see her again. He hoped she'd understand. Hoped she'd still be there when he did get back, and hoped she wouldn't hate him.

By the time they reached Fort Sill in the Indian Territory the weather had turned considerably colder and Noah knew winter wasn't far off. He hoped Carrie had plenty of food and plenty of firewood to last her till spring. Major Johnson said Noah's name again and laughed when Noah's head spun around.

"You were deep in thought," he said.

"Yeah, just looking around," Noah answered.

"We'll meet up with my men here. They've had a few days R&R in town, and I imagine more than a few of them will be hung over, or in need of a few stitches. We'll ride out to the post and pick up supplies and then head south to the Red River. The Comanche's have been raiding settlements along the river all summer and if we can't get results, I'm afraid the Army is going to call in every regiment in the area and go in shooting first, asking questions later. I'm hoping to save as many lives as possible, Indians and whites."

"I'm still not sure what you think I can do that you haven't been able to," Noah said. "I don't even know if I can get my own tribe to surrender and go peaceably to the reservation. I don't know if I'll be any help to you or not."

"Let's get my men rounded up, then we'll pick up supplies and winter gear. Snow's gonna fly soon, and you'll be wanting something warmer than those deerskin leggings there."

"I'll be fine, Johnson. I can take care of my own needs, including winter gear."

"Not a problem, Noah. But if you change your mind, let me know and I'll fix you up."

"Thanks, I'll keep it in mind."

Major Johnson kept his head facing forward, but he could see Noah in his peripheral vision. He was a young man, but there was enough anger and pain in the man's eyes for him to be eighty. He knew from his own experience how hard it was to be born a slave, but for Noah, he imagined it had been even more difficult.

Both of the Major's parents had been slaves, so even though he didn't belong in the white world, the slave world was his family. He had been raised with five brothers and four sisters, grandparents, aunts, uncles, and cousins galore. It was his family alone that tilled the soil, planted it, and harvested it down in Alabama.

It'd been a slave's life, but it wasn't hard like it must've been for Noah. Johnson knew the babes born to slave mothers fathered by their white masters lived a hard life. They weren't just hated by the whites, the slaves shunned them as well.

Elijah Johnson had seen slaves come and go over the years, had seen members of his own family sold, had seen others bought at auction and brought to the plantation. He'd seen young girls raped by the field masters; saw how they were cast aside when they became pregnant.

He'd seen some of those girls kill herself rather than give birth to a half-white child. He'd also seen some those half-white babies smothered to death by their mothers as soon as they entered the world. For the women who carried their master's children to term, and brought them screaming into the world, life was just as difficult.

The older slave women often tried to talk them into killing their children, would shame them for letting the world know a white man had bedded them, and if they still insisted on keeping their children, those children were tormented and taunted by other slave children.

Noah looked to have more white blood to Elijah than the mulatto children he'd known on the plantation, he couldn't imagine what it was Noah hid behind those strange-looking gold eyes. Those eyes were like looking into no-thingness, into the darkest pits of hell, and he imagined hell was exactly where Noah had been once or twice in his life.

But he saw something else in Noah as well, something besides the scars across his back. He saw something deep, something strong, something that could move men's hearts and minds to change, to follow him, to believe there was something more, something better in life than what they'd known. Elijah was a good judge of character and he expected Noah's character was better than most of the men he'd known.

They rode on toward the Red River the next day after rounding up the Major's men. They'd found most of them in the saloon and Noah laughed when he went inside.

The room was large and there was a bar on each end. On one side of the room were white soldiers and on the other were the Buffalo Soldiers.

They even had Negro women sashaying around dressed indecently on one side and white women in indecent clothing on the other side. And each side ignored the other as if they didn't exist.

Noah got more sideways glances from the Buffalo Soldiers than he did the white ones when he pulled up a barstool and took a seat. He ordered a shot of whiskey and tossed it back, then it occurred to him both sides thought he was an Indian and he laughed out loud.

~ ELEVEN ~

Carrie welcomed the cooler weather that finally arrived. It had even rained a few times and brought welcome relief to the land. She had a good crop of vegetables to harvest and put up for winter. The chickens reproduced at a rapid rate and the cow still gave milk.

Carrie had even managed to shoot a deer early one morning. While making coffee, she glanced out the window to see the buck standing in the clearing. She'd stepped quietly outside with the Henry's and fired twice, dropping the buck where he stood. She dressed him out as best she could and wished she knew how to prepare the hide, but her father hadn't taught her that, so she hauled it as far from the house as she could to let the wild animals take care of it for her.

By the time the first snow had fallen, Carrie was ready for winter, but she wasn't sure she was really ready for the baby.

On her way out of town when she'd gone in for supplies, she'd seen a sign above a door that read *Doctor Reynolds,* and she'd stopped in to speak with him. He insisted on making sure she was healthy and well, and hadn't even charged her.

She told him the same story she'd told Mr. Hopkins at the mercantile. She said her husband was away on business and she didn't know when he'd be back, but in case he wasn't back in time for the birth of the baby, she needed to know how to deliver the baby on her own.

The doctor tried to encourage her to stay in town until after the baby was born, but to no avail. Instead, he found a book on pregnancy and childbirth for her to read and let her take it with her, promising she'd return it when she came in for supplies again. He explained to her what would happen when she went into labor, during the birth, and how to make sure the baby was breathing, and how to tie and cut the cord.

Carrie had read the book through several times since she'd been back home, but she just couldn't see how she was going to be able to manage on her own.

Now that winter had arrived and snow began to fall, Carrie worked each afternoon into the evening knitting sweaters and booties, or cutting the material into little nightgowns for the baby. She also made Noah a shirt out of the plaid flannel and folded it up neatly and placed it in the trunk with the new baby clothes.

She still had to go out to the barn each morning to care for the animals, but she did as little as possible now that she was so big she could barely walk. She even put up the rope between the barn and the house just to have something to hang onto as she made the trip back and forth.

The snow wasn't sticking to the ground yet, but fell in swirls as the wind blew cold across the prairie and up the mountain. Carrie wore the old wool coat she'd had for the past five years, but it had no hope of buttoning around her middle now. Her back ached constantly and sometimes she thought she'd just fall over from the weight of her stomach.

Guessing the time of year must be nearing the end of December, she realized she was now twenty-one years old, and hadn't seen Noah in almost nine months.

Though she tried not to worry about him, and tried to believe he was alive and loved her, she wanted to believe he'd come back. Sometimes her resolve was so weak she wished she had never met him, then she'd cry and hug her pillow to her chest and be glad for every moment she'd had with him.

Rubbing her hand over her stomach, she felt the kick as the baby rolled slowly beneath her touch. He hadn't been really active the last few days, not like he had weeks before when he seemed to be using her bladder to bounce on. She read through the book the doctor had given her again and again, and didn't find anything that said it was abnormal for the baby to quit moving as much as he used to.

Sometime during the first week of January, Carrie woke up in the middle of the night. Her backache was worse than it had ever been before and she couldn't get comfortable. She got out of bed, stoked the fire to life, and made a cup of tea. As she paced back and forth, the pain in her back suddenly reached around her abdomen and squeezed.

Carrie wasn't sure she could make it back to the bed, but when the pain began to ease some, she made it and sat down heavily. She lit the oil lamp, picked up the book from the doctor and opened it to the chapter that told her how to tell when labor began. She read it quickly, and then paused when the next contraction began.

When it had passed, Carrie pushed herself to her feet and gathered together the things she'd need to deliver the baby, and hoped she could remember everything she was supposed to do. As the night faded into morning and the pain increased in frequency and duration, all Carrie could think was she was alone and Noah should be there with her.

By late morning, Carrie was exhausted and hadn't managed to rest much between contractions. By early evening, Carrie was sure she was dying and the book had been completely wrong about how this was supposed to work. But when her water broke it relieved some of the pressure she'd been feeling low in her abdomen. Shortly afterwards, the pain became so intense she couldn't resist the urge to bear down.

Carrie panted and pushed, screamed, and pushed some more. She felt as if she was being ripped in two and would never survive the birth of her child. After nearly thirty minutes of pushing, she couldn't endure the pain anymore and forced herself up, then stood facing the bed, bent over with her hands flat against the mattress.

The pain eased some and made her somewhat more comfortable, then suddenly she felt something happening. Reaching with one hand between her legs, she felt the baby's head. Carrie got onto the bed on her hands and knees, rocked back and forth, and a few minutes later, the baby was lying between her legs, screaming louder than she was.

Carrie managed to turn around and took the scissors and string, tied the cord and cut it, then wiped the baby's face with a soft cloth and wrapped it up. She hadn't even notice if it was a boy or girl because the afterbirth delivered and she had too much to take care of.

Holding the baby close, she slept and when the baby cried, Carrie woke and watched in amazement as the baby rooted at her breast until she'd found a nipple and began sucking greedily. When the baby finally went back to sleep, Carrie put her on her father's bed, then went about to the task of cleaning up herself and the bed.

By the time she was finished, she was exhausted and barely had the energy to slip a nightgown over her head. She lay down and went back to sleep until the baby woke her again. And that was how the next few days went, sleeping when the baby slept, feeding her when she was awake.

Carrie had finally rested enough to have the energy to unwrap the baby and sponge her off, put a diaper on her and wrap her in a clean blanket. She had a daughter, and she couldn't believe it. The baby had a mass of dark hair that clung to her head in tight ringlets, and she reminded Carrie of Noah.

She thought of his life, of all he had been through, and decided to name their daughter Sarah, after his mother. Carrie didn't know if she should use Noah's last name for her daughter since Noah wasn't there, and Carrie didn't want to be presumptuous. But after a few minutes of thought she decided she would give the baby Noah's name and if the subject ever came up in town, she'd just use Noah's last name as well.

Naming Sarah Ann Mosely after both her mother and Noah's mother, Carrie held the baby in front of her and said "Hello, Sarah Ann Mosley. I've been waiting for you." She smiled at her sleeping daughter, and then kissed her gently on the cheek.

Carrie spent the next several weeks getting to know her daughter and trying to keep up with her feeding schedule. Carrie didn't know how someone so small could eat so much, but the baby never seemed to get enough. And when she wasn't eating, she was filling her diaper.

Carrie washed diapers daily, and by the end of the second week she had managed to get Sarah to sleep long enough periods between feedings to get outside to the barn and take care of the animals.

It was full winter now and the snow had piled up in deep drifts against the cabin. Carrie knew it would be at least springtime before Noah would be able to make it back.

Carrie hoped he would be back by then anyway. She hoped he would be happy he was a father, and even though her heart told her he would be, her mind had a way of warping everything her heart said.

Her mind doubted everything she thought he felt for her, and everything she thought she felt for him. Her mind doubted if he had ever been there at all, and if not for the baby he left her, her heart might have wondered the same thing.

Carrie loved Noah. She thought she loved him from the first moment she had seen him, the first time she had held a gun to his head, and she smiled at the memory. She'd never known a man more determined, stronger in body or mind, than Noah. He was the finest man she'd ever known and she knew in her heart if he was able to come back to her, he would. No matter how her mind tried to convince her otherwise.

She picked up Sarah and held her close. She loved the way her daughter smelled, the way she felt, the way she sounded when she cried. She loved the way the baby scrunched up her little face, the way she looked when she yawned, and the startled look on her face when she sneezed. She loved the way Sarah wrapped her little hand around Carrie's finger and held it tight, and she loved the way Sarah smiled in her sleep.

Carrie cuddled the baby and stroked her cheek, gently pulled one dark ringlet out straight and let it go, then smiled as it snapped back into place like a spring. Sarah was a miracle that Carrie couldn't comprehend. She was a gift made from the love between Noah and herself, and she cherished every moment with their daughter.

The weeks turned into months and Carrie and Sarah fell into a perfect rhythm. Carrie's life was Sarah, and when spring finally pushed winter aside, Sarah was laughing, cooing and demanding her mother's undivided attention.

Carrie fashioned a sling to carry Sarah in. It hung across her chest and tied around her waist keeping the baby cozy and warm next to her mother's heart. Carrie was able to do her chores without leaving Sarah in the cabin, and she was afraid to leave her alone for more than a minute anyway. The sling had been made out of necessity, but was proving to be more than just a convenient way to carry the baby.

As Sarah grew larger, Carrie changed the design a bit and made leg holes so Sarah could sit upright while facing Carrie. And she left her dress unbuttoned so Sarah could easily access her breasts anytime she wanted.

By the time summer was in high heat, Sarah could sit up on her own and began getting up on her hands and knees attempting to crawl. Carrie took her to the pool at the creek every day and the two of them swam and splashed together in the cool water. By the time fall arrived again, Sarah could swim short distances by herself, and saying *Mama* in a very loud, demanding voice.

Carrie had begun feeding her daughter bites of vegetables cooked very soft, and Sarah loved feeding herself scrambled eggs. By the time winter had arrived again and Carrie was twenty-three, she couldn't believe she'd ever lived without her daughter in her life. She didn't know how she'd ever managed without her, and spent the evenings while Sarah slept making the growing baby new clothes, and used the leggings Noah had left for her over a year ago to make Sarah little booties and leggings.

When Sarah's first birthday arrived, Carrie baked a cake and covered it in fluffy frosting, then set it before Sarah and watched her eat with both hands. By the time she finished, she had frosting from head to toe and laughed as loudly as her mother.

Carrie missed Noah every single day, especially now that Sarah's coloring had finally evened out. She had liquid gold eyes just like Noah's, fringed with dark eyelashes and thin, arched brows. Her hair turned the color of brown sugar, shot through with pure gold that reflected brightly in the sunlight. It hung in loose curls past her shoulders and bounced when she attempted to walk.

Sarah's beautiful light caramel-colored skin turned golden brown when exposed to the sun. Carrie thought she was the most beautiful child in the world, and thought of how much her own mother would have loved being a grandmother.

During the winter weeks indoors, Sarah learned to walk and Carrie took her outside to play in the snow. She never allowed Sarah to stay out very long, and Sarah screamed and kicked when Carrie brought her back inside. She stood at the cabin door and beat her little hand against it as big tears rolled down her cheeks, and she looked so sad when she turned to see if her mother was watching. Carrie only smiled and picked her up, wiped the tears from her cheeks and distracted her with a bit of honey or pudding.

By the time spring came again, Sarah could walk and run like she had been doing it for years instead of weeks, and followed Carrie as she went about her daily chores. She showed Sarah how to gather eggs and if Sarah held one too tightly and screamed when it ran through her fingers, Carrie only laughed and hugged her close.

She also showed the little girl how to hold the cow's teat and pull to get milk, causing Sarah to squeal with delight. And except for Noah not being there, Carrie thought they had the perfect life.

Then one day in late summer while Carrie picked vegetables from the garden and Sarah squished a tomato in both hands, Carrie sensed, more than heard, someone behind her. When she turned around an Indian with long white hair stood very still observing her.

Carrie stood slowly, then moved toward Sarah and picked her up. She didn't know who this man was or what he wanted, and she didn't know his language. She looked at him and looked around for a weapon, but there was nothing. The Henry's was in the house hanging on the wall above the door where Sarah couldn't reach it.

"Do not be afraid," the man finally said in broken English.

"Who are you?" Carrie asked.

"Called White Bear. You are white woman where Dark Horse come."

Carrie remembered Noah speaking fondly of White Bear, and remembered his Indian name was Dark Horse. She sighed with relief. This man would not hurt her or her daughter.

"My name is Carrie," she told him. "This is Sarah."

He nodded and continued looking at them both with those intense, piercing black eyes. He didn't move and didn't speak again for the longest time.

Finally, he said, "Dark Horse has child."

He didn't say it as a question, but Carrie answered him anyway.

"Yes, this is Noah's daughter. He doesn't know."

White Bear nodded once, and then said, "You do not know where he is."

"No," Carrie said and shook her head. "I haven't seen him in over two years." She walked closer to the man, and then said, "He will be back. I know he will."

And she fought hard to keep the tears from falling. White Bear only nodded, and Carrie asked, "Won't you come inside and have something to eat with us?"

White Bear nodded and followed her into the cabin. He looked around and nodded again, then sat on the bed that had been Carrie's fathers. "You give medicine for Running Elk."

Carrie smiled and looked up at him as she prepared their meal. "He was hurt badly. I helped Noah take care of him. I hope he is well."

"He is."

White Bear nodded and Carrie went back to preparing the food. When she turned to check on Sarah, the little girl had fallen fast asleep sitting on White Bear's lap.

~ TWELVE ~

Noah spent months and months in Arkansas, Texas, and all over the Indian Territory combing through the mountains, the valleys, and places where no white man, or Negro, had ever gone. He sat in the lodges of one tribe after another, explaining the advantages of willingly stopping the raids on the settlers and giving up to the Calvary.

He doubted he did any good for anyone because he understood the Indians felt cheated, lied to, and robbed. The government had broken every treaty they'd signed with the Indians, had stolen their land, brought their diseases into the tribe, and allowed the People to starve.

They'd seen their men slaughtered, their women raped, their children murdered, and still the Indians had been willing to listen to presidents, governors, and military officers. But now the Indians were not willing to listen to anymore white men, they only wanted the white men dead.

Noah tried to reason with them, explained the whites were too many for the Indians to fight, had too many weapons the Indians didn't have, and no matter how many whites the Indians killed, they'd only be replaced with more whites. They weren't going to go away, they weren't going to stop until all Indians were either dead or on the reservations.

Noah didn't want to see any more Indians die, didn't want to come upon the remains of summer villages torn apart, littered with remains of children lying in the dirt. Nor did he want to see any more white settlements burned to the ground, women dead with their children cold in their arms. And he didn't know how to make either side see they were not accomplishing anything except creating more hostility.

Noah dressed as the Indians did, and most whites thought he was an Indian. The Indians never thought he was one of them, but word of him had spread throughout the Indian tribes. It seemed that for as remote and private as the Indians were, rumors moved as fast between the tribes as they did among the whites.

By the summer of 1870, Noah had become well known throughout both the white and Indian worlds, and he'd been to Washington with Major Johnson and General Harrington to meet President Ulysses S. Grant and Lieutenant-General William T. Sherman. He also met Jefferson Long, the first black man to be elected to the U.S. House of Representatives, and Hiram Revels, who was the first Negro U.S. Senator. Mr. Revels had finished Jefferson Davis's term in the senate when Mr. Davis resigned to become the first, and only, President of the Confederate States.

Noah didn't understand why he was there meeting truly important men when he was nothing more than a runaway slave who spoke the Indian language. He hadn't done much, as far as he saw it, to change the way things were going with the *Indian Wars*, as the whites called it. But he dressed in a suit, wore boots shined to a high gloss and shook the hands of those important men and thanked them when they told him what a fine job he was doing for his country.

He sat at their table and ate their fine meals, sipped their fine French wines. And sat in their library, smoked their cigars and drank their brandy. He gave his opinion when they asked him, and they asked him a lot. They spoke to him as if he were one of them and not as a slave, not as a field nigger, not as a Negro they had to placate. They spoke to him as if he had something valuable to share, as if what he thought mattered to them, as if he belonged there with them. And he had never been so glad to leave any place in his life.

He rode the train from Washington to St. Louis with Major Johnson and General Harrington. There they learned the Apaches had attacked settlers in New Mexico and Texas and were moving to the plains. They feared the Indians were forming an alliance against the whites and if that happened, there simply were not enough men in the Army to stop them.

As General Sherman had told the president, "We would need alone on the plains a hundred thousand men, mostly of cavalry... and we still could not protect the over five thousand miles of frontier clamoring for us to stop the raids."

As long as the Indians fought as individual groups, remained disjointed in their method of attacks, the Army had an advantage and would be able to bring them under control. If they ever united as a single entity and fought as a single Indian nation, they would win the war. The government knew it, the Army knew it, and at present, the only ones who didn't know it were the Indians themselves.

In Missouri, Noah spoke to the governor and then moved on to Arizona to meet with Apache Chief Bear Killer. Arranging the meeting was not an easy one, and Noah went in unarmed except for the Bowie knife he'd brought as a gift for the chief. He also brought blankets, pots for cooking, and ten stallions that'd never been ridden.

The Army refused his request for the gifts he wanted to give the chief but once the Governor of Missouri spoke on his behalf, he was given the items. Noah didn't want to bring worthless gifts—he wanted to give the chief something useful, something of value to show the Apache Chief he was sincere and truly desired to speak with him as an equal.

Chief Bear Killer was younger than Noah, and had been spoon-fed hatred of the white man all of his life. He was arrogant from the success he'd experienced at a very young age, and he made it quite apparent that killing Noah was always in the front of his mind.

Noah had an easy demeanor and never showed fear. He knew it was important to the chief he show respect, but never fear. He didn't talk down to the chief, and didn't treat him as if he didn't know what he was doing either. Noah was well aware of Chief Bear Killer's reputation and knew he had fought hard to get to where he was.

His mother was a *senorita* from south of the border, a captive his father had kept for some time, and though the real story might never be known, it was said that after Bear Killer's birth, his father killed his mother and then tried to drown the boy in the river. The story went that a female bear had found the wet and starving babe on the banks of the White River and raised him as her own.

Then, when he was twelve, and food was nowhere to be found, he killed the female bear, roasted her meat and used her fur as clothing. Then he went looking for his father. When he found him several years later, he slit the old man's throat while looking him in the eye, telling him who he was.

Noah knew the story had grown larger over the years with each telling, and he thought by now the chief might even believe it had happened that way. It didn't matter though—all Noah needed was for the chief to listen to him and let him walk away alive. Noah also knew walking away wasn't the problem, it was the *alive* part that worried him. But as things go sometimes, Chief Bear Killer had heard a few stories about Noah as well, and that was the real reason he had agreed to meet with him.

Noah's reputation as a man who was as big as a bear, and as strong as one, had preceded him. The chief heard Noah's mother was an Indian maiden who was out bathing in the river alone one day, and as she came out of the water she came face to face with the rare, and more rarely seen, black cougar. It was said the black cougar had spotted the Indian maiden and stalked her with the intent of eating her, but when she came out of the water he was mesmerized by the beauty of her naked body and the look in her strange blue eyes.

Instead of making a meal of her, the black cougar seduced her and mated with her instead, producing the golden-eyed son. Noah had been made aware of the story earlier in the year and shook his head when Elijah related it to him. Where such nonsense came from was a mystery to Noah, but if Chief Bear Killer believed it, then maybe he would walk away alive after all.

Noah sat cross-legged before the fire with the Apache braves between him and Chief Bear Killer as the pipe was passed around. Noah accepted the pipe and took a few token puffs, but he'd been forewarned about truly smoking the Apache pipe. The Apaches smoked the heart of a certain cactus found in the desert that induced hallucinations. Noah needed his wits about him, especially if a group of wild Apaches were going to be hallucinating.

It was a good sign the chief accepted the gifts with what seemed to be true appreciation, and he was especially interested in the horses. Noah waited an appropriate amount of time before speaking of the business at hand, and when he'd finished, Chief Bear Killer sat with a grim expression on his face, his jaw clenching and unclenching as he considered Noah's words.

"And what will happen if we agree to go back to our own land? Will the Army leave us alone? Will they never come after us again? Will they stay off our land?"

Noah shook his head slightly. "I cannot tell you they will. I can only tell you that you will die if you attack anymore settlements, or if you come against the Army."

"Then we will die," Chief Bear Killer stated with feeling. "We will not sit on our own land, sit in our lodge and wait for the Army to kill us and take our land from us. They may take it from us, but they will also die with us."

Noah understood this man, understood all too well, and when he left the next morning, he shook the chief's hand and wished him well. Chief Bear Killer's eyes held Noah's, and he knew the man before him had seen as much sorrow and grief in his life as he had. They may never be friends, but the chief knew they were of kindred spirits and presented his own bow and quiver of arrows as a gift to Noah.

Noah was touched by the expression, and accepted the gift without saying a word, as was Indian custom. But he ran his hand over the items, examined them as carefully as the chief had examined the horses, pulled an arrow from the quiver and notched it in the bow. He raised the bow, pulled the arrow back, inhaled, then exhaled slowly and let the arrow fly. It flew straight and true, hitting its mark, a flower that had bloomed atop a cactus.

Noah slung the quiver over his back, hung the bow on one shoulder and mounted his horse. He looked at Chief Bear Killer one last time and both nodded slightly to the other as Noah rode away.

When he met up with Elijah once again he said nothing for a long while. Then Elijah asked him what he thought about the chief and Noah smiled. What did he think of the chief? He thought the Army was in a whole lot of trouble.

But instead he said, "I think he's an intelligent man and I think he would rather fight than surrender. He's tired of being told where he can go, how he's supposed to live, and I really can't blame him."

Elijah grinned. "I thought you'd like him."

~ THIRTEEN ~

Carrie and Sarah had survived another winter and now that Sarah had turned two years old, she talked all of the time, even if Carrie didn't quite understand every-thing she said. Sarah constantly amazed her mother. Sarah couldn't quite believe her daughter's intelligence, inquisit-iveness, and her natural curiosity about all things around her. She kept Carrie busy throughout the days, and after she fell asleep at night, Carrie sat watching her child's peaceful face while she sewed or knitted.

Carrie thought about Noah, wondered if he was still alive, and wondered if she only waited for a ghost. She tried not to think the worst, but as the months and years slipped away, she found it more and more difficult not to.

White Bear appeared occasionally to visit, bringing fresh meat or furs. He seemed to adore Sarah, and Sarah was absolutely intrigued by him. She could now say *Bear*, and squealed with delight whenever he appeared. He picked her up and carried her in his arms or on his should-ers, and seemed quite proud.

White Bear had enjoyed being a father, and losing his wife and sons to the white man was the hardest thing he'd ever had to bear. Noah had been like a son to him, and now that Noah had a child, White Bear felt as if he were back in time twenty years. He enjoyed Carrie's company as well. She was a strong woman, like his wife had been. He admired Carrie's tenacity, her ability to go on alone, to raise her child, and to believe Noah would return.

It was high summer and Carrie and Sarah had waved good-bye to White Bear earlier that morning and then went out to do the chores. Afterward, they picked wild-flowers and Carrie left Sarah sitting outside holding the flowers on her lap while she ran inside to find a jar to put them in.

Sarah played with the pretty petals and giggled aloud as a butterfly landed on her knee. The man standing at the edge of the woods stopped and watched the golden haired child with flowers on her lap and smiled. He had been so sure of himself right up until the moment he reached the edge of the forest and saw the little girl.

He slid off his horse to the ground and looked around. Everything around the cabin looked the same to him, but when he saw the child, he wondered if Carrie had left, if someone else now lived there. But when he saw Carrie walk out of the cabin and kneel next to the child, his heart pounded in his chest.

Had she found someone else? Had she married another? Noah hadn't let those thoughts rear their ugly heads in his mind, even though they'd tried. But now he didn't know if he should continue on, or turn around and walk away. He took a deep breath and blew it out, then decided if she had found someone else, he was going to make her tell him to his face. He hadn't come all this way to turn around without so much as an explanation.

With his horse left to graze, Noah walked out of the woods and across the clearing on silent feet, watching Carrie and the child place the flowers in a jar. He was cautious, watching to see if there was anyone else about; he didn't want to get shot. He almost laughed, it would be funny for him to have survived all this time with warring Indians and white men only to be shot while walking across a clearing.

He was less than fifty feet from them when Carrie suddenly stopped what she was doing and turned her head slowly in his direction. Noah froze mid-step, and Carrie just sat and stared. They looked at each other for a long, suspended moment before Carrie came to her feet and ran toward him.

"Noah!"

She screamed and launched herself at him. He caught her and wrapped his big arms around her, crushing his lips against hers. Carrie cried and kissed him all over his face, saying his name over and over.

"Are you real? Are you really here?" She held his face in her hands and looked into his golden eyes.

"I'm real."

He kissed her again and tears streamed down both their faces. He held her as tightly as he could and continued to kiss her. He'd dreamed of this moment so many long, lonely nights. She felt so good, even better than he remembered, and he didn't want to let her go. Ever.

"Mama, mama. Mama!" Sarah shouted and tugged on Carrie's dress. "Mama, mama!"

Carrie pushed away from Noah, made him put her feet back on the ground and bent over to pick up their daughter. Noah looked at Carrie, then at the little girl she held and saw his own eyes staring back at him.

He couldn't speak. Staring, afraid to speak, afraid what he was thinking wouldn't be real, and even though he could see himself in the face of this child, he didn't want Carrie to tell him it wasn't true.

Carrie looked from father to daughter and wiped her face. She grinned broadly at the emotion in Noah's eyes, and she could see he knew.

"This is Sarah," she said softly. "I named her for your mother."

Noah's eyes flickered, looked from Sarah to Carrie and back to Sarah again. "Can I hold her?"

"Sarah, this is your papa," Carrie said to their daughter. "Do you want Papa to hold you?"

Sarah continued to stare wide-eyed at the man, and then she reached out and touched his face.

"Papa," she said softly, and Noah thought his knees would buckle beneath him. Sarah leaned toward him and he took her into his arms.

121

She laid her head against him and patted his shoulder with her little hand. Noah was afraid to breathe, afraid to move. In his wildest dreams, he'd not expected this. Had not expected to have a family waiting for him. He was only hoping to still find Carrie at the cabin, to find she still wanted him, but this? He was totally overwhelmed.

Later that evening Carrie tucked Sarah into bed and turned back to look at Noah. She couldn't believe he was there, finally, after all the time that had passed. Carrie was still afraid she'd turn around to find he'd never really been there at all.

Noah stood and took a step toward her, then she was in his arms again and she couldn't stop crying. All the months and years of loneliness poured out of her and Noah held her close, kissed the top of her head and let her cry. He picked her up, carried her to the bed, and sat down with Carrie on his lap, cradling her like a baby. And still she cried. It took more than twenty minutes before she had cried it all out and could speak again.

"I thought you were dead," she sniffled. "I tried not to think like that, but the longer you were gone, the harder it was to believe you were coming back."

"I'm so sorry, Carrie. I'm so sorry. I should never have left you."

"I woke up the night you brought the tunic and leggings and tried to catch you. I wanted you to know about the baby but I couldn't find you."

"I'm so sorry," he said again and held her even closer.

"Are you here to stay?"

"For a while, Carrie. I've been working for the government with the Indians, trying to help bring peace. I have more work to do yet."

"How long will you stay?"

"Till the end of summer. I had to see you, I couldn't stay away any longer but I felt so guilty for leaving you, guilty because Running Elk died, guilty because I couldn't do anything to help. Then I met Major Elijah Johnson and found Negroes all over the states are doing important work, even in Washington."

Then he told her the long story of how Running Elk and the others had died, and how he met Elijah Johnson.

"I'd been up in the mountains so long I didn't know what was going on in the world, and when I found out there was a place for me, I had to see. I don't mean that it's easy, because it's not. The whites still have a long way to go." He grinned.

"They still segregate their saloons, hotels and buildings, but I can see the war did a lot more than just free slaves and it gives me hope."

"What about us, Noah? Is there an us?"

"Oh, Carrie," he said and then kissed her slowly. "I wanted to take you to the tribe to marry you in an Indian ceremony because I know no white man will marry us. I still want to."

"Really?" Carrie grinned from ear to ear. "White Bear will be so happy to see you. He just left this morning."

"He's been here?"

"Several times. He showed up one day last summer, and when he saw Sarah, he knew immediately you were her father. He brings us fresh meat and furs, and Sarah adores him. I think he just missed you so much that he came here to feel closer to you."

"Will you go with me, Carrie? Will you marry me again?"

Carrie kissed him and caressed his face. "I'll go with you, Noah. I love you so much. I want nothing more than to be your wife again, and forever."

Noah moved her from his lap and reached into a pocket, then held up a small gold ring. He took her hand and slid the ring over her finger. He looked into her eyes and said, "Till death do us part."

123

"Yes, Noah," Carrie breathed looking at the gold band on her finger. "Till death do us part."

~ * ~

They left the next morning to go to the tribe's summer camp. Noah wanted them married, but he also wanted to talk to White Bear, to try and convince him that fighting the white man would come to no good thing.

They took their time, Noah on his horse, Carrie riding Nellie, with Sarah in front her father. When she became fussy, Carrie brought her to sit in front of her.

When they arrived at the tribe nearly four days later, White Bear didn't seem surprised at all to see the three of them together. Sarah ran as fast as her little legs would carry her when she saw White Bear. She giggled and squealed when he picked her up and swung her high in the air. White Bear held her in his arms and looked at Noah with a wide grin on his face.

"I knew you would come back," White Bear said in English, surprising Noah.

"I should've been back long ago," Noah said, his gaze shifting to Sarah. "I'm sorry to tell you Running Elk and the others were killed by the white men. There was nothing I could do. I tried." Noah took a deep breath and swallowed the lump in his throat.

"I know," White Bear said. "They are with the ancestors. They are happy."

Noah hoped they were. He thought of his mother and hoped she'd gone to be with her ancestors who had died in Africa before the white man came, and he hoped she was happy as well.

"I want to marry Carrie," Noah said.

"Good." White Bear nodded with satisfaction.

Just as the sun began to set they stood on a hill, bathed in golden light with all the members of the tribe and were married by the tribal shaman. The women had dressed Carrie in a traditional ceremonial wedding dress and decorated her hair with beads. Noah dressed in a long tunic and leggings complete with fringe, intricately beaded and worked with bone.

They feasted most of the night and danced in the firelight, and when dawn began to break, the women of the tribe led Carrie to the wedding lodge where they undressed and bathed her, then left her lying softly scented and nude on a pile of furs. Noah entered the lodge and smiled at his wife as he began undressing himself. He knelt on the furs beside her and let his fingers slide slowly down her body.

Her golden brown hair spread out around her, reflecting red from the dim firelight. She was even more beautiful now than she'd been when he first saw her. She'd become a woman in his absence, a mother, and her body had matured and rounded. He hadn't thought it possible, but her beauty seemed to cause her to glow, and it wasn't just how she looked or the shape of her body.

It was in everything she said, the gestures of her hands, the way she laughed. It was in the way she held Sarah, the way she looked at him with her bottom lip caught between her teeth, her green eyes glowing with passion when he touched her. She was everything beauty could be and so much more. And she was his. It was the last coherent thought.

They spent the night making love, talking of their future and Noah's role in the Indian wars. He'd had little success with White Bear, but had gotten him to agree there would be no more attacks on whites perpetrated by any of the men there. They could live in the mountains for years to come with no one knowing about them if they didn't draw attention to themselves.

Noah knew of things going on within the government he wasn't allowed to reveal to anyone else, not even Carrie, and he knew it wouldn't be long before the Indians would have no choice but to accept their fate and move to the reservations, or die resisting. Noah pushed all thoughts of the government and the Indian wars out of his mind and focused on the naked woman lying on top of him.

Carrie was gloriously happy while they were with the tribe and she wished they could stay right there forever. She wanted to pretend there was no world outside of the one they were living in right then. She wanted to be where Noah was, where Noah wouldn't go away again, where they could live together in peace and happiness.

She spent her days with the women learning how to prepare animal skins to be used for clothing, and furs for keeping warm in the winter. She learned how to prepare the meat, to dry it so it would last through the winter, and she learned how to keep pumpkins and squash fresh through the long, cold days as well.

Sarah played with the other children and her dark golden curls and liquid gold eyes were a novelty to the Indian children.

By the time the air began to grow cooler and the sun began setting earlier, Carrie knew fall had come and Noah told her they had to go back to the cabin. They packed their things and wound up leaving with furs and hides and meat hung over another horse that followed along behind Noah's.

White Bear wanted Carrie to have another horse in case she had to go into town for supplies again, and it would be easier for two horses to pull the wagon than it was for Nellie alone. Carrie hugged the women and children, and she kissed White Bear on the cheek. Sarah waved bye-bye as she sat in front of her father and they began the long ride home.

Less than a week later they reached the cabin, and as Carrie unpacked the horses, Noah went to work immediately chopping wood and working on the other things Carrie and Sarah would need in his absence.

Noah stayed with his family another few weeks, but by the end of October, he had to leave. The Army planned to bring some of the northern tribes in during the winter months when they were at their weakest and not expecting the Army. They would then escort the tribes south to the reservations. Noah told Carrie if all went well, he should be home by early summer.

They spent their last week together walking hand-in-hand through the woods with Sarah perched on Noah's shoulders. They made love when she slept, and by that time, Carrie knew she was expecting another baby who would be born in June. Noah promised he'd be home before the baby came. And he hoped he'd told her the truth.

He felt obligated to Elijah, obligated to the Indians, but he was responsible for Carrie and their children, and wanted to tell the major this would be his last service.

He kissed Sarah and put her on the bed, then held Carrie to him and kissed her long and slow as they said good-bye. She stood with Sarah on her hip as they watched him ride away, and Carrie didn't cry until he became a tiny speck in the distance and then disappeared.

~ FOURTEEN ~

As hard as it was to leave his family, Noah wanted to see to the business that lay ahead of him so he could be finished with it once and for all. He'd have his bonus from the government and he wanted to take Carrie somewhere new, build her a fine home like she had lived in before the war in Charleston. He wanted her to wear fine gowns and set her table with china and crystal. And he wanted his daughter to go to school and learn to dance and play the piano. He wanted to give his women the best he could, and he knew it wasn't going to be easy.

Noah knew the white men well, had seen how they treated men like him before the war, knew that even since the war Negroes still hadn't had an easy life. He also knew that because of his light skin, he was more readily accepted than most people of his race, and he knew because of his relationship with the Indians, the government treated him well.

However, he also knew that one day his services would no longer be required and he'd have nothing coming from the United States Government. Noah planned to do what he had to do now so when the time came, he could walk away with enough cash to provide for his wife and daughter.

Noah had never lived a fanciful life, had never dreamed of living any way except free, but Carrie made him want. He wanted her, wanted to give her more, and he wanted his daughter to have all she should in life without anyone judging her because of her mixed blood.

Now he had a second child soon to be born, a child he hoped would be a boy. He loved his daughter of course, more than he ever thought possible, but he wanted a son to carry on his name. And maybe his son would grow up to be an important man, one that might even change the world. Noah smiled at the thought, but he knew better than anyone that anything was possible. He was living proof and his only regret was that his mother hadn't lived to see it.

~ * ~

He rode to St. Louis where he met Major Johnson. The news of events that had occurred in his absence was grim, and Noah knew it was only going to get worse before it got better. The Army hoped with the coming winter the raids by Indians would decrease and give the Army a chance to rest as well. There had been many casualties over the summer and fall, supplies were running low, and they desperately needed more men.

Many of the freed men from the southern states were now moving into the plains states in search of work. The poor southern whites took over the field jobs once belonging to slaves, and white plantation owners hired white men before they hired Negroes. Also, white organizations had formed, such as the Ku Klux Klan, and Negroes were beaten and hanged for taking jobs when white men were out of work.

At Fort Louis there was a tremendous increase in black men wanting to join the Army. The pay was only twelve dollars a month, but clothing, food, horses and weapons were provided by the Army, and offered the freed men a sense of independence they'd never known before.

From November through January, Noah spent his time at the fort helping Major Johnson train new ranks. Noah tried to instill in the men what he knew of the Indian tribes and compared it to how they had been treated as slaves. The men seemed to understand much better than General Sherman suspected they would. Noah had a way with people – black, white and Indian, and the General had to admit, Noah made life at the fort run more smoothly.

However, on January 24, 1871 Comanche's attacked and killed Britton "Brit" Johnson, Major Elijah Johnson's cousin. Brit and two other Negro cowboys were hauling supplies for the troops and all three were killed. It was somewhat of a surprise that the men had been killed since Brit had often recovered Indian captives from whites, as well as from other Indian tribes, and he was one of the best shots Noah knew.

Noah thought maybe it was Brit's friendship with the Comanche's that had gotten him killed. Perhaps he'd not thought they would fire on him until it was already too late. Whatever the case, the murders sparked a series of attacks by various tribes and Noah headed back to Indian Territory.

It was March and Noah had chased rogue Indians near the Red River, but he'd found none of the guilty. The only thing he had found was a few burned out settlements, the bodies of white settlers, and a few people who actually managed to survive the attacks.

Noah sent some of the men to escort the survivors back to the nearest fort, then headed north, telling the major he'd rejoin them later. He didn't know why, but he wanted to make sure everything was all right and headed toward home. Toward Carrie and their daughter.

Nearly dusk when he arrived, Noah unsaddled his horse and left it in the barn with fresh water and hay, then went to the cabin and opened the door slowly. Carrie stood before the stove, fixing supper for herself and Sarah, and the cabin felt warm and inviting. Sarah looked up from where she played with a rag doll Carrie made for her. She squealed when she saw Noah, and laughed when he scooped her up and kissed her cheek. Carrie grinned at the sight and went to the pair. Noah wrapped one arm around her and leaned over to kiss her as he pushed the door shut with his foot.

"I wasn't expecting you," Carrie said as she leaned into him.

"There's been trouble to the south," he said. "I wanted to make sure you were safe."

He set Sarah on her feet and gathered Carrie in both arms and crushed her mouth beneath his. The scent of her filled his nostrils, the feel of her seeped into his blood and he took the kiss deeper. *How could I ever live without her?* He never expected to have her, but now that he did, he knew he'd never be able to survive without her.

Carrie loved the taste of him, the feel of his hard, powerful body against hers. She fell into the kiss, let it go on and on and wished they'd never have to stop. But then she put her hands flat against his chest and pushed gently, breaking the kiss. She grinned up at him, licked her lips as she looked into his liquid gold eyes.

"Dinner's going to burn," she said softly.

"We can't have that," he said with a grin and patted her swollen belly as she went back to the kitchen.

"How long can you stay?"

Noah sat at the table and lifted Sarah to his lap. "Long enough to eat some of your cooking."

"I wish you could come home for good," Carrie said as she turned the meat. "Will you still be able to be here when the baby comes?"

"Do you still think he will come in July?"

Carrie nodded. "The end of June or beginning of July, if I've figured it right. I went by what the book said, so I hope it's right."

"I'll be here in June and stay until you're well enough for me to leave, Carrie. There's nothing more important to me than you are."

Carrie's heart swelled. She went to him then, bent over and kissed him. She whispered, "I know."

Carrie finished making their supper, set the table and the three of them sat together, joined hands and prayed, then Carried served dinner. Afterward, she cleaned up Sarah and got her ready for bed, then Noah held his daughter and rocked her to sleep. He laid her gently on the bed and kissed her soft cheek as he pulled the bedcovers over her and tucked her in.

Then he turned to Carrie and smiled.

Lifting her hand to his mouth, he kissed the palm, then kissed her wrist and felt her pulse skittering beneath his touch. He kissed her hand again, then pulled her to him and stroked his hand over her cheek, into her hair, fisting itself in the silkiness, and then he lowered his mouth to hers.

The kiss was soft. Liquid. Warm. His tongue moved lazily against hers, and Carrie's hands moved up his arms to his shoulders. The heat spread through his blood, hummed in his ears, caused his heart to race at high speed. When she moved her hands beneath his shirt, and raked her nails over his skin, his back, and down his sides, the muscles rippled beneath her touch, and she heard a low growl rumble in his chest. The kiss went deeper, became more intense and Noah could hold back no longer.

Much later, Noah held her against him, breathing heavily while Carrie sighed with satisfaction. His hard body was warm against hers and she fell asleep in his arms. Carrie didn't know what time it was when she woke to find Noah sitting on the edge of the bed putting on his boots. He turned to her when he felt her hand on his back.

"I'm sorry, darlin'," he said as he stroked her cheek, "but I have to go."

Carrie felt her chest tighten, but she swallowed hard. "I love you, Noah."

Noah felt tears sting his eyes. He hated leaving her, but had no choice at the moment. He leaned over and kissed her softly. "I love you, Carrie. I'll be back as soon as I can."

Carrie nodded as Noah rubbed the pad of his thumb over her lips. Then he was gone again.

Carrie pulled the quilt up tight around her and buried her face in the pillow. Noah's scent was strong, mixed with the scent of their lovemaking, and Carrie inhaled deeply. It was almost dawn before she managed to shut her eyes again and go back to sleep.

~ FIFTEEN ~

Noah joined Major Johnson and rode with him to Fort Sill where General Sherman, along with the Tenth U. S. Calvary, waited for them. Seven settlers had been killed and forty-one mules stolen. General Sherman seemed determined to put an end to the raids, and had set a trap for the raiding Indians by sending an invitation to the chiefs of the tribes to come to the fort.

When they had arrived, all were arrested, including the leader of the raids, Chief Satanta, who was accompanied by Chief Satank, Chief Big Bow, and Chief Lone Wolf, from various bands of the Kiowa Tribe. Troop D of the Tenth Calvary came out of hiding with carbines and pistols ready, and Chief Lone Wolf was the only one who had attempted to fight. He threw back the blanket he wore, uncovering concealed rifle, and pointed it at General Sherman.

The general was alert and quick enough to be able to pull the gun from the chief's hands before the weapon could be fired. During the scuffle, Chief Big Bow attempted to escape, but was stopped before he got very far. While the Calvary dealt with containing the chiefs, hundreds of Indians already confined to the reservation took the opportunity to flee into the hills.

Noah headed up the company tracking the escaped Indians. They rode for three days rounding up scattered braves as they went, and dispatched escorts to return them to the reservation. Spring arrived and the Indians weren't hampered by cold or lack of game for food. It was well into May before they had finally rounded up the last of the escapees, or at least as many as they had any hopes of finding.

Those not found by that late date were supposed to have found their way back to their tribes, or joined forces with marauding bands of Indians. But they had at least chased them west, Noah thought, away from Carrie and Sarah. His biggest fear was that Indians would find the cabin with a woman alone with a child, and he would come home to find them gone and the place burned to the ground.

He knew June was coming to a close and he wanted to be back home with Carrie. He returned to Fort Sill with the last of the Indians they'd captured and asked Elijah to come outside so they could speak privately. Elijah was the only one who knew Noah was married to Carrie, but even Elijah didn't know she was a white woman.

"My wife is due to give birth any day," Noah said. "I have to be there for her. I wasn't there when our daughter was born, and I'm afraid if I miss this one, she'll have my head." He managed a grin as he turned his hat around in his hands.

Elijah looked at him for a few moments with a smile playing on his lips. "Noah, how long have we known each other now? Three years?" Noah nodded. "How is it that I've never been invited to meet your wife?"

Noah took a deep breath. He and Elijah were friends, and he'd met Elijah's family. They lived near Fort Louis and he'd eaten supper there on more than one occasion. Noah spoke of his wife and daughter often, and even though Elijah's wife, Mabel, had made him promise to bring them for a visit, he'd never told Elijah the reason he never got around to it.

He looked at the hat in his hands, blew out the breath he'd been holding, then looked at Elijah and grinned. "It's nothing personal, Eli, but I've got my reasons. I didn't want anyone to talk or cause problems for us." He shrugged and looked at Elijah for a long moment. "She's white."

~ * ~

Elijah didn't say anything for a long while as he thought of the consequences that could go along with such an admission. He wouldn't have told anyone either if it had been his wife and child at risk for the reprisals that could come. Marrying a black man wasn't unheard of, but it was far from being accepted by white society.

Elijah knew of a Negro man who had married an Indian woman, and he knew of a Negro man who had married a Mexican *senorita,* and even then, they were treated as all Negroes were treated.

He had also heard of a Negro man who'd been secretly seeing a white woman back east, and when the relationship was found out, the man had been beaten to death and the woman shunned from society. She eventually packed up and moved out west where no one knew her.

Elijah understood why Noah hadn't wanted anyone to know he was married to a white woman. It could possibly mean his death, or even the death of his wife. And they had a daughter to think of as well.

"I appreciate you telling me, Noah," Elijah said and clapped Noah on the back. "You don't have to worry about anyone finding out from me."

"I know that." Noah smiled and nodded. "You're welcome to come out anytime you're in the area. I know Carrie would be thrilled to have company."

"You better get yourself going so you don't miss the birth of that baby," Elijah said

"I'll see you in a few weeks."

Noah mounted his horse and rode off. He had another stop to make before he headed back to Carrie.

~ * ~

Carrie managed to get through the spring months, but now as summer settled in high and hot, her stomach grew even larger now than it had been with Sarah, and she moved slower each day.

The morning chores often weren't done until afternoon, and she only planted a small garden that spring, hoping it would be enough to get them through the next winter. She also hoped Noah would make it home in time for the baby's birth.

Her only relief the past few weeks had been the time she spent swimming in the pond with Sarah. It not only cooled them off, but it relieved the pain in Carrie's lower back and the pressure of her extra weight. Sarah swam like a pro now and Carrie marveled at how much the little girl had grown. She was three-and-a-half years old now and a big help to her mother.

Carrie led Sarah out of the water and dried them both off, then slipped their undergarments on before walking back to the cabin. Halfway there, Carrie felt a familiar sensation in her back travel around her mid-section, as the contraction gripped her. She stopped momentarily until the pain subsided, then hurried to get Sarah inside.

She tried to stay calm so she wouldn't frighten her daughter as she got everything she would need together to deliver the baby. When that was done, she made Sarah something to eat and lay back on the bed to wait it out.

~ * ~

Late that night, Noah finally arrived. He had a wagon pulled by a pair of horses behind him, having stopped in the small town of Mena and bought everything he thought Carrie and Sarah might need, and the wagon was piled high.

He went to the barn first and unhitched the horses and put them with his own in the corral with fresh water, hay and oats. He would unload the wagon in the morning, it was late, he was tired and wanted to be in bed next to Carrie more than he wanted anything else at that moment.

Quickly crossing the distance between the barn and the house while pulling his gloves off and wiping his face, Noah knew he needed a bath. He'd been on the trail for six days and was covered in dust and smelled like the horse he'd ridden. But that could wait till morning he thought with a grin, he just wanted to feel Carrie next to him.

He had covered half the distance to the house when he heard a scream, and felt his heart begin pounding as he broke into a dead run.

Hitting the cabin door at a full run, he went inside and found Carrie standing nude next to the bed, bent over with her hands flat against the mattress, obviously in the final stages of delivering their baby. He rushed to her side and put an arm around her.

"I'm here, Carrie, I'm here. Tell me what I can do," he said and brushed the hair back from her face.

Carrie panted. "Noah! Help me!"

Then she screamed again and Noah didn't know what he was supposed to do. Just then he saw a gush of blood and water run down her legs onto the floor. He grabbed a cloth from the bed just in time to catch the baby as it came into the world with Carrie's final scream.

Noah looked at the screaming baby boy he held in his hands, and then looked up at Carrie as she tried to catch her breath.

"I don't know what to do," he said softly.

"Help me onto the bed."

He held the baby, who continued to wail, in one arm and helped Carrie with the other one. When she was finally on the bed, she took the baby from him and told him how to tie and cut the cord. With that done, he delivered the after-birth, then helped clean up his wife and son. Afterward, he sat down heavily on the edge of the bed and stared at them.

"How did you ever do that on your own when Sarah was born?"

Carrie smiled at him as her new son suckled at her breast. "I had no choice," she said softly. "I'm glad you were here this time. I can't believe you made it. I wasn't sure you would."

"I'm glad I did, too," Noah said, as he caressed her cheek, then stroked the baby's head. "He's beautiful. Thank you."

Carrie could see tears in his eyes as she handed the baby to him. Noah took him from her, cradled him gently in his arms and looked at Carrie.

"What's his name?"

"I want to name him after my father if it's all right with you," she answered. "Noah Charles Robertson Mosely."

Noah grinned and nodded. "I think it's perfect." He held the baby boy in front of him and looked at the sleeping face, then whispered, "Hey, Charlie, I'm your papa."

~ * ~

Noah had been home since the 29th of June when Charlie was born and now August was coming to a close. Carrie hadn't asked him when he would leave and secretly hoped maybe he wouldn't if she didn't bring it up. Tired of living alone, and raising their daughter alone, she now had a baby son as well, and she didn't want to be alone anymore.

She dreamed of the four of them being a real family, of Noah getting up early to plow the fields, and coming in at noon for dinner. She dreamed of them adding on to the house, making another room, maybe two more rooms even, so they would have the privacy of their own bedroom. Sarah was getting older now and soon she would notice their lovemaking. Carrie blushed at the thought.

"Mama! Mama!" Carrie heard Sarah and rushed out of the cabin.

"What is... ?"

Carrie stopped where she was and shielded her eyes from the sun as she saw a man in a soldier's uniform dismount. She bent over, lifted Sarah into her arms and walked slowly out to the yard.

Noah had already come out of the barn and spoke earnestly with the stranger, but Carrie knew he wasn't a stranger to Noah, and her heart sank. She'd never met him, but she knew he was Major Elijah Johnson from the description Noah had given her. Noah liked the major and spoke of him often, but Carrie knew he wasn't here just for a visit.

"Carrie," Noah said. He could see in her eyes she expected the visitor wasn't bringing good news, and even though she was right, he wasn't going to tell her just yet.

"This is Major Elijah Johnson," Noah took her hand as he introduced her. "This is my wife, Carrie, and my daughter, Sarah."

Elijah removed his hat and nodded. "Pleased to meet you, ma'am."

"Nice to meet you, Major," she said and tried to smile pleasantly. "Won't you come in and have some sweet tea?"

"That's the best offer I've had all day," Elijah said with a wide grin, as he accepted the offer. "You have a beautiful daughter."

"Thank you, Major. I understand you have children as well," Carrie said as she set Sarah on her feet and opened the door to the cabin.

She entered first, followed by Elijah and Noah. She offered Elijah a seat and went to pour the tea.

"Yes, my wife and I have three sons and a daughter. The oldest boy is almost ten now, and the baby, well, she's hardly a baby anymore," he said with a laugh and accepted the tea from Carrie. "Her name is Abigail and she just turned five. She gives her brothers a run for their money, that's for sure."

Carrie set her tea on the table when Charlie began to cry. She changed his diaper and picked him up while opening the buttons on her dress. She sat on the edge of the bed and fed him while she listened to her husband and Elijah talk about the trouble with the Indians. None of the conversation comforted Carrie.

It was grim as Elijah told them Congress had recently signed an appropriations bill declaring no further treaties were to be signed with the Indian Nations or with individual tribes. It further declared Indians were to be treated on an individual basis, but since they were not considered U.S. citizens, they had no rights.

Carrie felt a shiver run up her spine when she saw Noah's reaction to the news and she knew it meant there would only be more bloodshed.

When Charlie finished eating, Carrie passed him to his father and went to the kitchen to start supper. Noah and Elijah went outside while Carrie cooked. She fried two chickens, boiled fresh ears of corn, mashed potatoes with cream and fresh butter, baked cornbread, made gravy and baked a peach cobbler for dessert. Then she went outside and wiped her face on her apron.

"Give me the baby," she said to Noah. "You two bring the table out here, it's too hot to eat inside. At least there's a breeze now."

"Good idea," Noah said and handed Charlie over, and kissed Carrie's cheek.

He and Elijah went inside and brought the table and new chairs Noah had brought home for Carrie outside into the shade. Then Carrie handed the baby to a surprised and delighted Elijah while she and Noah brought the dishes and food out to the table. Sarah helped by carefully carrying the dish of freshly churned butter outside for her mother.

When they had eaten and not a bite of dessert was left over, Noah walked Elijah out to the barn while Carrie put a sleeping Charlie down. She began clearing the table with Sarah's help, then washed and dried the dishes. Afterward she walked Sarah down to the creek for a bath and sat on a rock while Sarah played in the water.

The sun disappeared and the day hung in shades of purple between light and dark. A light breeze blew through Carrie's hair and brought scents of dried grass and late blooming flowers with it. Carrie drew her knees up and hugged them to her. Noah would be leaving in the morning with Elijah and she didn't want him to go. Not ever again.

She picked up the towel, wrapped it around Sarah and carried her back to the cabin and dressed her. She sat on the bed and held Sarah on her lap and picked up the book of fairy tales Noah had brought home for his daughter.

Carrie had told her daughter stories all of her life, but to now have a book full of fairy tales was as much fun for Carrie as it was for Sarah. Sarah turned to the section of the book she turned to every night since the first night Carrie read to her. She loved the story of *The Princess and The Pea*, and Carrie read it one more time. After she helped Sarah say her prayers, Carrie tucked her beneath the covers next to her brother and kissed them both goodnight.

Carrie left the cabin door open and went outside where it was cooler. Noah sat on a round of wood beside the cabin with his elbows on his knees. He looked up when Carrie walked toward him. He smiled and reached for her, and when she took his hand he drew her to his lap and wrapped his arms around her waist.

"Elijah's bedded down in the barn," he said quietly.

"You're leaving with him in the morning," Carrie said without looking at him. Noah didn't answer, but held her more tightly to him. "It seems like all I've done since I met you is tell you good-bye," Carrie said sadly.

"I know, but it won't be for much longer. By this time next year, I'll be home for good."

Carrie turned in his lap to face him. "Really? You promise?"

Noah kissed her. "I promise. I just want to stay long enough to get the bonus they promised me. Once I get that, we'll have enough money to move anywhere you want to. Enough money to build you a big house like you had in Charleston, and buy you all the things you want.

Sarah will be able to go to school and take piano lessons, and Charlie will grow up to be a fine gentleman. I was thinking of going west. I hear out in the Montana territory the land is rich and fertile and we could raise horses. What do you think?"

"I think I love you more every day than I did the day before," she said and curled into the crook of his arm. "I think I have everything I've ever wanted right here, and I don't need what I had in Charleston. That was my parents' dream, Noah, not mine. You, Sarah and Charlie are my dream. I don't care if we live all our life and die right here in this cabin. You are all I want."

Noah's heart swelled and his blood hummed as he moved his hands over Carrie's body. This woman was the only thing he needed, the only thing he wanted, and right now the want and need of her was overwhelming. He stood with her still in his arms and carried her inside to the bed and laid her down.

"Carrie," he said in a hoarse whisper as he drew back and looked into her eyes. "I love you, Carrie. I love you so much." And then he showed her how much in a very slow, methodical way.

~ SIXTEEN ~

By the time Noah and Elijah arrived back at Fort Sill it was near the middle of September. Troop D had return-ed to St. Louis with General Sherman and Troop B had re-placed them. Elijah was assigned to Fort Sill until further notice, and except that it kept him far from home, he didn't mind. It gave him time to be with Noah, to question him about his thoughts on the future, not only the future of the United States, but Noah's future as well.

Noah didn't know, but he thought if he and Carrie could move west and start the horse ranch he wanted, maybe they'd be able to live in peace. Maybe they wouldn't have to worry about what people would think, or the racism their children would have to live with.

Noah couldn't bear the thought of Carrie or their children being taunted because of the blood in his veins. He hoped someday people could live wherever they want-ed no matter what race they were, hoped one day child-ren could play with other children without being called names, or being belittled because of skin color.

He didn't think Sarah would have much of a problem because she looked white. True, she had his golden eyes, and her hair hung in tight spirals, but that was where the resemblance stopped. She had beautiful golden skin, beauti-ful full lips, high cheekbones and a delicate chin. Her bones were fine like her mothers, and he imagined she'd resemble Carrie a lot once she was grown. She had an exotic look about her, but she didn't look like she had Negro blood running through her veins at all. Charlie on the other hand, looked very much like Noah.

Charlie had the same golden eyes as Noah and Sarah, but he had Noah's same black, curly hair. His skin was even darker than Noah's, and he had the same broad fore-head, wide nose bridge, high cheekbones and a prominent chin. Carrie said he was much bigger than Sarah had been

144

at the same age. Of course, Charlie was still an infant and Carrie told Noah Sarah's hair had been just as dark until she was much older. They would just have to wait and see, but Noah thought he could see his own face every time he looked at his son.

Noah also thought if they couldn't live peaceably in America, maybe they could move to another country. He'd had a chance to talk with men he'd met in Memphis and St. Louis who traveled all over the world by ship, and he'd learned there were some places where people didn't care about race.

He had heard of islands where the weather was warm year round, where land was free for the taking and men of all races lived together in peace. Noah wasn't sure if all the stories were true, but he thought he'd like to see those places just to find out.

They had been at the fort only a few days when news that a detachment of Troop B had been attacked by an Indian war party. The rider rode hard most of the night and came into the fort exhausted and wounded. After a healthy shot of whiskey, the seventeen-year-old soldier was able to tell the story while a medic tended the wound to his arm.

Private Jimmy Wilson was near tears as he told the story. He had only joined the Army last May and this was his first assignment. He'd heard about the Indians of course, but that had been part of the appeal of joining the Army. It sounded exciting and fun, and life on the farm in Indiana had been anything but fun, so he'd told his mother and father he was going to be a soldier so he could go out west and fight the savages.

He sat in the captain's quarters now with no less than a dozen men looking at him, listening to his story, and the fleeting thought that Indiana wasn't such a bad place after all went through his mind.

When he finished, the captain sent him with the medic, and when he was gone, Captain Williams turned to the other men and took a shot of the whiskey himself. He looked at Major Johnson, then at Noah and knocked back another shot of whiskey. "How soon can you leave?"

"Immediately," Elijah said and looked at Noah. Noah nodded and the two men walked out together. They readied their horses, checked their rifles and ammunition, then slung themselves into their saddles and rode out of the fort.

Jimmy had given them an idea of where the attack had occurred, but he'd also been rattled and neither man was sure the boy really knew how far away they had been. He said he had ridden all night, but according to the detachment's orders, they shouldn't have been more than a five-hour ride away. Of course, they realized to a scared youngster like Jimmy Wilson, riding hard through the dark for a few hours might seem like a full night's ride.

It took Noah and Elijah less than five hours to reach the area where the battle had occurred, and it wasn't quite as bad as they'd expected. Only one soldier had been killed, along with one horse, though several men were wounded, none seriously. Three Indians lay dead and Noah kneeled next to them. It tore at his heart to see the dead warriors, but he was doing what he could to prevent bloodshed and he knew that was really all he could do.

Noah stood and looked at Elijah. "Kiowa," he said, shaking his head. "They aren't going to give up, and after losing three of their braves, this won't be the last attack either."

He was right. A few weeks later in October, the Kiowa ambushed another detachment of Troop B who had been scouting along the Red River. One trooper was killed, but none of the Indians lost their lives and none were captured, though the troop gave chase. Noah knew the Indians would take this raid as a victory and it would only encourage them into further attacks. But Mother Nature intervened and winter fell hard and early that year.

By the first of November a blizzard blew in and covered the land in several feet of snow. The wind howled and the temperature dropped rapidly. Noah knew the raids wouldn't resume until the land thawed, and it gave him the perfect opportunity to go home.

He was concerned about Carrie and his children and didn't want them to be alone through such weather. He wrapped his buffalo coat around him and it was long enough that it covered his legs as he rode. It took him more than a week to make the trip since the snow was so deep, and even deeper in some places where the wind had blown it into drifts.

He walked and led his horse through some of it, and had to wrap his horse's nostrils and eyes against the pelting ice. But finally the cabin came into sight before him and both he and the horse breathed an audible sigh of relief as they went into the barn.

Noah built up the fire in the wood stove to warm the barn for the animals, after he'd unsaddled the horse and put him in a stall with water and fresh hay. He found the rope tied to the barn lying in a coil on the ground and picked it up. The storm had blown in so unexpectedly and quickly, so he wasn't surprised Carrie hadn't put the line up between the house and barn. He brought it with him as he made his way slowly from the barn to the cabin. He attached it to the hook fixed in the wall, then shook the snow from his hair and coat, stomped his feet to shake it off his boots and opened the cabin door.

Noah felt a chill run up his spine as he opened the door and went inside. The fire was no more than fading embers on the hearth and the air was filled with a stench that nearly made Noah's stomach revolt. He found the oil lamps in the dim light, lit them and looked around.

Carrie laid on their bed, looking very pale. He went to her quickly, kneeling beside the bed, and put his hand on her forehead. Burning with fever, she couldn't even speak to him. Next, he went to the other bed where Sarah and Charlie were both asleep. Charlie was wet and needed a bath, but Noah didn't think he was ill.

Sarah's eyes fluttered open when Noah touched her face. She smiled at him, "Papa."

He picked her up and held her. She had a fever as well, but she didn't seem to be as ill as her mother. "Are you sick, Sarah?"

Sarah nodded. "I'm hot. Mama's sick and she can't wake up. I took care of Charlie, see Papa?"

Noah laid her back down, and brushed her hair back. "You did a great job, Sarah." He smiled and ran a finger down her cheek.

Then he went back to the bed where his wife lay and picked up the thunder mug and bucket she'd vomited into. He took them outside and left them there, then built the fire back up in the fireplace. Finding a rag, Noah dipped it into the water bucket and began bathing Carrie's face.

She was so hot, he didn't know what else to do except strip her clothing off and bathe her body in the cool water. She shivered at the contact and moaned, but Noah continued bathing her. He knew he had to get her temperature back down to normal, but she was so ill, so hot and limp, Noah became frightened. He knew if he could get her to the tribe, they had herbs that would cure whatever was wrong with her, but with the storm still roaring outside, he knew there was no way to get her there. He would just have to do what he could, and hope she recovered.

Noah spent days and nights bathing Carrie's body with cool water, and taking care of Sarah and Charlie. He slept very little, ate very little, and had a hard time feeding the baby. He was only a few months old, and even though he could eat some soft foods, he wanted his mother's breast.

Noah tried with little success to get him to drink milk from a cup, and finally, out of desperation, turned Carrie onto her side and laid Charlie next to her so he could nurse. Noah watched his son suckle and hoped he wouldn't become ill as well, but since he'd been in the cabin with her and Sarah both sick, and hadn't already become sick, Noah thought maybe he would be spared. When Noah managed to get Sarah and Charlie to sleep at the same time, he slipped outside to the barn to care for the animals.

Finally, after ten days, or at least Noah thought it had been ten days, though he wasn't really sure, Sarah seemed to recover rapidly and was able to help him care for Charlie. Two days later Carrie's fever finally broke and she slept peacefully. Sometime late into the night she called Noah's name and he jerked awake from where he had dozed off sitting on the floor next to the bed.

"Carrie," he said softly as he sat on the edge of the bed and held her hand. "How do you feel, darlin'?" He placed a hand on her forehead, relieved to find it cool.

"I'm thirsty," she whispered hoarsely.

Noah went to the kitchen and poured her a cup of water, then helped her sit up and held the cup to her lips. She drank a few swallows and lay back down, the activity seeming to exhaust her.

"You've been very ill," he told her, stroking her hair. "I was worried about you."

"How are Sarah and Charlie?"

"They're sleeping. Sarah was sick as well, but she's all right now. Charlie never did get sick, and he's been a handful wanting his mama," Noah smiled and smoothed his hand over her hair again.

"Poor baby. How did you feed him?"

Noah grinned. "I didn't, you did."

"I did?" Confusion crossed Carrie's still-pale face as she tried to remember.

"I laid him next to you and he did the rest," Noah explained. "Plus I fed him boiled vegetables and bread soaked in milk. Sarah's been a big help since she's been feeling better. Are you hungry?"

"Not just yet." She closed her eyes and went back to sleep.

Noah looked over at his daughter and son who were still asleep. It was early morning, but it hadn't gotten light out, so Noah climbed onto the bed beside his wife and fell asleep. He woke again sometime later with Sarah standing beside him watching him with patient gold eyes.

She whispered, "Are you awake?"

Noah smiled and nodded. "Are you hungry?" Sarah nodded. "Is Charlie still asleep?" She nodded again. "Okay, let's see about getting you something to eat."

Noah swung his legs over the edge of the bed and scrubbed his hands over his face, then stood up and stretched. He glanced out the window and saw it still wasn't light out. He went to the door and opened it to find the sky dark gray with clouds, and snow falling heavily.

He'd never seen a winter like this one, and it was only November. He shut the door when he heard Charlie begin to cry and turned to see Sarah had already gone to pick him up.

"Here," he said as he reached out. "Let me take him so your mama can feed him, then we'll get your breakfast made."

He changed Charlie before taking him to Carrie, and as much as he hated to wake her, he brushed his hand over her cheek and whispered to her. "Carrie, wake up, darlin'. Charlie's hungry."

Carrie's eyes fluttered open and she smiled when she saw her husband and son beside her. She rolled to her side and Noah laid the baby beside her and he began to nurse immediately.

"I'm going to cook some eggs for Sarah, do you think you can handle some?"

"I'll give it a try." She smiled weakly.

"You've lost weight," he observed. "You need to eat as often as possible so you'll gain your strength back."

"I know. I hope it hasn't hurt the baby any with me being so sick," she said.

"He looks fine to... what?" Noah looked at Carrie as her meaning began to dawn on him.

Carrie almost managed to laugh. "Yes, I'm pregnant again."

Noah shook his head and rubbed a hand across his face. "What am I going to do with you?"

"Love me?"

He smiled and leaned over to place a chaste kiss on her forehead. "I already do."

He went to the kitchen and began preparing scrambled eggs for Sarah, then scooped them onto a plate and set them before the little girl at the table. He took a plate to Carrie, and since Charlie had fallen asleep again, Noah moved him to the other bed, and then helped Carrie to sit up. He fed her as if she were a child, even though she insisted she could do it herself.

"When is the baby due?"

"In the spring. May, I think," she replied between bites.

"What flavor do you want this time?"

Carrie smiled. "I don't care. As long he's healthy and looks like you, it doesn't matter."

Noah shoveled the rest of the eggs onto the fork, then into Carrie's mouth. "I don't care either, just as long as you're all right. You are too thin. Do you want something else to eat?"

She shook her head. "Not right now. I would like some water, and I need to lie down. Being upright seems to wear me out."

Noah brought her some water and helped her lay back down. He spent the day cleaning the cabin, washing dishes, and heating water so he could bathe Sarah and Charlie. Then, when they were sleeping after supper, he heated more water and helped Carrie into the bath. She sat for a long time in the steaming water, and when she was done, Noah used the water to bathe.

"That was the best bath I've ever had." She smiled as she put on a fresh nightgown and sat on the edge of the bed watching him bathe.

"I thought you'd enjoy it," he said as he poured water over his head and washed his hair.

When he was through, he dried and slipped naked into the bed with Carrie. He held her close to him with her head resting on his chest and listened to her even breathing while she fell asleep.

He'd been so scared when she was sick, so worried she wasn't going to get well. He felt panic trying to rise within him and it had taken sheer will power to push it back down, push it away, so he could take care of everything without feeling overwhelmed.

And now, with her recovering, he was still worried because she'd lost so much weight and she was pregnant again. He could kick himself for that. He'd never thought about her being pregnant again, but he sure would think about it in the future. Three was enough and he wouldn't put her through that again, even if he had to go to the tribe and ask about herbs or something else to prevent it.

~ SEVENTEEN ~

Noah stayed home throughout December and January, but in February the weather finally broke and the sun shone brightly, reflecting off the snow. Noah shielded his eyes with his hand and looked around. He knew he needed to get back to the fort, knew Elijah would be worried about him, but he didn't want to leave Carrie again.

Even though she seemed fully recovered from her illness now, she never really gained back the weight she'd lost. Even though she was six months pregnant, the only part of her that had any weight was her stomach, and he still worried about her.

Noah took the shovel off the nail on the side of the cabin, and began shoveling snow to clear a path between the cabin and the barn. He'd done it countless times this winter and he'd be glad when spring finally broke through and the snow melted.

He didn't want to leave Carrie now, but he saddled his horse early the next morning and got his gear together, then went back inside. He picked up Sarah and kissed her cheek.

"You be a good girl and help your mama, all right?"

"I will, Papa," she said, smiling brightly and kissed his lips with a loud smack.

Noah set her on the floor and tickled Charlie's chin. The baby laughed and grabbed his finger. Then Noah went to Carrie and gathered her close and kissed her passionately.

"I'll be back just as soon as I can get here, but I promise to be here before this guy is born," he told her, rubbing a hand over her swollen stomach.

Carrie smiled and looked up at him. "It would be nice if you didn't cut it as close as you did when I had Charlie."

153

"I'll try," he said and kissed her again. "I love you, Carrie."

"I know. I love you, too." She followed him outside and he kissed her one more time, then mounted his horse and rode off through the melting snow.

~ * ~

The weather held for the first two days of his journey, but Noah arrived at Fort Sill in the middle of yet another snowstorm. Major Elijah Johnson was among those who came out to greet him and when he'd dismounted, one of the privates came to take his horse to be fed and watered. Noah went inside with Elijah and Colonel Grierson, gratefully accepting the glass of whiskey they offered.

"It had been a quiet winter up until a few days ago when the sun came out," Colonel Grierson said as he poured another whiskey. "As soon as it did though, the raids started again. To tell the truth, I was glad to see this new storm blow in. At least we should have a few weeks peace and quiet now."

He looked at Noah and held the whiskey bottle up, and Noah extended his glass for the refill. "I thought you were either frozen to death or had an arrow through you," the colonel said and poured more amber liquid into Noah's glass.

Noah laughed and sipped the whiskey. "Neither. Just snowed in. It took me a little longer to get there because of the snow, and when I did, my wife and daughter were both ill. I thought the snow would never stop."

"Is everyone all right?" Elijah looked concerned.

Noah nodded. "They're fine, just fine. And there's another baby due in May."

"Well, that's good news." The colonel laughed and filled their glasses again. "Congratulations, Noah."

"Thank you, Colonel." Noah grinned.

"I would congratulate you," Elijah said wryly, "but I think I should ask Carrie how she feels about it first."

"She's thrilled, as usual." Noah laughed. "But I think this is all for us. She was so sick and lost a lot of weight. I didn't want to leave her. Though she's recovered from the illness, she hasn't gained enough weight back if you ask me."

"We could send some men out with you to bring her and your children back here to the fort," the colonel offered. "It'd ease your mind to know she was close by and the doctor could look after her."

Noah and Elijah exchanged glances, and then Noah shook his head. "Thank you, Colonel but I don't think it would be a good idea to try and move her through the cold and snow this late. I'd be worried the trip would just make her ill again and she's really had it rough. But I appreciate the offer."

"I suppose you know best, but if you change your mind, just let me know," Colonel Grierson said.

"Yes, I will. Now, Major," Noah said, looking at Elijah. "I believe it's chow time. Would you care to walk over with me?"

"I would, thank you," Elijah said and finished his drink, setting the glass on the cupboard. Both men thanked the colonel and left his quarters together.

~ * ~

The troops were bored to death by the time the snow stopped and the sun came out again. It had snowed for three straight weeks and no one remembered ever seeing a winter with so much snow before. It was March 1872 and the morning routine was broken by the sounds of guards shouting that another troop was coming through the main gates. Colonel Grierson slid his plate back and rose from the table where he was having breakfast with Elijah and Noah, and the three men went outside.

Lieutenant Colonel Davidson was just dismounting with a troop of men behind him. "Colonel Grierson," he said and offered his hand. "I'm Colonel Davidson. I have orders here for you from General Sherman. You and Troop D are to report back to St. Louis, sir."

Grierson shook the man's hand and accepted the papers from him. He read them over, and then looked at Noah and the major.

"It looks like I'm going back to St. Louis. I've apparently been named Superintendent of the Mounted Recruited Service. I leave tomorrow morning with Troop D."

"Congratulations, Colonel," Noah said and shook his hand.

"Yes, congratulations," Elijah said with a smile.

But Noah could tell Elijah wished he was going back to St. Louis as well. His wife and children were there and he hadn't seen them in nearly a year.

"Colonel Davidson," Colonel Grierson said, "this is Major Elijah Johnson and our Indian tribe liaison, Noah Mosely."

"Major," Colonel Davidson said. "Glad to meet you, but you have orders to return to St. Louis as well. I've re-quested only my own staff remain here and everyone associ-ated with Colonel Grierson will return to St. Louis."

Elijah looked at Noah, and they both looked at Colonel Grierson, who asked, "Where does that leave Noah?"

Colonel Davidson looked at each of the men and then settled his gaze on Noah. "Well, it appears I have no choice where Mister Mosely is concerned. The governor made it quite clear you answer only to President Grant. I don't know how you managed that, considering..."his voice trailed off, but they all knew exactly what he was thinking.

Elijah took a deep breath and blew it out, he managed not to laugh but the corner of his mouth twitched anyway. Noah looked at Elijah and grinned broadly, he'd had to deal with a lot of men like this new colonel, although it had been quite a while since he'd encountered one out here in Indian Territory. Noah looked at Colonel Grierson and then at Colonel Davidson.

"I suppose the fact I'm not regular Army is what's bothering you, Colonel?" Noah said, still grinning.

The colonel looked from Grierson to Johnson, then back at Noah. A large man, the colonel stood well above the six-foot mark, but Noah was still a few inches taller and had at least fifty, or more, pounds on the man. Noah's long, black hair hung past his waist and he hadn't bothered to tie it back, so it now hung over one shoulder as well.

His gold eyes peered at the colonel, unblinking, like cat's eyes, and Noah noticed the colonel shifting uncomfortably from one foot to the other. The colonel blinked, looked at Grierson and Johnson, as if trying to find a little help. When he found none, he looked back at Noah, and cleared his throat.

"Of course, regular Army. What else?"

Early the next morning Noah said goodbye to Colonel Grierson, then stepped aside with Elijah. "If any of us survive this new colonel, it'll be a miracle," Noah said with a smile.

"Don't worry about him. As soon as I get to St. Louis, I'll contact the governor and get this straightened out. You take care and give Carrie my love. Take care of that new baby."

"I will. And you tell your wife I said hello."

They stood looking at each other for a long moment, and then Elijah mounted up and rode beside Colonel Grierson out the open gates with Troop D behind them.

Noah spent the rest of March and the first week of April training Troop B at Fort Sill. They had no idea how to handle the Indians out here, and Noah didn't want to see any of their young faces lying dead with an arrow or bullet through them. Colonel Davidson steered clear of Noah

most days, and only addressed him when absolutely necessary. Noah thought it was funny, but he didn't mind. He
didn't have much to say to a man like that anyway.

By the end of the first week of April the sun was
warm and there was no sign of the snow that had covered
the ground for the past several months. It also brought a
courier from Tulsa with a message for Colonel Davidson
and one for Noah. The colonel's superiors in St. Louis had
met with Major Johnson and Colonel Grierson and made
the decision that Colonel Davidson's assignment to Fort Sill
was temporary; therefore, he had no authority to replace
the staff Colonel Grierson had set in place. The colonel
was to be replaced by the first of July, and until then, he
was to make no more changes.

Noah, on the other hand, was summoned back to
Washington to meet with President Grant once more.
They had received notice that Chief White Horse and Chief
Big Bow of the Kiowa tribes in Indian Territory had joined
forces with the Comanche's. They had requested, and
were granted, a meeting with the president. They were
also guaranteed they could come and go without fear of
arrest.

Noah took a deep breath and exhaled heavily. What
the government took as a good sign from the chiefs, Noah
saw as the beginning of a long summer of raids on white
settlers. Neither the Comanche's, nor the Kiowa's, were
partial to peace, and Noah saw this visit to Washington
simply as a ploy on their part. He wasn't sure what they
hoped to gain, but he was sure it had nothing to do with
peace.

Noah left that afternoon to make the trip to Tulsa
where he'd catch a train to St. Louis. There he met with
Major Elijah Johnson and spent the night with Eli's family.
Noah always enjoyed the time with Eli's wife and children.
The boys were growing fast and Eli's daughter was becom-
ing a beautiful young woman. At seven years old, she smiled shyly at Noah from beneath long, thick black eyelashes.

Her chocolate brown eyes sparkled and her mouth formed a perfect pink bow when Noah picked her up onto his lap and kissed her cheek.

They ate roasted pork, peas, baked yams, potato salad, cornbread, gravy, fruit with fresh whipped cream, and apple pie outside on a wooden plank table with benches on either side. The warm evening air offered a slight breeze as they ate and Noah answered questions from Eli's sons.

After supper, Eli's sons ran and wrestled with one another, and when they ganged up on Noah, he was more than happy to roll around in the yard with them.

Elijah and Noah boarded the train in St. Louis the next morning and settled in for the long trip to the capital. Uncertain what would be expected of him, Noah wasn't sure he would be particularly helpful in this situation anyway. He could, of course, tell the president and his cabinet what he knew about Chief White Horse and Chief Big Bow. He had a lot of experience with the Kiowa Tribes over the past year, but it wasn't the Kiowa that worried Noah – it was the Comanche's they joined ranks with.

Noah had enough experience with other tribes to know the Comanche's. They had begun in northern Mexico and moved into Texas, running the Apaches into Arizona. The Comanche's were vicious and showed mercy to no one. Rape was the least of the atrocities perpetrated on women in the settlements they raided, and those they didn't kill after-wards, became hostages and were successfully assimilate them into the tribe, using force, intimidation, and fear.

The women of the tribe treated the captives abominably, forcing them to perform menial tasks and beating them with sticks if they did not cooperate. They were taught the native language in much the same fashion, and if any attempted escape, they were beaten the first time and killed if they attempted to run away again. The ones who survived, and were successfully assimilated, wound up married to one of the tribe's braves.

Cynthia Parker was one such captive. She had given birth to a son, Quanah, who later became chief of the tribe. Quanah led many raids on settlers and Army divisions alike, including an unsuccessful raid a year earlier on Fort Sill. Three weeks later, Quanah led a raid in St. Louis against General Sherman and nearly killed him. Quanah Parker would also be a guest in Washington with White Horse and Big Bow, and that didn't set well with Noah.

He hadn't met the Comanche Chief yet, but had heard a great deal about him. Quanah spoke English he'd learned from his mother, and he often dressed like a white man. He was intelligent, well spoken, and he could read and write. Noah heard he was quite charismatic, which was obvious since it was he alone who had been able to convince the Kiowa Tribal Chiefs to join him against the white armies.

The Comanche's alone were a dangerous group, but with the added strength of Kiowa warriors, Noah doubted they could be defeated in the manner the Army continued to use. He also feared that if the Comanche and Kiowa coalition proved successful, it would only encourage other tribes to join them, and the Army's fear of a united Indian front would become reality.

~ EIGHTEEN ~

When Noah and Elijah arrived in Washington they were greeted by General Sherman himself, and escorted to the Hampton Inn, the finest establishment in the city. They were shown to their rooms, which were next door to each other, but the bellman let it slip that it was a shame that officers of the United States Army only warranted a single room each while the "savages" were given the entire third floor.

Noah and Elijah looked at each other, tipped the bellman and shut the door behind him. Then they both laughed out loud. Noah left Elijah and returned to his own room to bathe and dress for the meeting to come.

Their escort, Corporal Thomas met the men at seven and took them to the White House to join the president, vice-president, General Sherman, the Indian chiefs, and assorted other dignitaries for supper. The chiefs had already been brought to the White House and stood regally in the rotunda where the reception line formed.

Chief Quanah Parker dressed in a black tux with tails, a top hat and white gloves. His knee boots were polished to a high gloss and he had one long braid down his back. Chief Big Bow and Chief White Horse were both dressed in traditional ceremonial garb, complete with colorful head-dresses, bone and bead breastplates, and the traditional two red stripes painted across one cheek. The trio stood with straight backs, eyes forward, unblink-ing, with their arms crossed over their chests. Their faces didn't change expres-sions when they were introduced; they only nodded their heads almost imperceptibly in silent acknowledgement.

Dancing followed the formal dinner for those who were simply invited to the White House to fill the seats, while the president and his entourage, followed by the chiefs and the members of the Army, retired to the library for cigars and brandy.

Noah, dressed in a black suit over a black silk shirt, with a black tie, and highly polished black boots walked with Eli down the long hallway, bringing up the rear. Eli wore his dress uniform with gold braiding on the shoulder and his ceremonial sword in a scabbard on his side.

They all took their places on the high-back cherry wood chairs upholstered in red velvet. The room had high shelves along the length of one wall filled from floor to ceiling with books. Another wall were windows draped in red and gold velvet that overlooked the rose garden. A third wall held portraits of every president that had walked the coveted floors of the White House.

Though old, the furniture was comfortable; the rugs were heavy and ornate. Tables of cherry and mahogany were arranged artfully and held busts of various historic figures, as well as gifts that had been brought to the White House by dignitaries from other countries, and governors invited for one occasion or the other. Beneath the presidential portraits was a long chest that held crystal decanters filled with French cognac, Kentucky whiskey, and various bottles of wine from Italy and France.

Trays with crystal snifters, shot glasses, and wine flutes, were filled with wine and brandy, and servants offered a glass to each guest. The low table in the middle of the rug held leather and wood boxes filled with cigars that were offered to the guests, and when everyone had settled com-fortably with a glass in one hand and cigar in the other, the servants quietly left the room.

Quanah Parker felt as comfortable in this room with these men as he was with his own people in his own village. He held a snifter of brandy with the stem between two fingers, while the glass rested in his palm to warm the amber liquid. He swirled the drink absently as he smoked his cigar and gauged each man by the expressions on their faces.

Quanah looked around, but he knew the men he watched couldn't tell because he continued to look straight ahead and when he moved his eyes, it went unnoticed. He regarded General Sherman, who had looked at him several times, and never with a smile. He wondered what the great white warrior was thinking, wondered if he wanted to kill him in retaliation for the assault at the fort. Quanah knew if it had been the other way around, he would kill the man where he was, no matter who was present.

That was the difference between the white man and the Indian, Quanah thought philosophically. The white man concerned himself with being civilized and would never consider shooting a man in such a setting. It would be so undignified, uncivilized, and utterly messy. The Indian didn't consider things like being civilized or dignified.

An enemy was an enemy, and to allow one to live was inviting one's own death and destruction. Quanah drew on the cigar and swirled the brandy once again. He didn't think Indians and whites would ever manage to see things in the quite same way.

`His eyes moved over the other men and he paused when he looked at Noah. He understood Noah, though they had never been formally introduced until tonight. He had known Noah by reputation for some time now, had heard of the work he'd done with some of the other tribes, as well as the story about his mother being an Indian maiden and his father the rare black cougar.

Quanah pondered the story, considered Noah's golden eyes and thought perhaps it could be true. But it wasn't Noah's paternity that intrigued Quanah Parker—it was his reputation. He knew most white men thought Noah to be Indian, but Quanah could see it wasn't true. Even though Noah had lived with an Osage tribe, Noah wasn't Indian, but, Quanah thought, Noah wasn't white either.

That was probably why Noah managed to walk into the tribal villages, and more importantly, why he was allow-ed to walk out again. Quanah heard Noah had even able to manage a pow-wow with Chief Bear Killer of the Apaches in Arizona. And that alone was enough to impress him.

Quanah knew Bear Killer very well and had nearly been killed by him when the Apaches were still in Texas. He'd only survived and succeeded because of sheer numbers. His men outnumbered the Apaches two to one. Even though the Apaches remained in Arizona and had never tried to come back to Texas, Quanah knew it was only because they chose to. And he was glad of it. Chief Quanah Parker had no desire to face Chief Bear Killer in battle ever again.

Noah had been sitting in his chair sipping brandy, smoking a cigar and listening to the various conversations going on around the room. It was casual, with no talk of the Indian Wars, or of anything along the lines of a serious nature at all. Noah answered questions posed to him, and smiled politely, even laughed at a joke or two, but he used the time to observe each man in the room, and spotted Quanah Parker doing much the same thing.

Noah had never met the chief before this evening, but knew him by reputation, of course. And he had been at Fort Sill when the Comanche's raided and Quanah at-tempted to kill General Sherman. He had been with the troop when they gave chase to the marauding band of Indians, but they hadn't caught any of them.

Noah noticed Quanah observing General Sherman in the room tonight, and wondered what he was thinking. He wondered if he was trying to calculate whether or not the general was going to retaliate. If it had been the other way around, Noah knew Quanah would kill the man where he sat, no matter who was in the room.

It was past midnight when Noah and Elijah were delivered back to the hotel, but were expected back at the White House the next day for a late luncheon, followed by a round table discussion about the Indian Wars and stopping the raids on the white settlements.

Noah knew it would actually be an attempt to talk the visiting chiefs into peace and surrender, and he also knew it would be largely unsuccessful. The Comanche Tribes had no desire for peace with the white man, and now, joined by the Kiowa, their forces were strengthened. It would be an exercise in futility, and in the end the government would simply increase their efforts to contain Indians on the reservations.

After three days of meetings there was no agreement between the Great White Chief and the Great Indian Chiefs. The Indians demanded their lands returned, with the settlers gone. They also wanted the forts closed and the Army removed. President Grant actually laughed out loud at the idea.

He countered with the offer of supplies and horses, as well as farming implements for the tribes with the Army serving as instructors to teach the Indians how to use them. If they agreed to surrender and went peaceably to the reservations, that is.

Noah and Elijah boarded the train back to St. Louis. They were both tired and felt the trip had done nothing but put another rift between the two factions. Noah was anxious to get back to Carrie, it wasn't much longer before she'd be having the baby and he was determined to be there before she went into labor this time. Walking into the house with Charlie already coming into the world was cutting it a little close as far as Noah was concerned, and he would like a little more time to prepare for this one.

Noah spent the night with Eli and his family when they finally arrived in St. Louis. He rose early the next morning and Eli took him back to the train station. They said good-bye, but only temporarily since Eli had been ordered back to Fort Sill by the first of July. In the meantime, he intended to spend the weeks ahead with his family.

Noah arrived in Tulsa in the middle of the night and took a room at a hotel near the livery. His horse had been left there and as soon daylight broke, he headed out. Riding hard with only the thought of Carrie on his mind, Noah arrived home in less than three days.

Carrie had been preparing for the birth of their newest addition, but she gained much more weight with this pregnancy than the previous two and was terribly uncomfortable. She also had a four-year-old and Charlie had just had his first birthday. He was not just walking, but running everywhere he went. Carrie depended on Sarah to help keep up with the toddler since she now had a hard time getting around, and just keeping up with the chores was nearly more than she could handle alone.

She missed Noah more than ever and resented the Army and the Indians both. She wanted her husband home with her and their children, and the fact his time was monopolized by the government made her more irritable. Leaving Sarah to entertain Charlie nearby, Carrie went to the barn to care for the animals.

"Papa! Papa!"

Sarah saw him first and ran laughing and shouting toward him. Charlie followed her as quickly as his little legs could carry him and Noah scooped them both up into his arms.

He walked toward the barn and met Carrie just as she came out. His grin broadened when he saw her.

He set the children on their feet and went to his wife, gathering her in his arms and kissing her softly. "You look great. I'm so glad to see you've gained back the weight you lost. I missed you," he said looking into her beautiful green eyes.

"I missed you, too," she said, savoring the feel of him. It didn't matter how many times he'd held her or kissed her, Carrie's heart did somersaults each time, just like it had the very first time he kissed her. "How long can you stay?"

"I don't have to be back until the mid-July," he told her. "I thought I'd spend the time adding another room on to the cabin. What do you think?"

"Oh, I'd love it, Noah," she said and kissed him again. "Are you hungry? It's nearly noontime."

"I could eat something," he said and draped his arm over Carrie's shoulder, as they walked to the cabin with Sarah and Charlie following along chattering noisily.

Noah already made arrangements in Tulsa for the necessary lumber for the room addition, and a few days later, wagons began arriving with the wood.

"Stay indoors until they've gone. We don't need any news going back to Tulsa with those men," Noah told Carrie.

He hated having to hide their marriage from everyone but Elijah, but it was a necessity if he was going to keep them all safe from retaliation, and the petty judgments of narrow-minded people.

Later that afternoon, after the delivery wagons had left, Noah rode southeast to a small settlement less than a day's ride from them across the Arkansas line. A few Negro families settled there after the war and Noah needed to hire help in order to finish the addition to the cabin quickly. He found two young men, brothers who were eighteen and nineteen and hadn't been able to find work.

They were more than eager to accept Noah's offer and Noah left half of the promised payment with the boys' mother. She explained how her husband died during the war, leaving her with the two boys and two young daughters. It had been a struggle for them to even eat, and if not for the other families in the settlement helping out, their mother hadn't been sure they would have survived.

The boys, James and Roland, were hard workers and Noah was happy to have their help. They worked from sunrise to sunset and slept in the barn at night. Carrie cooked large meals for them and she thought they ate every meal as if they were starving to death, when in fact, that was much closer to the truth than Carrie realized.

The room they added was large and would be the bedroom where they all slept, making more room in the main part of the cabin. The new room would be divided so Noah and Carrie could have privacy. But before it was finished, she went into labor.

Sitting in a chair Noah had moved outside to the front of the cabin for her, Carrie enjoyed the cool breeze that almost always blew. With Charlie on her lap, Carrie felt the first pain, and set him on the ground beside her. She took a slow, deep breath and waited for it to pass. When the second one came only a few minutes later, she sent Sarah to fetch Noah. He came running, sweat streaming through the dust on his face.

"Do you need to go inside?"

Carrie shook her head. "Not yet. But I think it will be soon. The pains seem to be coming much quicker than they did before."

"I'll have the boys take Sarah and Charlie down to the creek." He kissed her quickly and picked up Charlie. "Come on Sarah," he took her hand, "let's see if James and Roland want to go swimming."

The boys were more than happy to get off work so early and be able to go swimming as well, and having two younger sisters of their own, they didn't mind watching over Sarah and Charlie. Noah walked with them down to the creek and washed up. He kissed Sarah's cheek and patted Charlie's head, then went back to the cabin. He found Carrie doubled over in pain as blood ran down her legs, soaking her dress.

"Something's wrong," she panted as he helped her inside to the bed.

"What do I do, Carrie?"

"Get the book," she said, breathing heavily. "I don't know what's wrong." She screamed as the next pain gripped her.

Noah found the book and flipped through it with shaking hands. He couldn't find anything to help Carrie and now his vision began blur as tears tried to force their way through. Carrie screamed in agony and Noah felt panic rising like bile in his throat. He flipped through the book one more time and suddenly his eyes fell on a page that made his blood run cold.

Scanning the pages quickly, he read that bleeding and severe pain such as what Carrie now experienced could be fatal to the mother and the baby. The book said the pain could mean the placenta had separated and the baby wouldn't have enough oxygen, and would suffocate if not immediately delivered. When he read that the only way to deliver the baby was by a surgical method called a *cesarean section*, that was rarely successful and often resulted in the death of the mother, Noah threw the book across the room.

Noah rolled up his sleeves and went to Carrie. He remembered delivering a mule once that was turned wrong and the mare experienced much the same symptoms as Carrie. He had put his hands inside the birth canal up to his shoulders and turned the baby mule around. It had worked then, and it was the only thing he could think of now to save his wife's life. He hoped he could save the baby as well, but Carrie's life was the most important thing to him at the moment.

"Carrie," he said loudly, "listen to me. I only know one thing to do and it's going to hurt, but it's all I know."

She wasn't paying attention. Sweat soaked her hair and rivulets ran down her face. She screamed and writhed in pain, unaware of what Noah said or did. He took a deep breath, ripped her dress as he tried to get her bare and in a position where he could work. Blood ran everywhere, but Noah didn't hesitate. He knew every minute counted and if he lost her, he would never be able to survive.

He inserted a finger into her vagina, felt around, then put more fingers inside of her until he could stretch her enough to get his hand inside and feel for the baby. It was a foot that he found, and the thought of the mule he'd delivered crossed his mind again. Finding the other foot, he hung on to both of them and pulled gently, but the baby didn't move. He looked at Carrie, her face contorted with pain, but he needed her help.

He shouted at her, but she didn't hear him. He reached up and slapped her face hard, then felt like a heel for doing so. She looked at him then.

"Carrie, I need you to listen to me. The baby's turned wrong and I can't get him out. You have to help me or he'll die."

The realization her baby would die snapped her attention back to the task of getting him out quickly.

"Take a deep breath and push as hard as you can," Noah instructed her.

With both of the baby's feet in his hand, Noah pulled as Carrie pushed and slowly the baby began to move downward.

"Again, Carrie!" He shouted when she fell back to the bed.

Carrie panted, took another breath and began to push again. The baby continued to move downward until the feet and legs were out.

"Okay, Carrie. One more time, darlin', and make it a good one."

The abdomen and chest appeared, but Noah had to maneuver the head around to get it out, but finally, with the baby born, Carrie fell back against the bed.

The baby boy was limp and lifeless. Noah didn't want Carrie to see him, so he turned slightly and smacked the baby's behind, but there was no response. Noah felt the cold hand of fear grip him, but he would not give in. He stuck his finger in the tiny mouth and cleared some of the mucous, then smacked the baby again. He still didn't cry, but Noah refused to give up. He turned the baby and took a breath and blew directly into the baby's mouth, then turned him over again and smacked his bottom one more time.

Noah closed his eyes and offered up a prayer on behalf of his son. He knew Carrie would be beside herself when he told her the baby died. He'd never *not* wanted to do something so badly in his life. He turned back toward her and looked at her as she continued to try to catch her breath, then he heard a sound so soft he thought he imagined it.

He stopped and looked down at the baby, and saw the small chest move as the baby took another breath. He placed his fingers on the baby's chest and felt his heart beating. Then Noah began to shake. He handed the baby to Carrie and she smiled.

Noah tied, cut the cord, and delivered the afterbirth, then as he looked back up at Carrie and their new son, he saw her face suddenly go pale and she looked at him.

"Noah, I'm having another contraction!"

"No, no you're not," Noah insisted. "It's just the afterbirth."

"No, it's not, Noah. It's a contraction," she said as she took a breath and began to push.

Noah stared and then, with a gush of water and fresh blood, he watched another dark head begin to crown. He snapped back to reality and helped the baby's head through, then the shoulders, and the body slipped easily into his hands. Noah wiped the tiny face and the baby began to wail. Noah had never heard such a welcome sound in all his life.

He stared down at the wriggling, squalling child in his hands and looked up at Carrie with tears streaming down his face.

"We have another son," he whispered.

~ NINETEEN ~

The days moved quickly into summer and Carrie recovered from the birth of the twins, but trying to nurse two babies at once exhausted her. With the bedroom finished, Noah finished up the interior and began moving their beds into the new room.

He had taken James and Roland back to their mother, but he had talked to them about joining the Army. They decided to join knowing they'd be able to send their mother money every month, and without them at home there'd be more food for their mother and sisters. Noah spoke with their mother as well, and once she agreed, Noah told them he would return for boys in a few weeks and they could ride back to Fort Sill with him.

Noah also worked in the barn making a bed big enough for him and Carrie both, since the two beds in the cabin were small and Sarah now slept in one and Charlie in the other.

Taking the wagon into town, he bought supplies for his family, and found two cradles for the twins. Carrie was delighted to be able to rock one twin in his cradle with her foot while she fed the other one, and then switch them.

They had named the babies Matthew and Mark after the first two books in the New Testament of the Bible, and Carrie insisted both their middle names be Noah. Noah laughed at her reasoning that since Charlie was named after him, the twins would feel left out if they weren't named after him as well. But they both agreed Matthew and Mark would definitely be the last children they had. The twins' delivery had scared them both badly enough they didn't want to take the chance again.

Toward the end of June White Bear suddenly appeared. Carrie hadn't seen him since the previous summer and wondered if he and the tribe were all right. White

Bear was thrilled to find Noah at the cabin, and he grinned with grandfatherly pride when he saw the four Mosely children. White Bear stayed for five days, then one morning when they woke, he was gone. Noah told Carrie not to take it personally; that was just the way of the Indian. They were free and came and went as they pleased. It was one of the reasons they balked so badly at going to the reservations.

All too quickly it was time for Noah to leave again. He had ridden to the settlement across the state line and brought James and Roland back with him and they slept in the barn for the next two nights. Then it was time for them to leave for Fort Sill. Noah promised not to be gone very long this time. He was almost thirty years old now and feeling his age. He wanted to be home with his wife and children and didn't like leaving Carrie to care for all of them by herself.

He planned on speaking with Elijah as soon as he could. He had fulfilled his promise and the government owed him five thousand dollars. He wanted to collect it and go home. He talked to Carrie again about moving, about the horse ranch, and when he returned they would make plans together.

When they arrived at Fort Sill Noah was informed plans had changed and he was wanted at Deer Creek Fort instead. It was over two hundred miles away and wouldn't be an easy ride for James or Roland, who weren't used to being in the saddle for such extended periods. It took them five days, but when they arrived it was evening and chow was served. James and Roland were sent to the chow hall to eat, while Noah stayed with Elijah, and the two friends caught up on each other's lives.

"Twins? Well, that's a miracle isn't it?" Elijah shook his head in amazement.

"Now I have as many as you do. I have three sons and a daughter like you do." Noah realized.

"No, you don't," Elijah said as he shook his head and refilled the whiskey in their glasses. "We've got number five coming next spring!"

Noah laughed out loud. "Well, it's settled then. You win. After the scare Carrie and the twins gave me, we've decided four is all we want."

Eli laughed as well and looked at Noah. "That's what we said, too."

Noah's face lost all humor. "That's not funny. I swear if I had to go through that again, I think it'd kill me. I have never been so scared in my life. I'd rather do battle with Bear Killer than go through that again."

Eli slapped Noah on the back. "I'm sure it'll be fine. And speaking of Bear Killer, the Apaches are at it again. They killed almost everyone on a wagon train going west up in the Texas panhandle."

"You sure it was Bear Killer?"

Noah asked with concern. He liked Bear Killer, understood him and knew a raid on a wagon train would likely put a price on the chief's head.

"Yeah." Eli nodded. "One of the survivors is a Sioux scout who knew Bear Killer before. He'd hired on as a guide for the wagon train and recognized the Indians as Apache right off, but he saw Bear Killer, too. Sherman wants you back out there, Noah. You're the only one he's ever listened to without killing."

Noah swallowed the rest of the whiskey in his glass and set it on the table. He looked at Elijah for a moment, then leaned back in his chair and locked his hands behind his head. His long legs stretched out before him, crossed at the ankles.

His gold eyes held Eli's black ones, then he said, "No."

"No? What do you mean *no*?"

"I mean exactly that. I'm not going to do it. My service contract is up and the government owes me five thousand dollars. I want my money and I want to go home. I'm tired of this, Elijah."

Noah pulled his long legs up till his feet were flat on the floor. He leaned forward and rested his forearms on his thighs. "I have four children and a wife. You know what it's like. I want to be home. I want to see my sons grow into men. I want to raise horses."

"And you think you can walk away, just like that?"

Noah nodded. "I'm sure of it." He stood and paced around the room, paused to look out the window as darkness began to fall. "This isn't our fight, Elijah. This is the white man's fight and we got sucked into it out of desperation because we had no choice. The white man brought our grandparents here against their will, and they kept us as their slaves, no better than an animal. Then they started a war over it, but it wasn't even really over slavery, it was over money and they used slavery as an excuse. Then when the war was over, they left us to fend for ourselves."

Noah turned back to Elijah. "You and I would have been able to survive no matter what, but look at everyone who didn't. Everyone who isn't, like those two boys I brought with me. They were lucky to have beans in the evening, their mama barely able to take care of them and their sisters, and probably wouldn't have for much longer.

"Now, this government owes me five thousand dollars and it's going to buy my children a future I never would have dreamed of. My children are going to grow up to be something more than a nigger that can't do nothin' but work themselves to death in the fields of a white man. They're going to go to school, maybe even to college.

"And they're going to make something of their lives. Maybe they'll be doctors, or maybe they'll sit up there in the White House like Jefferson Long or Hiram Revels. Maybe they'll be great men, or maybe they'll be average men. I don't really care as long as I know they had the chance to make the choice for themselves. I want my daughter to have the chance to marry whoever she wants to and not have to marry a man who can't give her anything but a dirt floor to sweep and a dozen children she has to listen to crying every night because they go to bed hungry. She might not marry a rich man, but I want her to have the chance, the choice, the *right* to marry any man she falls in love with. Don't you want that for your children too, Elijah?"

Elijah remained in his seat with his fingers linked together before him, staring at the floor. "Yes," he said quietly. "I want that for my children as well. But I made a commitment to the Army and because of that commitment my family has it better than I'd ever expected any of us would. I made major, and I know one day I'll be a general, too. I also know this life isn't for everyone, Noah. I know it's not for you, I knew that the day we met."

Elijah looked up at his friend and smiled. "I'll speak with General Grierson as soon as he arrives and get you a bank draft for your money. But I'm asking you as a friend to speak with Bear Killer one more time."

Noah grinned. "Get me the draft first and I'll go."

"Grierson will be here in the morning." Eli laughed. "I'll have your bank draft by noon and I expect to be heading for Arizona with you the following morning."

"No problem, except I want it to be the day after tomorrow before we leave. I want to take the draft over to the bank so I can set up an account in Carrie's name." Then he added, "Just in case." Eli nodded. He and Noah both understood the risk they were about to take.

Deer Creek Fort was only a few miles from the town of Deer Creek and Noah rode to the bank and set up the account. He wrote a note to Carrie that would be delivered to her if he was killed before he could get back to pick up the money himself and go home. It was just a precaution, he told himself. He wasn't particularly superstitious, but he felt gooseflesh rise on his skin as he wrote that he loved her and asked her to make sure their children would never forget him. He signed it with love and folded it into the envelope and addressed it to his wife. The bank manager put it in the safe with Noah's money and promised he had nothing to worry about... either way.

On June 12, 1872 Noah and Elijah prepared to head for Arizona. The early morning sun bore down and promised to bring oppressive heat later in the day. As they mounted their horses a bugle sounded a rider through the gates.

Troops A and L had been attacked at Deep River, about twenty miles away from the fort. Noah and Eli looked at one another, and then waited for General Grierson to give the orders. They headed for Deep River with Troop B. It would be James' and Roland's first assignment and Noah rode next to the boys and told them what to expect. He didn't want them to arrive on what might be total carnage without warning.

When they finally reached Deep River Bend, they found a few stray Army horses and rounded them up. Further down they found two bodies floating face down in the river and pulled them out, then strapped them onto the horses and continued down river. As they followed the curve of the river, they found the attack site and Major Elijah Johnson called the troop to a halt. They dismounted and began check-ing to see if there were any wounded survivors. Nearly half of the bodies on the ground were dead or close enough there was no hope of survival, and the rest were wounded, but would recover.

After they buried the dead, some of the troops were sent to round up the rest of the horses that had wandered off, while others were ordered to assist the wounded and get them ready to transport back to the fort. Noah scouted the area and concluded it was Comanche and Kiowa who attacked. He had suspected them to begin with, but now he was sure.

He clenched his teeth and followed tracks they had tried to camouflage, but Noah could track them even when they crossed the river to the opposite bank. He returned to where Eli shouted orders to one task or another, and told him what he'd found.

"I'd be willing to bet the raid was led by Quanah Parker," Noah said.

Eli nodded. "I guess we'll go back to the fort and file a report, then see what they want to do. I'm thinking they'll send an attachment after Quanah, but you and I will still be heading to Arizona."

Noah said, "I'd rather chase Quanah. It's closer to home."

~ TWENTY ~

Noah rode alone into the area of Arizona where he knew Chief Bear Killer posted unseen scouts. He raised his hands and rested them on top of his head. The Arizona heat made Noah feel like baking in an oven and he could feel sweat trickling down his back. There wasn't a breeze to be found and even Noah's horse hung his head.

They walked slowly across the hot sand and Noah could see Eagle's Rise in the distance. Eagle's Rise was a group of rocks formed by time and weather that rose out of the desert like sentinels. The six giant monoliths rose more than thirty feet into the air and formed nearly a perfect circle in the sand providing the only shade for a hundred miles in any direction. Somehow small cedars and other bushes had managed to plant themselves around the rocks and formed a natural barrier all around the structure. Noah knew they'd wait for him there.

Continuing his ride toward the rock formation, Noah kept his hands on his head, but he had his sidearm, and a rifle was in the scabbard. He didn't leave his weapons behind this time because this wasn't an arranged meeting and Bear Killer hadn't known he was coming. This wasn't a meeting for peace talks like the last one, and Noah wasn't bearing gifts.

Bear Killer knew the Army would be looking to retaliate for the settlers that killed up north, and if the chief thought Noah was there to arrest him, he might not be willing to let Noah walk in, or out, alive. And Noah wasn't going to die out here in the god-forsaken desert without a fight.

Still a hundred yards away from the mammoth structure, Noah spotted a Comanche scout with a rifle standing between two of the rocks, mostly concealed by brush. His instinct told him to reach for a weapon, but his good sense told him to keep his hands where they were.

The horse plodded forward, weary from the heat and in need of water. Fifty yards from the rock enclosure a Comanche brave came toward him on horseback, guiding the animal with his knees since his hands were otherwise occupied with the rifle he leveled at Noah.

Noah's heart rate increased slightly, but he kept himself relaxed, kept the hands on his head loose and ready. When Noah and the brave met, Noah kept his eyes forward and the horse walking. The brave kept the rifle trained on Noah and turned his horse to follow.

The scout standing beside one giant boulder stepped forward with his rifle also pointed at Noah and watched him all the way in. When Noah's horse reached the scout on the ground, he came to a halt and waited. The scout motioned for Noah to dismount, which he did while his hands remained on his head. He swung his right leg over the saddle and slid to the ground, and the scout took the reins and led them both through the opening between the rocks. The brave on the horse slid to the ground and followed them through the aperture with his horse following close behind.

When they reached the inside of the stone circle, Noah saw Chief Bear Killer sitting on a rug on the ground in the shade. He stood when he saw the men and looked warily at Noah. He motioned with his head and Noah's sidearm was removed, then the two escorts lowered their rifles and went back to their posts.

Chief Bear Killer offered Noah a seat on another rug and a young brave brought water in gourds for the two men to drink. Noah accepted gratefully and drained the gourd, only to have it immediately refilled.

"I did not expect to see you here again," Bear Killer said.

"I did not expect to be here again." Noah took another drink of the water.

"Why have you come Dark Horse?" Noah's Indian name had made the rumor circuit as well, and he wasn't surprised Bear Killer used it now.

"Because of the wagon train attacked up north in the Texas panhandle. The report I received came from a Sioux scout who said you and your men attacked the white men. Women and children were killed. I have come to ask if it was you."

Bear Killer looked at Noah and Noah thought he saw the corner of the man's mouth curve slightly. Finally Bear Killer nodded. "It was."

"Why did you go into Texas and kill those people? The Army now has a price on your head. Men will come looking for you, they will come to kill you."

"I did not go to kill them. I did not know they were there. The wagons go further north now, not into Texas. When we came upon them, we stopped to let them move on. One of their men saw us and shouted. They began firing on us. We killed them."

"I believe you, Bear Killer," Noah said, knowing he did. Bear Killer would not lie, it was not the kind of man he was and Noah respected him for it. He knew if Bear Killer had attacked the wagon train first, he would have admitted it proudly. "The Great White Chief probably will not. I will try to tell him, to make him believe your words. But you must stay out of the Texas territory. There is much war there with the Comanche and the Kiowa. Stay on your own land."

Bear Killer watched Noah intently for a long moment before he spoke. "We will not cross into Texas, Dark Horse. Tell your chief we will stay on our own land, but they must stay away. If the Army comes, we will fight."

"I understand," Noah nodded. "You must understand I cannot tell you the Army will stay off your land. I do not work for the Army. I am going home."

Bear Killer nodded and lit the pipe. He passed it to Noah who put it to his mouth. He sucked on the stem, but refused to inhale. Still, he had to smoke with Bear Killer; refusal to do so would see him dead where he sat. When he passed the pipe back, he stood and Bear Killer stood with him.

They nodded and Bear Killer signaled to the scouts. They brought Noah's horse and he led the animal out of the stone enclosure. He paused for a moment as he looked back to see the scouts, and Bear Killer, watching him. He saw Bear Killer nod his head slightly and Noah did the same. It was the last time they would see one another.

The following November General Crook, along with Captain John G. Bourke, led his men into Arizona and waged a full-fledged war on all bands of the Apache Indians. In December, seventy-six Indians were killed at Skull Cave. Most of the dead were women and children. By the following spring most of Arizona's Indians realized the Army could not be defeated and either surrendered and were placed on reservations, or they continued to resist and were killed.

Counted among the dead were Chief Bear Killer and his men.

Noah returned to the camp where he left Elijah waiting. He reported the conversation he had with Bear Killer and Noah knew the chief would never surrender, or go willingly to the reservation. Noah hated the position his job put him in. He hated that he had to be away from his family most of all, but the fact that he felt he betrayed the Indians in some way didn't help. Elijah told him he was doing more for the Indians than most people would.

"I've never known a more compassionate man than you, Noah," Elijah said, as they sat around the campfire drinking coffee. "You didn't start this war, Noah. I don't think anyone remembers who did. There's no use in beating yourself up over it either, you're not the bad guy here. God knows there are enough of them to go around. There's bad men everywhere—bad Negroes, bad Mexicans, bad white men, and bad Indians. Our duty is to help end these wars as peaceably as possible, and sometimes it's not possible. That's just a fact of life."

"Elijah, I know you have this all straightened out in your head, but I don't. I ran away from the plantation in Mississippi and if it wasn't for the Indians that found me, I wouldn't be here right now. That same tribe was nearly wiped out by the white man but they managed to escape into the mountains where they still live. Until I met Carrie, they were the only family I knew, the only home I had, and I can't reckon it all in my mind so that it seems right they should be forced onto a reservation. And to tell you the truth," Noah paused and stared into his nearly empty cup. He looked at Eli again, and said, "To tell you the truth, Elijah, if it comes to it and the Army tries to force them to the rez, I'll fight with my people against the Army."

Elijah stood and stretched, then shook out his bed-roll, rolled it up and tied it behind his saddle. "Noah, my friend, the sun will be up before long and we have a long ride. You have a longer one if you still plan on going home."

Noah and Eli mounted their horses and began riding across the desert of Texas toward the Indian Territory. Noah glanced over at Elijah now and again and wondered what all went on inside that head of his. Eli was dedicated to the Army and planned to either die or retire with his uniform on. He thought there was no finer a life for a man than being a soldier and he hoped his sons would feel the same way. Noah knew Eli had been a slave and so had his wife. They had been on the same plantation together and married with the blessings of the slave owner. The plantation owners often encouraged marriage between slaves; it was cheaper to breed slaves than to buy them.

Noah didn't understand why Eli remained a soldier, even though he fully understood why he'd become one. It had been for much the same reason Noah had gone to work for the government-self-preservation. But Eli had a wife who was the same race he was, and their children had the same skin as their parents. In Noah's case, that wasn't true. And as much as Noah loved Carrie, and loved their children, he couldn't help but feel guilty sometimes.

He'd known how things were before he ever laid a hand on Carrie, which was the reason he left her after his leg healed. He'd had feelings for her then, but he knew what that might bring for them both if anyone ever found out. And he'd done everything he could since then to keep anyone from knowing.

But one day their children would be old enough to go out into the world alone, as much as he hated to think about it, but he couldn't very well keep them locked up in the barn. *Could he?* Noah chuckled to himself at the thought.

He and Eli almost made it into Indian Territory when the first arrow struck Elijah in the chest. Noah didn't even have time to draw and fire his weapon before an arrow pierced his thigh and his horse was shot out from under him.

"Elijah!" Noah shouted as he looked around for his friend.

He held one hand over the bleeding wound in his thigh. With his good leg and arm, he pushed himself toward Eli, but the Indians were on him before he reached Elijah's side. Noah felt their rough hands as they grabbed his arm and he gritted his teeth as they jerked him to his feet, but he still looked at Eli, who still hadn't moved.

One of the Indians grabbed Elijah's head and pulled it back, grunted, and let it drop. Elijah was dead, and Noah was a prisoner. One of the braves tied a strip of leather around his leg to slow the bleeding, then tied his wrists together and tethered him to one of their horses.

The pain caused Noah to feel sick. The heat was unbearable, but coupled with the pain and loss of blood,

Noah stumbled and it wasn't long before he fell and refused to get back up. One of the braves kicked him in the ribs, but another one grabbed the brave's arm and pulled him back. The second brave helped Noah to his feet and motioned toward a horse. He helped Noah mount the animal and walked beside him to make sure he didn't fall off.

They continued for three more days, heading south and then east. Noah thought they must be somewhere near Wichita Falls. It was only hours later when they were met by the other members of the tribe, and Noah was escorted to a lodge and seen to by one of the elders. His leg was cleaned and cauterized with the blade of a knife heated in the fire, and he was given herbs in a tea to make sure he didn't get an infection.

And Noah slept.

He dreamed of Carrie, dreamed of being home with her. He could feel her body next to him, could hear her voice whispering in his ear. She was an angel in white with her hand cool on his brow. She was the fever raging in his mind, the heat that spread through his body. He called her name, reached out for her and felt her slipping through his fingers. He called her name again, but she only laughed and ran away from him. She laughed, looking back at him over her shoulder. She ran farther and farther away from him and his legs wouldn't move. They felt like clay as he tried to go after her, no matter how he tried to make them move. He looked up to see where she went, but she was nowhere in sight.

Noah sat up fighting the darkness, screaming Carrie's name. When he looked around, he saw he was in an Indian lodge. At first he thought he was with the People in the mountains of Arkansas, but when he moved his leg the pain brought the memory back to him. He'd been shot and had somehow survived. Elijah, his best friend, lay dead and like carrion on the hot sands of Texas. Noah lay back down and closed his eyes.

The flap of the lodge door opened and a woman came in. She looked at him, but her face remained expressionless. Helping him to sit up, she gave him water and a bowl of stew with flat bread. She nodded as she watched him eat, and when he finished, she took the dishes away and left him alone.

When the flap opened again, a man came in. Noah couldn't see his face, but he seemed familiar for some reason. When the man came closer and his features were illuminated by the dim firelight, Noah clenched his teeth. His golden eyes were hard as they met Quanah Parker's hard black ones.

Quanah sat across the fire from him and settled comfortably on a rug. He said nothing for some time and Noah silently held his gaze. When Quanah finally spoke, his voice was soft.

"I am sorry you were shot," he said in perfect English. "I would not have allowed my men to hurt you or your friend if I had been there. I do apologize also for the death of your friend."

"Am I your hostage?"

Quanah nearly smiled. "I would prefer to call you my guest."

"A guest that cannot leave at will I take it?"

"That is unfortunate, but true for the time being. You are valuable to the Great White Chief and I am in need of a bargaining chip at the moment. The Calvary has been chasing my people, has made our life difficult."

"Your braves have been raiding settlements all along the Red River, along Deep River Bend, and at Deer Creek. They attacked a troop of soldiers a few months ago and left most of the soldier's dead. As long as your people keep raiding, the Army will keep chasing you."

"And as long as they keep chasing us, we will keep raiding." Quanah shrugged.

"Believe me, I understand how you feel, but this will come to no good, Chief Parker. And once Elijah's body is

187

found, they will be more determined than ever to hunt you down. Quanah, let me go. Come with me to the fort and I will do everything I can to stop the slaughter of your people."

"I know you want to help. I know your history with the Army, your history with the Osage. I know you do want to help Indians everywhere, but it is out of your hands now, Noah. This is a war that cannot be undone. It will stop only when the Indian people give up and go to the reservations, or when the Army has killed all of us."

Noah knew of no reason to continue this line of conversation. Quanah would not bend, yet Noah understood what Quanah had said was true, and if he were in the chief's place, wouldn't he do exactly the same thing?

"Chief," Noah said, shifting positions to try and relieve the pain in his leg. "I have quit the Army. I am my way home, and when your men stopped me. I had been in Arizona with Bear Killer and it was my last assignment. I am tired, as I am sure you are. I only want to go home to my wife and children. I, too, desire peace."

"The white woman in the small house is your wife?"

Noah felt his heart thud and his blood went cold. His eyes narrowed as he looked at Quanah. "How do you know about my wife?"

"Do not worry, Dark Horse. Your wife and children are safe. They will not be harmed, not by the Comanche or the Kiowa."

Noah measured the chief carefully, never had the man called him by his Indian name. "Why do you use my Indian name? And how do you know of my family?"

Quanah grinned then. "I met with your chief less than a moon past. We have been meeting with as many of the People as we can. We want to bring the People together as one nation against the white Army."

"I know he did not join you."

"No, but he will not go to the reservation either. If the white man comes to him, he will fight."

Noah knew that was a true statement but decided to change the course of their conversation. "Quanah, your mother is white. Don't you feel some loyalty to her people?"

"Your father was white, Dark Horse. Do you feel loyalty to his people?"

Noah clenched his teeth again and stared unblinking at Quanah Parker.

~ TWENTY-ONE ~

Carrie stood with her children around her as she looked at Colonel Grierson. She couldn't believe what he was saying, even though she knew he wouldn't be there if what he said wasn't true.

Troop C found Major Elijah Johnson as they patrolled the borders of Texas. Although still in Indian Territory, in a few weeks they would be heading to the San Carlos Reservation in Arizona. They thought Eli was dead When they found Eli, they though him as dead as the horse lying nearby.

If he hadn't been wearing his uniform, he would have buried him right where they found him, but when they picked him up, he moaned and they realized he was still alive. After pulling the arrow from his chest, they bandaged him up as best they could with the few medical supplies they carried. Fashioning a makeshift stretcher, they carried the major to the nearest town, and fetched a doctor to take a look at him.

It would be at least two weeks, or more, before he could be moved, and the troop had gone back to Fort Sill to report to Colonel Grierson, leaving Major Johnson in the good doctor's care.

Colonel Grierson immediately rode with an attachment to the small prairie town and waited until the doctor said Elijah could be moved to the fort. Still weak from the loss of blood, Elijah knew how lucky he was to be alive since the arrow that entered his chest managed to miss his vital organs.

He explained to the Colonel what happened, or as much as he knew. It all happened so fast Eli only clearly remembered the force of the arrow and hitting the ground hard.

Managing to catch a glimpse of Noah falling to the ground along with his horse, Elijah blacked out with only vague memories of day and night, being investigated by a coyote, and vultures watching him from a short distance. He still wasn't sure how much time passed while he lay in the hot sand, and he couldn't say for sure whether Noah was dead or alive.

~ * ~

"He's not dead," Carrie said firmly as she raised her chin and glared at the Colonel. "My husband is *not* dead! You are all wrong. I know it. He would not leave me, Colonel. He would not leave his children. He's leaving all of you, leaving the war, and we're going to buy a horse ranch. He wants to raise horses."

Her voice became shriller with each word she spoke, and then she began to sob. The colonel offered her his kerchief as she collapsed against his chest, and he patted her back gently while her children observed him. He gave them a half smile and continued to pat Carrie's back until her sobs subsided.

She wiped her nose and face with the borrowed kerchief, then said, "I'm sorry, Colonel."

"Don't be Mrs. Mosely, I understand how you feel. It's a shock for you. Major Johnson would have come himself, but he is not yet fully recovered enough to travel. He said to tell you as soon as he can manage, he'll be out to see you. I suspect he will take a few months to go home to his own family as well," the colonel's voice trailed off.

"Thank you, Colonel." Carrie regained her composure. "You were kind to make the trip, and I'm sure you're hungry. Will you join us for supper?"

"I appreciate the offer, ma'am, but my men are waiting. We're on our way to the Red River," he explained. He tipped his hat. "If there's anything we can do for you, ma'am, just send word to Fort Sill and I'll get it."

"Thank you. I will, Colonel."

Carrie watched as the colonel disappeared in the distance, and then looked back at her daughter, who held one of the twins, and at Charlie, who played in the dirt.

Colonel Grierson hadn't known Noah's wife was a white woman, and although he'd been surprised, he hadn't been shocked. It explained why Noah had been so closed-mouthed about his wife and family, and that was something Grierson could understand perfectly. He smiled as he thought about his own blue-eyed, blond wife who was now very close to delivering their first child. No one knew the colonel was even married, much less to a white woman, and he planned to keep it that way.

~ * ~

Carrie look around, automatically counting heads, then asked, "Where's Mark?"

"He's still sleeping, Mama," Sarah answered.

Carrie took Matthew from her daughter and forced a smile. "Let's go inside and see about supper, shall we?"

Sarah nodded and took her brother by the hand. "Come on Charlie. You have to get washed up for supper." They walked toward the cabin together, and just as they reached the front door, Sarah asked, "Mama, do you think Papa will come back?"

Carrie felt her breath catch in her chest and she swallowed hard to push down the lump in her throat. "Of course he will, Sarah. Don't you worry, your papa will always come home to us." She opened the door and followed Sarah and Charlie inside, hoping she had not just lied to her daughter.

~ * ~

Noah recuperated while at the Comanche camp and spent quite a bit of time with Quanah Parker. The Kiowa chiefs, White Horse and Big Bow, joined them occasionally as well. Noah asked questions of all of them, trying to understand these formidable men. He thought perhaps if he knew them better, knew their mind and how they thought, he might be able to provide Colonel Grierson with a clearer picture of how to end this war without committing genocide. And he was afraid that at the rate the con-

flicts between whites and Indians were escalating, genocide might not be that big of a stretch for the Army.

Noah felt winter coming, but this far south it would
not be as bad as in the northern part of Indian Territory.
The women of the tribe had been getting ready for the
colder months all summer and fall. They had stores of
pumpkins, squash and cactus apples that were picked from
a certain cactus in the desert. The fruit was really quite
good once it was learned how to get past the long barbs on
the plant that pierced the skin like an arrow.

Noah would always be amazed by the resiliency of
the Indian people, by how efficient they were, how self-
sufficient they were. He thought of the white people he
knew who lived in cities with their gas lamps, fine homes,
and some even had indoor plumbing now. He thought of
how they bought their goods at the mercantile, and no
longer raised their own meat or grew their own vegetables. They would never be able to survive out here in
this wild land.

Noah thought a lot about Carrie as well, and he
thought about his children. He knew Carrie was capable of
taking care of them, of taking care of everything like she
always had, but he knew this time it would be different
for her. He knew someone must have already gone out to
the cabin to tell her of Elijah's death and that he was
missing.

Sure the Army thought he was dead by now, Noah
wondered if the bank had delivered the money he left
there for his family. It gave him a sense of relief to know
that even if she thought he was dead, at least she would
have enough money to last her for a long while.

Noah also left money in the leather pouch in the
trunk. He never told her, and he doubted she ever checked since he brought supplies home with him each visit.
There should be close to ten thousand dollars in the trunk
and with five thousand in the bank, he knew Carrie and his
children would want for nothing.

He didn't know how long his captivity would last, but he hoped if it continued on for any length of time, Carrie would use the money to ensure their children's education. Noah could read and write, could even do sums, but he wasn't an educated man and he wished he were. He wanted his children to have the best education that could be found because he knew it was the only way they'd ever be able to rise above the lines of racism that stretched across the land.

Many Negroes now held important jobs in Washington, and their were men who were judges and lawyers. The United States Naval Academy had even admitted John H. Conyers earlier that same year. A Negro at the Naval Academy. Noah smiled, satisfied that even though it was slow, the world seemed to be changing for the better.

Noah's head shot up when he heard commotion from outside the lodge and went out to see what happened. Noah was not bound hand and foot during the day—Quanah had too much respect for him for that. At night however, Noah was confined to the lodge and guarded by four warriors. He had not tried to escape, and even though he was sure he could during the daylight hours, he never forgot that Quanah knew where his wife and children lived. Quanah was an honorable man, but he was a warrior first, and vengeance was just as much a part of him as breathing.

Noah stood in front of his lodge and watched as two men rode into camp. Women stood back watching. Some wept openly. The children and dogs ran around, with laughter and barking sounding in the air. The braves stood, looking very proud. Quanah grinned from ear to ear. As the two men on horseback drew closer, Noah could see their smiling faces more clearly and recognized them.

Chiefs Satanta and Big Tree rode into camp. They had been imprisoned for the raid on Fort Sill, but now they'd returned and Noah figured they had either escaped or been paroled. Later he found out it was the latter. But knowing the men the way he did, Noah wasn't sure that had been sound judgment on the government's part.

It was a paradox. The government declared Indians were not citizens of the United States, and the Indians did not recognize the legitimacy of the United States Government, or the laws thereof. Why the government paroled the two men, expecting them to adhere to the guidelines and regulations of their parole conditions, was beyond Noah. He knew the two would be leading raids against settlers and soldiers alike in no time.

Winter came and time rolled on into the next year. Noah remained a guest of Chief Parker, albeit unwilling as he was. Spring came early in 1873 and Noah accompanied the chiefs on various and numerous trips to other tribes for meetings with those chiefs. Noah had to give White Horse credit. he had come up with a plan that, if he could get the other tribes to agree, just might bring the Army down.

By the summer of that year an intertribal council formed deep in the badlands of Texas where no white man lived, and no Army likely to patrol. Gathered together were all of the Kiowa, Comanche, Cherokee, Cheyenne, Shawnee, Arapahoe, and other tribes from miles around.

Noah was witnessing something no other non-Indian would ever see, perhaps something no Indian had seen either, or would again. As the days and nights progressed, so did the arguments, fights and brawls. But from what might appear as mayhem, arose a united Indian front the Army could not even imagine. Noah knew the consequences to the Army, government, whites, and to the country itself, would be swift and severe.

He also knew the fatalities would be numerous on both sides, and as much as he didn't want to see that happen, he knew the Indians were willing to continue the fight until every last one lay dying, as long as the white man was annihilated. It would be a blood bath beyond any nightmare the white man had ever had.

After a month in the heat of the desert, Noah was happy to leave it behind and head back north where the weather would be somewhat cooler. He remained with the Comanche tribe throughout the rest of the year, accompanied them on raids, and continued to try and reason with Parker, though he knew it was useless.

~ * ~

Carrie waited for more than a year after Elijah came to see her. He stayed for two days and apologized so many times, she wished he would stop. A few days later, she received a visit from a banker who handed her a letter and an envelope of cash Noah left her. She signed for the items with shaking hands, but managed to wait until the man rode away before she ripped the letter open.

My Dearest Carrie,
I write this letter hoping you will never read it, because if you are reading this, then I am no longer among the living. I cannot bear to think that we will not grow old together, watching our children grow, watching our grand-children play together. I have tried to be a good husband, a good father, and a good American, although I feel I have failed at the first two. I only did what I did with the hopes that I could provide well enough for you and the children. I hoped those efforts would not only provide us with the money we would need to start our horse ranch, but also that our children would live better lives than we have. I had such dreams of seeing them go to college, become great men, and for Sarah to live the life of a princess, because she is one and deserves the best life has to offer. I wanted you to have a fine house, fine clothes, to have the life you had before the Yankees ruined it for you. I want you to know that you are the only woman I have loved. You were a dream I had that came true, and I know I never deserved you or the child-

196

ren you gave me, and I know that even in death, my love for you will never die.

You deserve so much more, Carrie, and I know you could have had any man you desired. Why you wanted me, I'll never know, but I know that I never told you enough how much I love you, how much you mean to me, how grateful I am for you and for your love. I never told you thank you, but I mean it, Carrie. Thank you for your love, for standing by me, for the children we made together, for the life you made for us. I want you to be happy.

I want you to go on with life. I want you to find another love, someone who is worthy of you, and will care for you and our children, and will cherish you and love you with all of his heart. Please remember me sometimes, don't let my children forget their father, but don't let them mourn me either. Use the money I am leaving for you to make a life for yourself and our children. Move into a fine house, make friends, teach our sons to be gentlemen and our daughter to be a lady.

I am so sorry I had to leave you, so very sorry, Carrie. I know you are hurting now, but please don't dwell on the sorrow, and don't allow it keep you from living your life. You are so young, so beautiful, and have so many years left ahead of you. Be happy, Carrie and know that if it is possible, I am keeping watch over you from Heaven. I love you, Carrie, with all my heart.

Your loving husband,
   Noah-1872

Carrie sobbed hot, scalding tears that shook her entire body. She read the letter again as she wiped tears from her face, only to be replaced by new ones. She read the letter again and again, held it to her heart and cried.

Sarah sat next to her mother holding one of the twins on her lap while Charlie played on the floor with the other twin. Sarah knew the only reason her mother would cry like that was because her father wasn't coming back. Sarah had tears in her eyes, but she didn't cry. Even though she wanted to be strong for her mother, she didn't cry because her heart didn't hurt. She was sure if her father was never coming back, her heart would hurt, and since it didn't, it must mean he would return.

Sarah couldn't imagine anything could keep her father from coming home to them anyway, no matter what the men from the Army said, and no matter what the man from the bank thought. Her heart didn't hurt, therefore her father would come home. Sarah was a bright and intelligent child, and she had the faith of a child of five as well. She could not imagine never seeing her father again, and if she couldn't imagine it, then it must not be real.

~ TWENTY-TWO ~

Noah was simply outnumbered. There were too many chiefs, he mused, and not nearly enough Indians. None of the chiefs would hear any more talk of peace or cessation of raids, even though the Army had sent the Fourth Calvary under the command of Colonel Ronald S. Mackenzie to track and subdue the marauding Indians.

Even so, Noah had great respect for the chiefs and the way they organized their tribes and led the attacks. They were fearless, precise, and determined to succeed. And by late summer, after Quanah had personally led a raid on the Calvary camp and stolen all of their horses, Colonel Mackenzie took his troops back to the fort.

As 1874 approached, the raids decreased due to weather and cold, much to Noah's relief. Tired and lonely, he missed his family, and thought he might strangle the chiefs one by one as they slept. He wanted to go home, but Quanah wasn't finished with him, and Noah thought it was probably more that Quanah hadn't really decided how to best use him to the advantage of the tribes. So for now, he waited, he watched, and he dreamed of Carrie.

~ * ~

Carrie looked around the cabin and swallowed hard so she wouldn't cry. Everything they were taking with them had already been packed in the wagon and Mr. and Mrs. Walter Forsythe would arrive at any time. They moved west because there were too many people in Philadelphia, and they wanted the wide-open space of the prairie. Carrie sold them the cabin for much less than she could have gotten for it, but she didn't have the heart to ask for much.

This was her home. Her sister and father were buried there just beyond the barn. This was where she'd met Noah, had tended him when his leg was broken, and fell in love with him. This was their home, where they'd laughed and loved and had their children. How could she put a price on that? How could she sell their memories? The tears came anyway, and Carrie wiped them away when she heard Sarah calling to her.

"Mama, Mister and Mrs. Forsythe are coming."

"Thank you. Help your brothers into the wagon. We'll be leaving very soon."

With all of her children loaded into the wagon, Carrie slapped the reins against the horses and they started the long trip that lay ahead of them. Carrie left all of their furniture, animals and farm tools. She took her trunk, their clothing and the children's toys. She packed the cookware and other items she'd need along the way, and found herself shaking as they got farther and farther from the cabin.

Sarah helped with the packing, had been such a help to her mother that Carrie didn't know what she'd have done without her. The boys helped as much as they could, but they were still so small they weren't really any help at all. Sarah, six, Charlie, four, and the twins were nearly two, yet Carrie regretted her decision not to have any more children. If she'd known the last time Noah came home was the last time forever, she would have tried to get pregnant one more time. Having his children was her greatest comfort, and she would always be grateful for that.

Elijah Johnson visited on a few occasions and tried to talk her into moving near his home in St. Louis, but Carrie simply smiled and declined. She was going to live Noah's dream and raise horses in the Montana territory. She had no idea how to run a horse ranch, but she would hire some hands and ask other ranchers. She would learn the how of it like she did everything else—by doing it.

Eli convinced her to stop at Fort Sill on her way so he could send a couple of men with her for protection. He knew an Indian who would be able to protect her from the wild Indians, and had a friend who was a sharpshooter and a friend to the Indians to send with her. He was concerned for her safety of course, but lately, the raids had been concentrated in Texas, the Indian Territory, Missouri, and Arkansas. However, the Apaches were still causing problems in Arizona, New Mexico, and the Colorado territory. The least he could do for Noah was help keep his family safe.

The trip was long and arduous and Carrie was almost sorry she had made the decision to drag her children halfway across the country just so she could keep her husband's memory alive through owning a horse ranch, and making his dream a reality.

The rain fell for days at a time, and everyone was soaked and chilled, and Matthew became ill. There were flash floods, broken wagon wheels, rivers and creeks to cross, and trips around gullies and canyons that added weeks to the length of the trip. They ran into wild animals, a few wild Indians, and were even held up by two men who thought being outlaws was an easy way to make a living. They had been young and brash, and the sight of a woman with four children, an Indian, and a nigger, seemed to them an easy target. They were already dead before they realized they were outmatched.

When the group of travelers could finally see mountains in the far distance, it was late summer and Carrie was so weary of the trip that she wished she had never left Indian Territory. They had lost one horse that stumbled into a gopher hole and broken a leg. It took several days to locate a town where they could purchase another one. The twins were fussy and whining, Charlie was grumpy and irritable, and Sarah refused to speak to her mother at all.

Then finally, after having to take a southerly detour around a lake before heading north once again, and passing through the Bighorn Mountains Pass, and crossing Crow land, they made it to the small town of Billings,

Montana. Carrie had never been so happy to see civilization in her life. She made arrangements for the horses and wagon, and paid the Indian scout, but when she tried to pay Mr. Drake, the man Elijah had sent with her, he only smiled and looked at her.

"If it's all the same to you, ma'am, I'd like to stay on and help you get settled. It's rough land and a woman alone is apt to find more trouble than help out here in the west."

Carrie smiled and was more than a little relieved. "Thank you, Mister Blake. I'll pay you now for your time escorting us here, and then you'll receive the usual wages for a ranch hand. Whatever that may be," she added with a wistful smile.

Mr. Blake laughed. "I'll help you figure it out, Mrs. Mosely."

"Thank you," she said and handed him the money she owed him.

Mr. Blake escorted her to the hotel and helped with the large trunk she'd packed their clothing in, then said he would see her in the morning after everyone had a good night's rest. Carrie thanked him again and rented a room for herself and the children, ordering baths and food to be sent up for them as well. She was exhausted and didn't think she could manage going to the dining room just yet. A bath, clean clothing, and a real bed would do them all well. And as soon they had eaten and she had gotten the children bathed and asleep in the bed, Carrie looked around and sighed. They had made it, she thought, and realized it surprised her to know they had.

After a long bath in clean, hot water, Carrie put on a clean nightgown and lay down. She was so very tired, and slept without dreaming for the first time since Noah had left her. And she still referred to him as being gone, not dead. She just couldn't bring herself to say the words out loud because saying it aloud would make it real, and Carrie wasn't ready for it to be real.

By the time fall had begun to turn colder and winter was promising to come with a vengeance, Carrie had been able to locate the perfect place to start a horse ranch. It had belonged to a family previously, but the lawyer in town had told her the man only lasted through one Montana winter before packing up his family and moving back to the plains where they'd come from.

He told her the winters were harsh here, much harsher than it was in Indian Territory, and it wasn't so much the long, snowy days, but the wind howled and blew icy and cold enough it could freeze a person to death in a matter of minutes. He wanted her to understand that before she invested so much money into the place, but Carrie seemed determined and paid him in full.

Then she set about purchasing furniture and other items they'd need to get them through the winter. She wasn't worried about horses, or any other animals just yet, that could wait till spring. For now the only worry was making sure they would have plenty of food, wood for the fireplace, warm clothing, and quilts for the beds.

The ranch house was large with three bedrooms, a kitchen the size of the cabin Carrie's father had built, a separate dining room, a living room, and another room that could be used as another bedroom, an office, or whatever Carrie thought she might want it for. The front yard had a white picket fence with flowerbeds all around it.

The barn was three times the size of the one at their old home, with stalls for twenty horses. There were corrals and training pens, a chicken coop out back, a place for cows and pigs, and a garden area Carrie couldn't wait to see plant-ed and growing. There was a bunkhouse where Mr. Blake had already stored his gear, had built a fire in the wood stove to warm the place up, and had bedded the horses down in the barn.

Carrie stood looking out the kitchen window at the vast land beyond, all of it was hers, and her heart ached for Noah. This was his dream, the life he wanted to live so he could give his children everything life had to offer. Carrie had checked to make sure a school was nearby, and a church. She hadn't been to church in so long she'd forgotten what it was like to meet with other families after services on Sundays, to gather in the churchyard and share the dishes they had all brought for dinner. She smiled sadly and turned around when she heard Mr. Drake calling to her.

"You don't have to knock, Mister Blake. Just come on in whenever you need something," Carrie told him as she ushered him inside.

"I just wanted to let you know I got the wood chopped and want to know where you want me to stack it for you. There's a good place right out back, but I don't see no wood box in here. I'll see to that just as quick as I can. Winter's coming real fast too, and we don't have much time to get ready for it."

"I appreciate your help, Mister Blake. I really don't know what I'd do here if you hadn't stayed. Thank you."

Carrie smiled at him and she could have sworn he blushed. He did look down quickly at the hat he was twisting around in his hands.

"I knew your husband, ma'am. He was a fine man and I know he'd want someone to make sure you and your children are taken care of."

Carrie felt her breath catch as he spoke so fondly of Noah, but she was determined not to cry again.

She took a deep breath instead, and said, "Thank you. You're very kind."

They made it through the winter months and into the following spring. With Mr. Drake's help, Carrie began buying horses. She bought thoroughbreds, and though it took several weeks, she thought she'd done well and had a good start on the horse ranch.

She had bought fifteen mares and three young studs. Mr. Blake would be in charge of the breeding and keeping

track of which mares were impregnated by which stud,
and to keep the foals separated as well. He was an excel-
lent horseman and the animals seemed to respond to him
in a way that surprised Carrie. He told her he thought with
his connections to the Army, he might be able to arrange
for them to purchase horses from Carrie, and Carrie beamed at him. She wanted more than anything for the ranch
to thrive, to be able to fulfill Noah's dream, and have a
legacy to leave for their children, and their children's
children as well.

Mr. Blake—Carrie insisted on continuing to address
him formally even though he'd asked her several times to
call him by his given name, William, or Billy as most
everyone else called him—also helped Carrie hire two
ranch hands, Mr. Cummings and Mr. Wilson, who both had
horse and cow experience. She bought five cows and two
good bulls on the two men's word and hoped they would
be able to not only have beef for the table, but be able to
breed and sell them as well.

By the next fall the ranch was running smoothly, the
bulls and studs appeared to be doing the job they were
purchased for, and Carrie looked forward to spending the
winter months making new curtains for the house. She was
happy here in Montana and the children seemed to be
thriving.

Charlie had taken to the men and they were teaching him to ride. They spent time in the evenings with
Matthew and Mark, and had made a swing for them out
back on the old oak tree. Sarah was learning to knit and
crochet, and Carrie planned to teach her the fine art of
cookie baking during the cold winter months. Carrie cooked for everyone and during the warm months they'd eaten
outside at the table the men had made with long benches
on each side so there was room for everyone. Carrie planned on sending Sarah to school the next spring, but had
already taught her to read and write and figure numbers.
Charlie might even be old enough for school too, and

Carrie knew how proud Noah would be to know his children were getting an education.

Life was perfect, Carrie thought, as long as she kept pretending Noah was at the fort and would be home any day now. Her days were busy enough that she only thought of him ten or twelve times a day, but in the evenings when the dishes were washed and the children bathed and sleeping in their beds, and the house was quiet, she thought of him constantly.

She had finally gotten to the point she could think of him without bursting into tears, most of the time. But she continued to make him shirts and store them in the trunk, although she told herself they were really for the boys when they got older.

They were growing so fast, she could hardly believe they were the same sons she'd given birth to. And while Sarah matured as she grew older, grew more beautiful, and looked so much like Carrie at that age, it was quite obvious she was going to be a petite young lady.

Charlie was two years younger and already as tall as his sister. Although all of the children had wound up with Noah's golden eyes, and the boys all had features that strongly resembled Noah's, Carrie could see some of her own father in Matthew and Mark that wasn't evident in Charlie.

She could see more and more of Noah in Charlie every day. He looked amazingly like his father, with the same golden eyes, the same facial features, the same silky, curly, long black hair. But it was more than just Noah's appearance that Carrie saw in her son. He had the same mannerisms, the same gestures, and the same laugh. He carried himself like Noah did, and Carrie often caught him looking at her, or one of his siblings, with the same bemused expressions as Noah had.

November became December and Carrie and the children decorated the Christmas tree Mr. Blake had brought inside. He had also brought candy canes and a clear glass ornament with a horse and sleigh in the snow painted on both sides of it. Carrie invited the men inside the house on Christ-mas day and gave them each a present. She'd made them all a pair of wool socks, and a scarf to wrap around their necks beneath their coats while they were outside in the cold.

They gave Carrie a new trunk, since they'd noticed the one she had brought to Montana was charred on one side like it had been in a fire, and it was fairly battered all the way around. Carrie knew they didn't know the story of how the Yankees had burned her home in Charleston, and the trunk was among the few things that survived, but she was very happy with the new one.

They gave Sarah a new dollhouse they had built and painted together. For Charlie they had a pair of cowboy boots so he would be a real cowboy when he was riding his pony. They gave Matthew and Mark each a new hat and stick ponies and the twins were happily riding around the house on their steeds.

Carrie baked a ham for Christmas dinner, and served it with all the trimmings and three kinds of pie for dessert. She and Sarah had made oatmeal cookies and fudge, and after supper they all sat together in the living room with the fireplace crackling merrily, drinking tea and sampling the cookies. Carrie laughed at the stories being told and sighed as Mr. Wilson told of his favorite Christmas memory.

It was just as it should be, Carrie thought, looking around the room. They had a fine home filled with laughter and love, a warm fire, good food, good company. Her children were happily playing with their Christmas gifts, and Carrie had everything Noah wanted to give her. Everything except him.

~ TWENTY-THREE ~

Noah had been in the middle of this conflict for so long he was no longer certain where he belonged anymore. Or if he had ever belonged anywhere except where Carrie was. The year had started off with the Indians confident and successful in their raids on the white settlers and the Army, but by late spring things took an unexpected turn for the worse and they began suffering setbacks.

They took a couple of months to regroup and reassess their methods and then, sometime in the weeks that followed, they made plans to attack Adobe Walls again. The first time, they'd been denied the thrill of victory since the Calvary had chosen that place and time to rest and pick up more supplies. The intertribal alliance was not prepared to take on the Calvary and retreated. A second attack, they reasoned, would not be suspected, and the Calvary would be long gone as well.

They arrived in late June, seven hundred strong—a combination of Cheyenne, Arapahoe, Kiowa, and Comanche warriors. They attacked the twenty-eight men and one woman there, but the raid was a disaster. The hunters at Adobe Walls had superior weapons and a seemingly endless supply of ammunition. Wave after wave of warriors attacked, yet the hunters were able to fend them off, and in the end they only suffered one casualty. The warriors however, lost fifteen men, and many others were wounded. Including Quanah Parker.

The Indians retreated into a disorganized, defeated, and deflated group. With Quanah severely wounded, the leadership began to fall apart and by early fall, the alliance had crumbled. With the Army now in hot pursuit and rounding up fleeing Indians on a daily basis, it was only a matter of time for all of them. Quanah's wounds were severe and he wasn't recuperating very well. Noah stayed with him and tended to his wounds and by the middle of November he was able to convince Quanah to give up.

Noah took Quanah's horse and rode hard until he found an Army patrol that immediately took him into custody, refusing to hear any explanation from him. They bound his wrists behind his back and led him on his horse to the temporary Calvary headquarters near the Red River.

It was late night when they arrived and the sentries all looked at Noah with curiosity. He was dressed like an Indian and riding an Indian pony, but there was something strange about him they couldn't quite identify. They pulled him from his horse and led him roughly to the makeshift holding cell, then shoved him inside the cage and locked the door. He sat down in the middle of the space and crossed his legs. There was no use in trying to convince them now of who he was—he'd just have to wait until a superior officer came around.

Noah didn't sleep. It was only a few hours till dawn, and the camp would be full of noise and activity as the soldiers were roused from their tents. Noah stood as dark disappeared and the thin, wintry light allowed Noah a look around. There were tents set up in one area where the soldiers slept, a large mess tent had been set up west of the sleeping area, and the horses were corralled to the east. He could see officer's quarters beyond the enlisted men's tents and he waited patiently for someone to come speak with him.

A young private arrived a few minutes later with a tray of food and looked nervous as he opened the gate and handed it to Noah.

"I don't know what you injuns eat for breakfast, but we civilized folks eat ham and eggs. The Army feeds us mush, so just eat it and don't cause a fuss."

The young man was trying to sound tough, trying to pretend the fear Noah could see in his eyes didn't exist, but Noah couldn't resist the opportunity to frighten him just a little more.

"Our tribe usually has room service send up breakfast with hot coffee and warm buns," Noah said, sniffing the mush.

The private almost tripped over his own feet as his mouth fell open and he stared openly at Noah, but Noah didn't change expressions, he just continued to stare the young man down.

"You better get on back to your duties, son. Before I decide to take your scalp."

Noah dropped the tray and took a step toward the gate. The boy ran away without looking back and ran straight into his commanding officer.

Noah couldn't see much more than the top of their heads since there were tents between him and where the boy and the officer stood talking. He could see the boy turn back toward him occasionally, all the while waving his arms wildly. Noah chuckled aloud and kicked the tray out of his way.

When the boy had finally quit waving his arms, the officer said something and the young soldier went about his business. The officer began walking toward Noah and as soon as he walked between two of the tents and into full view, Noah began to grin. Colonel Elijah Johnson stopped dead in his tracks when he recognized the "Indian" his men had captured during the night. He thought Noah was dead, and of course Noah thought Eli was dead as well, and for a long moment they just stood staring at one another, grinning like fools.

"Well, are you gonna let me outta here or not?"

Elijah walked to the gate and shook his head. "I don't know. It might be safer to keep you right here."

Noah threw his head back and laughed. "Look at you! A colonel no less and I thought you died out there in the desert, Eli."

Elijah opened the gate and the two men embraced and slapped each other on the back. "Yeah, they felt sorry for me I guess, so they slapped a few more stripes on me."

210

Elijah looked his friend over and shook his head. "I thought you'd been separated from your scalp, Noah. I shoulda known you'd be all right."

Noah stepped back and looked at Elijah for a long moment before speaking again. Then he took a breath and asked the question he wasn't sure he wanted an answer for.

"Elijah, where's Carrie?"

"Noah," Eli said and looked away. "Carrie hung on for a long time. She refused to believe you were dead and she waited for you to come back. I saw her a few times and kept telling her she had to let go, she had to live even if it was without you, and finally, earlier this year..."

Noah's heart slammed in his chest as fear rose with the thoughts running through his head, "She..." Noah stopped and cleared his throat, afraid to go on. He took a breath. "She remarried?"

"No, she didn't remarry," Eli said and saw relief flood Noah's face. He grinned. "She took the money you left her in the bank and went to Montana to buy a horse ranch. I tried to talk her out of it, but she wouldn't hear it. She said it was what you wanted and she was going to see it happen. I sent two men with her, Little Eagle, and William Drake. You know they're both good men. And Drake decided to stay and help her. I got a wire from her not too many months ago. She said she's doing well and hired two more hands to help Drake."

Noah looked at the ground and felt more love and pride in his wife than he ever had before. She was stubborn and determined, he knew, and she hadn't listened to what he'd written in the letter about meeting someone else and getting married again. *Thank God*, he thought and exhaled heavily.

"Look, let's get this other business cleared up so I can get to Montana, all right?"

Elijah nodded and they went to the tent they were using as a war room. It had a table in the middle of the floor that had maps piled on it, and a few chairs sat around it. Eli called the lieutenant and captain in and Noah briefed them all on the raid at Adobe Walls and the events that had occurred since. He told them Quanah Parker had been wounded and was in need of medical care. He told them where to find White Horse, but he wasn't sure if Big Bow, Satanta, or Big Tree had survived the raid or not, and didn't know where they'd gone afterward.

After the briefing, Colonel Johnson provided Noah with a change of clothing, and then ordered an attachment to go with them as Noah led the soldiers to Chief Quanah Parker's ragtag group of warriors. The medic said it would be several days before his patient could travel by horseback, tended to Quanah. Elijah sent the rest of Quanah's men with some of his men back to the camp at Red River, leaving the rest of the soldiers with the medic and Quanah. Elijah rode with Noah north and west across Texas into New Mexico, and there they said good-bye.

It was the middle of December and Noah wanted to get to Montana as quickly as he possibly could. Winter was already upon the land and snow fell heavier and heavier the further north he went. By the time he reached Crow land, the snow was more than three feet deep in some places and made the going slow and dangerous. He was not unfamiliar with the Crow Indians, although most had gone to the reservation the year before. There were some that had fled into the mountains, but Noah wasn't worried about them now, he only knew the urgency to be with Carrie grew with each mile he put behind him.

~ * ~

He reached Billings and found the only business in town still open was the saloon, so he stomped the snow from his boots and stepped inside. After he'd spent a few minutes warming up next to the wood stove and had a shot of whiskey, he asked directions for Carrie's ranch, then was on his way again.

The ranch was about five miles northwest of town and blanketed in snow. He could see lamplight glowing through the windows and could smell smoke from the fire burning warm inside. Noah had never been so nervous in his life as he was when he left Quanah's pony in the barn and walked toward the house. He wasn't sure what he'd say or how he'd explain the past two years to Carrie, but at that moment he couldn't think of anything at all except that inside the house was his wife and children.

He saw a trail tramped through the snow from the barn to the back of the house, so he followed it to the back door. He didn't know if he should just walk in or knock first, and it took him a full minute to decide. He raised his hand and rapped on the door three times. He could hear laughter from inside and he knocked again more loudly. A few seconds later the door opened and the man stood staring at a ghost. William Drake stood with his mouth working like a fish out of water, staring at a face he recognized, but his brain wasn't accepting as being possible.

Noah looked at him and grinned. "Hey Billy boy, you gonna let me in?"

Blake continued to stare, speechless, but he moved aside and Noah came inside. He had to shut the door himself because William seemed to be frozen where he stood. Noah shook the snow off and wondered if Carrie was going to kill him for getting the floor wet. He took his gloves off, then his hat and coat, and hung them on one of the hooks in the wall next to the door.

"Noah?" Blake finally managed.

"I see you haven't forgotten me after all." Noah grinned.

"We thought you were dead. My Lord, Carrie is going to faint!"

"Yeah, I know." Noah's grin faded. "I don't know how to do this, Billy. Should I just go in, or what?"

Billy didn't get a chance to reply because just then Carrie came into the kitchen to see who had been knocking on the door, more, to see who was mad enough to be out this time of night in such a storm. She looked as if she was about to say something to Billy when her gaze landed on Noah and she stood frozen in her tracks. The teacup in her hand shattered on the floor at her feet and she didn't even seem to notice.

Noah glanced at Billy, who was already excusing himself from the room, and then he looked back at Carrie. He couldn't move, and his voice didn't seem to be working either. She was the most beautiful woman in the world. Now she was standing there in a fashionable green velvet gown with white lace, her hair piled on top of her head with ringlets framing her face. He thought she looked like a vision, like something from his dreams but couldn't possibly be real. Nothing that soft and beautiful could be real, but there she was, with just a few feet of floor space separating them.

He took a deep breath and very softly said her name. "Carrie, it's me, Noah."

Then he thought of how ridiculous that was to say to her. So he took a step toward her, but she still didn't move or speak.

"Carrie, I'm so sorry you had to go through all of this," he said, taking another step toward her.

Then he was in front of her with less than a foot of space between them. He reached up slowly, so very slowly, with one hand and touched her face. It was all he could do to keep from taking her into his arms right there in the kitchen. But he didn't. He only stroked a finger over her soft cheek again and again.

It was Noah, Carrie thought as she stared at him. It was really Noah, wasn't it? She was afraid to move, afraid to speak, afraid if she did she'd wake up and discover he was just a dream. But now he was touching her and she could feel his fingers, still cold from the frigid air outside, moving over her skin. She inhaled, his scent filling her nostrils, filling her senses. She moved her hand ever so slowly, wanting to touch him, but afraid if she moved too quickly she would break the spell and wake up. She had dreamed of him often, but she had never had one this real, one where she could feel him and smell his scent.

She placed her hand on his chest, felt his heart thumping as wildly as her own. She looked up at him, saw his golden eyes watching her, and could see his pulse beating in his throat. Then she saw his lips begin to curve and he was smiling at her, his white teeth glinting in the lamplight. She could feel his hand moving along her jaw line, down her neck, and over her shoulder. And then she was leaning into him and her arms were linked around his neck as their mouths came together.

Noah's lips were warm and demanding, his tongue was in her mouth and the flavor of him was seeping into her degree by slow degree. *He is real*, she thought. Noah was real and he was standing here in their kitchen and he was kissing her and his hands were in her hair and moving down her back and... then she jerked away from him and began screaming. Emotion crashed over her, wave after wave, and it was too much. She couldn't quit screaming, and suddenly felt sick to her stomach. She felt as if she couldn't stand on her own two feet, and then Noah picked her up and carried her into the living room.

He set her down on the sofa and looked around. Everyone in the room stared and Carrie continued to scream, though she did try to stifle it behind both hands. Noah looked at the children on the floor and felt his stomach lurch. He knelt down and smiled, then Sarah threw herself into his arms, followed by Charlie and the twins.

"I knew you'd come home, Papa!" Sarah threw her arms around his neck and kissed him on the cheek. "See,

Mama." Sarah beamed at her mother. "He came home just like I said."

Carrie continued to stare with both hands covering her mouth, though she had managed to stop screaming.

Noah felt the tears coming and didn't try to stop them as he held his daughter close to him. He looked at Charlie, who was now as tall as his sister and Noah was amazed to be looking into a face so similar to his own.

"Hey, Charlie." Noah grinned and caressed the boy's cheek. "How are you, Son?"

"I'm good, Papa. I knew you'd come home, just like Sarah," Charlie said with a grin.

"Are you Matthew?" Noah looked at one of the twins, who only grinned shyly at him.

"I'm Matthew," the other twin spoke up, and Noah tousled his hair.

"I'm your papa," Noah said quietly, looking at the identical faces.

He looked at all four of his children and hugged them close, then set them back and stood. He looked at Billy again and grinned. He offered his hand and Billy shook it.

"Thank you for helping, Billy. I owe you."

Billy shook his head. "No you don't, Noah. You're home and that's all that matters now."

Noah turned to the other two men. "I'm Noah Mosely."

"Jim Wilson," the taller of the two said and shook Noah's hand.

"Walter Cummings," the other one said. "Welcome home, Noah."

Then all three men said goodnight to Noah and his family and headed to the bunkhouse.

~ TWENTY-FOUR ~

Noah followed Carrie and his children to their bed-rooms and kissed each of them goodnight. Carrie looked up at him as she blew out the lamp in Sarah's room and shut the door.

"Would you like to see the rest of the house?" Carrie asked as she moved past him.

Noah nodded. "I guess so."

He followed Carrie through the house, but he saw only her. He couldn't get over how beautiful she was, so much more now than she was when he'd last seen her. She was soft and gentle, with an elegant grace that made her seem regal. And dressed as she was, in a new dress she told him she'd had made in town just for Christmas, he thought he'd been right before when he thought of her living in a fine house wearing fine clothes. She was suited for it, suited for luxury and the finer things of life.

She's done well, he thought. Done well in raising his children, done well in selecting this house, and he was just as sure she had done as well in selecting the stock she'd bought.

They had wandered through the house and were back in the living room, where Carrie offered him a brandy. He accepted it and saw the way her hand shook slightly. She was as nervous as he, and Noah didn't quite know what to do about it. For either of them. He sat on the sofa beside Carrie and sipped the brandy, then rolled the snifter between his palms, took another sip and set the glass on the table beside the sofa.

"Carrie," Noah said softly, but she jumped anyway.

She had her hands in her lap fidgeting with the material of her dress. He reached for her, a finger under her chin to turn her face toward him.

"Carrie," he said again when he could look into her eyes. "I don't know what to say to you." He took an unsteady breath, "except that I love you. I thought of you every moment I was away and I never stopped trying to get back to you."

Carrie's hand moved up to his and slid over his arm. "I thought you really were dead, Noah. I tried not to believe it when they told me. Even when Elijah said you'd been shot, I couldn't believe you were dead but after the first year and you didn't come back..." she wiped at a tear with her other hand. "What else could I believe, Noah? You weren't coming back and I made the decision to come here. It wasn't easy but I knew it's what you wanted for our children and me. I'm sorry I didn't wait longer."

Noah smiled and stroked her cheek. "I'm not. I'm glad you came here and bought this place. I love you so much."

"I love you, Noah. I could never love anyone else," she said just before his mouth found hers.

And then her arms were around him and every lonely night she'd spent without him was fading away.

Noah broke the kiss, smoothed the pad of his thumb over her lips, then stood and pulled her up the long, hard length of him. She fit perfectly against him, he thought as he lifted her in his arms and found her mouth again with his. He carried her down the hallway to the last door, which, he surmised, had to be Carrie's bedroom since the other doors had led to their children's rooms, and this one was the only room he hadn't yet been in.

He pushed the door open with his shoulder and saw an oil lamp was already burning as he carried his wife across the threshold to the bed. He set Carrie on her feet and pulled back so he could look at her lovely face. His heart thumped hard against his chest and his blood thundered in his head. He breathed, just concentrated on drawing air deeply into his lungs, trying desperately to gain some control over himself.

His hands shook as he reached for her. He caressed her cheek, then moved his hands into her hair, fumbling with the pins that held it. Carrie smiled and reached up to help him. When the pins were out, she shook her head slightly and the long cascade of hair fell down her back and onto her shoulders. Noah sank his fingers into the strands of silk, fisted them there, and used it to pull her to him.

On his side, he rested on his elbow, his face cradled in his hand as he looked at her. She was still lying with her eyes closed, her chest rising and falling with each breath she took, the thin sheen of perspiration on her body glowed in the dim lamplight. Her hair fanned out on the pillow above her head, reflecting gold and red that shined like a halo around her.

Noah couldn't resist touching her face and smoothed his fingers over her cheek. She reached up and held his hand in hers, pressed it to her face and kissed the palm. She rolled toward him and opened her eyes, a slight smile curved her lips as she looked at him. Carrie couldn't believe he was home. Couldn't believe he was alive. Alive and home. It couldn't get any better than that.

"I'm starving," Carrie said when she could finally speak.

Noah leaned over and kissed her. "What would you like to eat?"

"Well... " she said, then clamped her bottom lip between her teeth.

She looked at him with a gleam in her eyes that caused the muscles in his stomach to clench into a tight ball of desire. He pulled her to him and held her to the bed with one arm while he ravished her mouth.

"What were you saying?"

Carrie giggled and bit his lip. "I was saying I'm starving and there's a pumpkin pie in the kitchen that hasn't been cut yet."

Noah bounded over her and off the bed. "Why didn't you say that earlier? I've been lollygagging about with you when I could have been eating pumpkin pie!"

Carrie chased him down the hallway and into the kitchen. He grabbed her and kissed her again, then lifted her onto the counter. She traced her fingers over his face and kissed him softly.

"I love you."

"I love you, too."

"I'm so glad you're home." She wiped at a tear that rolled down her cheek.

"Hey," he said against her ear. "Weren't you going to get me some pie?"

Carrie laughed and nodded. "Yes. We are definitely having some pie."

Noah grinned and kissed her with a loud smack as he set her on her feet. Carrie cut two huge pieces of pie and handed one of the plates to Noah. They took them back to the bedroom and sat in the middle of the bed eating and talking and laughing until it was nearly morning, and they fell asleep exhausted in each other's arms. And long before Carrie was ready to leave the warmth of Noah's body, their children were standing beside the bed wanting breakfast.

Carrie smiled sleepily at them and whispered, "Go into the kitchen quietly so you don't wake your papa. I'll be there in a moment."

When they were gone from the room, she slipped her nightgown over her head and pulled a robe around her. With her feet covered in slippers she'd knitted just a few weeks earlier, she padded to the kitchen and began mixing batter for hotcakes while sausages sizzled in the skillet.

Noah stood in the doorway of the kitchen watching Carrie help Sarah to flip a hotcake, while Charlie showed the twins how to set the table. The grin on his face widened as love and pride rose within him.

And when the twins saw him, they shouted, "Papa!" and wrapped themselves around each of his legs. Carrie turned to him and smiled.

Sarah said, "Look, Papa, I'm making hotcakes!"

Charlie looked up and grinned. Noah was still amazed his son looked so much like him. Noah swallowed hard, trying to remove the lump in his throat. He was home, he thought, home with his family, and he had no plans of ever leaving again.

~ TWENTY-FIVE ~

Present Day-
        Emily Williams gently shut the album and put it away in the bottom drawer of her grandmother's trunk. She wiped her eyes. Looking at the old photos always made her cry, but reading the old journal written by one of her ancestors made her wish love could really be like that.

        Emily had just turned twenty-five and there wasn't even a glimmer of hope she would find Mr. Right anytime soon. She'd dated so much, she felt like there should be a turnstile just inside her apartment door. Everyone she knew had set her up with their brothers, their friends, cousins, and once she'd even been set up with the widowed father of one of her co-workers.

        She had even thought of signing up with an online dating service, but that really seemed a little desperate to her. If an intelligent, twenty-something woman with a college degree and a great job couldn't get a date the old fashioned way, then Emily thought she'd just be single for the rest of her life.

        She walked from the den into the kitchen where she and her grandmother had spent so much time when Emily was young. She remembered coming here on holidays, spending summer breaks from school at her grandmother's ranch in Montana and smiled. She could almost see Granny standing at the stove transferring freshly baked cookies from the cookie sheet onto a plate. This was where Emily learned to make chocolate chip-oatmeal cookies, where she learned to ride horses, milk a cow, and gather eggs.

        It was so much different than her life growing up in California had been, so when Granny died last winter and left the house to Emily, she had come to look the place over and thought she would probably sell it. For some reason though, she had never gotten around to contacting a real estate agent, and now, as she stood at the window behind the kitchen table, she knew she never would.

As a matter of fact, she thought, she was going to leave L.A. and move here permanently. The cows still needed milking, the chickens were still laying eggs, and a few of the thoroughbreds Granny had raised were still grazing out in the pasture.

Emily hadn't felt this light or carefree in a long time and knew this was what she'd been looking for. It wasn't that she couldn't have found a man to marry—it was that she hadn't *wanted* to marry and settle down in L.A. She didn't want the life her parents had in the city she'd been raised in. She didn't want to fight traffic every morning of her life to get to work. She didn't want to breathe brown air, and she really didn't want to be divorced after only a few years of marriage like most of her friends.

This, she thought, as she looked out at the open space beyond the house, was where she wanted to be. She could breathe here, could relax here, and she wouldn't mind if she never heard the sound of traffic again.

She could run the ranch herself, she thought with a nod of her head. She could raise thoroughbreds like all the generations before her had raised right here. Maybe that was why Granny had left her the ranch instead of leaving it to her father, Granny's only child. She'd known her son wasn't suited for raising horses and living in the middle of nowhere, although they were really only a few miles from Billings. And she had known her granddaughter *was* suited for the life of raising horses. Emily picked up the phone and booked a flight back to L.A.

A month later Emily was back in Montana. She had driven the entire way in her Jeep Cherokee with all of her personal belongings stuffed in every available area of the Jeep. It was stacked from floorboards to ceiling, front seat to rear window, leaving barely enough room for Emily to sit comfortably and drive.

Now, she thought as she carried boxes inside the house, she was going to get a dog. She had always wanted one, but never did because she lived in an apartment and wouldn't make a poor animal live indoors with no yard to run around and play in. But she had plenty of room now, and she was going to get the biggest dog she could find, maybe one of those big sheep dogs with long hair and floppy ears. She smiled to herself and went out to get another box.

When all of the boxes were inside, Emily flopped down on the couch with a glass of iced tea in her hand and ran the frosty glass over her forehead. It was hot out even though the sun had disappeared behind the mountains in the distance, and there wasn't a breeze to be found.

She flipped the switch on the oscillating fan and sank back onto the sofa. How Gran had lived here all those years without air conditioning, Emily didn't know, but she lived here now and there would be air conditioning by next summer. She took a long drink of the tea and closed her eyes, only to be startled by a knock on the door.

Emily opened the door and smiled warmly at the man standing on the other side of the screen.

"Hi, may I help you?"

Deep black eyes gazed into hers and Emily suddenly felt a little nervous. It was a long moment before he said anything, then he cleared his throat and looked away from her.

"Yes, ma'am. I'm looking for Granny Williams. Is she home?"

Emily took a deep breath. She didn't recognize this man, but it was obvious he hadn't been around in a while because he didn't know her grandmother had passed away. "I'm sorry, Mister...?"

"Blade," he said quickly. "Nick Blade."

"Nice to meet you, Mister Blade. I'm..."

"Nick, it's just Nick," the man interrupted her.

"Nick, then. I'm Emily Williams. I'm sorry to have to tell you my grandmother passed away last year, just after Christmas."

Nick looked at the ground with his hat in his hands and Emily could see the muscles in his jaw working as he clenched his teeth. After a few moments he looked up at her and sighed.

"I'm sorry to hear that. Thank you, ma'am." He turned away and started down the walk.

Emily pushed the screen door open and walked outside onto the porch.

"Nick, wait," she called after him. When he stopped and turned toward her, she hurried down the steps. "Why did you want to see my grandmother? Maybe I could help you."

His hat was back on his head and made it difficult to see his eyes, but Emily thought he was very handsome, and she could feel his eyes on her, even if she couldn't see them.

"I never met your grandmother but my father used to work for her. He was here before your grandfather died and stayed on afterward to help your grandmother."

"Jake was your father?"

Nick nodded. "You knew him?"

Emily said, "I used to stay here all summer when school was out and Jake taught me how to ride, how to rope and brand. I was sorry when he died. I don't remember he was married or had a child though, I'm sorry."

One corner of Nick's mouth twitched. "No need to be sorry. He wasn't married. And I only saw him a few times when I was a kid. He sent money for my mother and me, but he didn't mean much more to me than a name."

"What does my grandmother have to do with it?"

Nick pulled off his hat again. "My mother died a couple of months ago," he said. Holding his hat in one hand, he reached into his back pocket and pulled out a worn envelope. "I found this letter in my mother's safety deposit box. It's from your grandmother. She wrote to my mother to tell her my father had died. She said he wanted her to know how sorry he was and he wanted my mother

225

to tell me he loved me, and he would understand if I hated him. She said if I ever wanted to know about my father I should come here and she'd give me a job." He held the letter out to Emily. "You can read it if you want."

Emily looked at the letter in his hand, and then back at Nick. "Why don't we go inside first?" She took the letter and led him back inside the house.

They went into the kitchen and Emily poured a glass of iced tea for Nick and refilled her own glass as well, then sat at the table across from him. Emily turned the letter over and looked at the address on the front. Her grandmother's familiar loopy handwriting stared back at her, and she noticed it had gone to Phoenix, Arizona.

She took the letter from the envelope, unfolded it and began to read. She smiled as she read, and could almost hear her grandmother's voice saying the words aloud. She wrote exactly like she spoke. After a few minutes, Emily folded the letter and replaced it in the envelope, then slid it across the table to Nick.

"I'm sorry about your mother."

Nick shrugged. "Thanks, but it wasn't sudden. She had cancer and knew she was dying. She was strong though and fought for nearly three years, but in the end, the cancer was stronger."

"That must've been difficult for you watching her die day by day. I still have both my parents. I can't imagine what I'd have done in your position."

"You do what you have to do. You don't really think about it, you just do it."

"You took care of her yourself?"

"For the most part. In the end a nurse came in a couple of times a day to check the I.V., make sure the morphine drip was right, that kind of stuff. I think it was to check on me too, but she was a nice lady and she was with me when Mom died."

Emily's heart was nearly breaking in two for him, but she didn't think he wanted her sympathy. So she offered him a job.

"I need help here," she told him. "I just got back from L.A. with my stuff today and I want to make a go of this place. If you want a job, you can stay in the bunk house and start in the morning."

Nick nodded slowly. "Just like that?"

"You do know how a ranch works don't you? How to tend cattle and raise horses?"

"I could tell you I do, but then you'd just have to take my word for it. So I'll put my gear in the bunk house and by tomorrow night, I guess you'll be able to tell if I know what I'm doing or not."

He rose from the table, pushed his chair neatly back under the table, nodded once in Emily's direction and strolled out of the house. He waited until he was outside before he put his hat back on.

Emily didn't miss the way his jeans fit over his bottom, or stretched over his muscular thighs. She hadn't missed the way his T-shirt stretched over his chest, or how his biceps bulged, stretching the thin material to its limits, either. His hair was black and thick, and it hung much longer than Emily was used to seeing a man wear his hair. He had high cheekbones, a broad forehead, and a sharp nose. His lips were full and he looked exactly as Emily imagined an Indian would look. She knew he was an Indian, or at least half Indian, because Jake Blade was an Indian. She laughed at a memory that suddenly filled her head.

She was about six years old, she remembered, and she had climbed the gate of the corral so she could watch Jake ride one of the young Thoroughbreds for the first time. It bucked and leaped, reared up and pawed the air. Then it bucked some more, but Jake hung on like he was glued to the saddle. Pretty soon, the horse accepted the fact it was going to carry the man upon its back no matter how hard it objected, and settled down to trot around the corral. Jake pulled on the reins and the horse stopped, even though it continued to prance and paw the ground, and Jake threw his leg over the saddle and slid to the ground.

"What are you doing there, Little Bit?" Jake asked as he climbed over the gate and tugged on Emily's braid.

"Watching you," she answered with a wide grin.

"Oh yeah? Well, what did you think?"

"I think you ride real good!"

"That's because I'm an Indian, and horses know better than to mess with an Indian," Jake said with a grin and a wink.

"You are? A *real* Indian?" Her eyes were wide with astonishment.

"Yep, I'm a real Indian." He winked again.

"Then maybe you can tell me something," Emily said with a very serious expression.

"What would you like to know, Em?"

"Just how *do* you scalp somebody?"

With that Jake had thrown back his head and laughed out loud. He gave her his Bowie knife and told her when she could throw it straight and true and make it stick in a tree at twenty paces, he would tell her how to take a scalp.

Emily laughed at the memory. She'd spent all summer throwing that knife at a tree, every tree she saw in fact, but she hadn't been able to stick it in the bark even once. By the next summer when she came back to the ranch, she had completely forgotten about taking scalps.

~ TWENTY-SIX ~

Nick was already working when Emily came into the kitchen to make coffee the next morning. She watched him from the window above the sink as she ran water in the coffee pot, and then poured it into the reservoir of the machine. She added the paper filter and freshly ground beans, swung the compartment shut and switched on the machine. In a matter of seconds the machine began to hum and coffee began dripping into the pot. Emily thought it was probably her favorite scent, there was nothing like the aroma of fresh coffee in the morning. She looked back out the window and watched Nick as he carried a sack of feed on his shoulder, walking as if it weighed nothing, when she knew it weighed at least seventy-five pounds.

Emily couldn't take her eyes off of Nick. The way he walked, the way he carried himself, pulled at something inside of her. He walked as if he wasn't subject to the laws of gravity, and he carried himself with such confidence, as if he didn't care what others might think. Maybe he really didn't care, she thought, and how nice that must be.

Emily had grown up worrying about what others might think. Had grown up trying to overcome her heritage—a genetic malfunction that left her looking as if she were an adopted child.

Her father was tall and handsome with wavy blonde hair and her mother was a golden haired beauty who had been a runner up in the Miss America Pageant when she was just nineteen. With so much blond hair and those deep blue eyes possessed by both, they looked like America's golden couple and surely, they would produce the perfect golden child. Not!

Emily had hair the color of brown sugar that hung to her shoulders in tight, springy ringlets, and skin so bronze everyone on Muscle Beach would have lain in the sun for days and poured gallons of lotion over their bodies in order to sport such beautiful skin.

The only thing golden about Emily, she sighed, was her eyes. She had been told they were beautiful, and they reminded people of the big cats at the zoo. But she'd been looking at them for twenty-five years and would have given anything to be the blue-eyed blond her parents had been so sure they'd produce.

It wasn't until she was nine years old that she had asked her mother about the difference between her looks and theirs. Annie Jamison had brought it to Emily's atten-tion one day in school when she had suggested Emily was probably adopted. Emily insisted she wasn't adopted, but Annie told her children always looked like at least one of their parents, and Emily looked nothing like either of hers. Therefore, she had to be adopted. Emily thought about it all the rest of the day and on the bus ride home, and when she came into the house, she immediately asked her mother if she'd been adopted.

She remembered her mother's shocked look, and then her gentle smile as she sat on the sofa and brought Emily to sit next to her. Emily explained Annie Jamison's theory to her mother, and then her mother had explained about a thing called jumping genes. It was something that happened sometimes and brought certain traits out in people from their ancestors who'd died years and years ago.

In Emily's case, her several times great-grandfather had been a slave in Mississippi, and his father had been a white man. Her mother had said he'd run away and lived with the Indians. Then he'd fallen in love with a white woman and Emily's own Granny was one of his descen-dants.

As Emily had gotten older she became more and more aware of the trick genetics had played on her. And she became more and more aware of the fact that people knew she was of mixed blood. For the most part, it hadn't bothered her overmuch, but children could be cruel, and sometimes they made fun of her. True, it was mostly boys who taunted her, but it still hurt her feelings. She knew she wasn't ugly, but she thought she was very average looking at best, and plain at worst. Then, as a teenager she became curious about the great-grandfather that had loaned her his DNA, and that summer when she came to stay with her grandparents, she had asked Granny about it.

That was the first time Gran had shown Emily the photo album and the journal. The pictures went all the way back to the kinds that were printed on metal plates instead of paper. There were some paintings of other ancestors Gran had kept protected in an old trunk up in the attic, and Gran had said the trunk was from the 1870's.

So was the house. Of course it had changed considerably over the hundred and fifty-some years since it had been built. Indoor plumbing had been installed, electricity wired in, and insulation and interior walls had been added as well. Another bedroom had been built on, and a laundry room added off the back door, and the appliances had changed with the times as well. The barn had been struck by lightning and burned down sometime around 1900 and then was rebuilt but other than that, it was the same place.

From the first time Emily had read the journal written by Sarah Anne Mosely-Washington, her fourteen-year-old heart had fallen in love. Sarah had written the journal for her children to have a record of their heritage, and the story she told of her parents had been the most romantic, exciting adventure Emily had ever heard.

Sarah had also written about her own life with Amos Washington, as well as the lives of her brothers. Charlie had stayed on at the ranch in Montana after the death of their parents, who'd died only months apart. Emily nearly swooned when she read that part. Even now she couldn't imagine a love that would last a lifetime, a love so deep and strong that after one had died, the other couldn't continue living without them.

Charlie had never married, Sarah had written. He had only been in love once, but the girl jilted him for a rich man from back east after she'd found out Charlie's father had once been a slave. Sarah had written that of her three brothers, Charlie most resembled their father, with the same facial features, black curly hair, and golden eyes. But, Sarah had noted, she and all three of her brothers had inherited their father's golden eyes.

Her younger brothers were twins named Mathew and Mark, and had looked like their mother. Mathew became a lawyer and moved back east where he married and had a successful law practice. He became a judge later on and had three children, all of whom looked like their redheaded Irish mother.

His twin, Mark, had also married and moved back east near his brother. Mark had become an engineer and designed bridges and dams. He and his wife had a set of twin boys that looked like him. Later his wife gave birth to a set of twin girls who Sarah said looked more like her than their father. She described them as having hair the color of brown sugar with lighter blonde streaks, and golden eyes.

It had been through Sarah's son, Henry, that Emily's granny had eventually come, and since Sarah's husband had been a black man, the blood ran a little stronger through Sarah's descendants than it did through her brothers. Of course, times had changed over the century and a half since Sarah's parents had lived. Being of mixed blood wasn't the taboo it had been back then, or even in the first half of the twentieth century. Unless of course you had blonde hair, blue-eyed parents.

Emily watched Nick through the kitchen window and heard the coffee maker hiss, bringing her attention back to the twenty-first century. She pulled a mug from the hook and filled it, then brought it to her nose and inhaled the aroma before she sipped from the steamy liquid. Movement caught her eye again as Nick walked back to the barn. Emily lifted another mug from a hook and filled it, then carried a cup in each hand and went outside.

Nick was cleaning a water trough when she walked up to him and said, "I thought you might like some coffee."

He looked up and grinned before wiping his wet hands on the legs of his Levi's. He reached for a cup and inhaled the aroma before he sipped from it.

"Thank you," he said.

"I didn't know if you take anything in it. I can go—"

"No," Nick shook his head. "I take it black."

"Good, I can remember that. I'm going to fix breakfast, it should be ready in about thirty minutes."

"You're inviting me to breakfast?"

"No," Sarah smiled at him. "Three hots and a cot are part of the deal. My grandmother cooked for all the hands. During the summer they set a picnic table and benches up under the old oak and ate there. In the winter, they all came inside the house. So, breakfast will be ready in about thirty minutes," she said again.

"Yes, ma'am." Nick took another drink of his coffee and went back to scrubbing the water trough.

Emily opened the refrigerator and pulled out a carton of eggs, a pound of bacon and the jug of milk. She didn't know why she felt so excited about cooking breakfast for Nick, but her stomach was fluttering. She made biscuits and put them in the oven, then fried the bacon, made gravy from it while a pan of hash browns sizzled on the stove. She set the table and put the food on it, and just as she pulled the biscuits from the oven and was placing them on a plate, the door opened and Nick came in. He hung his hat on a hook in the wall next to the door and stood looking at the table.

Emily put the plate of biscuits on the table, and sat down. Nick took a chair as well and sat, but didn't start filling his plate.

"Aren't you hungry?" Emily asked just to break the silence.

"Yes."

"Then dig in." Emily picked up a biscuit and reached for the butter.

"I'm just used to saying grace before meals," Nick said with a shrug.

"I'm sorry. We can pray if you want to."

Nick folded his hands and bowed his head. He said a short blessing and Emily echoed his *Amen*, and buttered her biscuit.

Nick said, "I know most people don't pray, and think it's ridiculous that I do. My mother insisted we pray before each meal and before I went to bed at night. She took me to church every Sunday, too. I don't go to church anymore, but I still pray before I eat. I guess you never outgrow some things."

"We prayed, too. I mean when I was here with my grandmother we did. My parents never did, so every summer my grandmother would have to remind me, but by the time I went home, it felt natural. Then I'd expect my parents to pray when I was home—very confusing." Emily grinned as she popped the last of the biscuit into her mouth.

Nick had a piece of bacon between his fingers, but when Emily grinned at him, his hand froze halfway to his mouth. She was the most beautiful woman he'd ever seen, he thought. She was tall and lithe, had the thin, graceful body of a dancer. Her fingers were long and slender with perfectly manicured nails. Her hair was the color of honey and warm sunlight and hung just past her shoulders. It was a tangle of tight curls that made him want to pull one of them straight and let it go just to see if it would bounce like a spring.

Her lips were full and sensuous and, he noticed, she had a habit of flicking her tongue out to moisten them that made his stomach clench. Her forehead was broad, her nose was straight, but the most striking of her features were her golden eyes. They reminded Nick of a mountain lion he'd seen once and he had a hard time not staring at her.

Her eyes were fringed with dark, thick lashes, and her brows were thin arches above them. Her neck was long and slender and Nick couldn't help but think what she might taste like right there where her shoulder curved into her throat. He could see her pulse beating there and the impulse to run his tongue over it was almost more than he could control.

He tried not to notice the way her chest moved with every breath. They rose slightly with each breath she took, and fell as she exhaled. Her baggy sweats made it difficult to see her shapely body, but he could see it in his mind's eye as he'd seen it yesterday.

She had been wearing a pair of tight low-rise jeans and a tank top that didn't quite reach her belly button. He had noticed the bare skin, but he also noticed the gold ring she wore in her navel. And when he followed her into the house, he noticed the tattoo of a dragonfly in the middle of her lower back as it rose above the waist of her jeans.

He had wanted to reach for her last night while they were sitting at this same table while she read the letter her grandmother had written, but he had gone to the bunkhouse instead. It would've probably gotten him fired quickly if he had followed through, but the desire hadn't dissipated after he'd gone to the bunkhouse. If anything, it'd gotten worse as he unpacked his single bag and put his things away.

"Aren't you hungry? Or is my cooking that bad?"

Nick jumped. "What? What did you say?"

Emily giggled. "Where were you? A million miles away it looked like."

"Yeah." Nick took a bite of the bacon. "Just thinking about everything that needs done around here."

"Is it in bad shape? I know Gran didn't keep it up the past few years, and I wasn't here to help her."

"Not in bad shape, just neglected. I'll get it back good as new in no time," he said, picking up a biscuit.

"If you need anything just make a list and we'll go into Billings and pick it up. I wanted to bring this place back to the way it was meant to be. I want to raise Thoroughbreds, breed them and sell them like they used to do here."

"Was it very successful?"

"It used to be up until your father passed on. After that Gran hired several hands, but none of them worked out the way Jake had. By then, she was getting so weak and old she couldn't do it herself, so she let most of the horses go. She sold them for half of what they were worth, but they'd done very well before that. And it was success- ful when my however many times great-grandfather and grandmother lived here. I'd like for it to be again."

"Your family has always lived here?"

"Yes," Emily said through a bite of eggs. "My original grandparents, Noah and Carrie, bought the place some- time around 1872 or '73, I think, and then their oldest son ran it, but he didn't have kids, so his sister's son took it over and it's been handed down like that ever since. My dad never wanted it, so it came to me."

"And you'll pass it on to your own child," Nick stated.

Emily breathed in deeply, then exhaled and pushed her plate back. "I hope so, but at the moment it looks like I'll be more like Charlie and never marry and have kids."

Emily caught the look Nick gave her and thought he must be thinking how pathetic she sounded. "Don't get me wrong," she added quickly. "I chose not to get married before. I was in college and getting my career started, so marriage wasn't really a top priority. Besides, I'm only twenty-five, I have lots of time for that."

Nick only looked at her and ate another piece of bacon. "I only meant that you planned on keeping it. That you wouldn't sell it or anything."

"Oh," Emily felt her cheeks heat. "No, I won't ever sell it."

~ * ~

Nick went back outside after setting his dishes in the sink, even though Emily told him she'd take care of it. She cleaned the table, ran hot, soapy water in the sink and watched Nick as she washed the dishes.

~ TWENTY-SEVEN ~

Emily didn't know what it was about Nick, but he made her feel all fluttery inside, as if butterflies had taken flight in her stomach. Her brain didn't seem to work properly around him, and her tongue always felt thick and too big for her mouth. Her blood seemed to heat and bubble in her veins, and she felt a warm ball form somewhere deep within her every time she looked at him. That was ridiculous, she chided herself.

A man, albeit a sexy one, didn't cause a physical reaction. She had dated. My, how she had dated, and never had she felt this way around a man. She'd had boyfriends as well and had kissed them and made out with them, but they'd never made her stomach flutter, or her blood sizzle and heat.

That was the reason she was still a virgin, she sighed sadly. Not that she'd planned on being the world's oldest living virgin—it had just turned out that way. And not that she wanted to be one of those girls who slept around. And she often heard Granny's words in her head talking about waiting for the wedding night and how she would feel if she saved herself. Granny of course, preached to her about how God wanted everyone to wait until marriage and if everyone had, there wouldn't be the problems there are now.

Emily could see that point but to have slept with only one man in her whole life, that was kind of old fashioned. She had tried to lose her virginity to Chad when she was in college, even going so far as to getting stripped down to her bra and panties with him. Then his roommate came home, totally ignoring the red sock tied to the door handle, and the moment was ruined. Afterward, she decided it hadn't been all that exciting anyway, and then the semester ended and so did her relationship with Chad.

She thought Michael would be the one to do the deed, or un-do it, whatever the case may be, but that hadn't gone so well either. They had dated for four or five months and had gotten along so well that when he asked her to come back to his apartment with him, she agreed. He was gorgeous, sexy, a real GQ cover model, and he never spared any expense on their dates. He always brought her flowers when he picked her up, and held doors open for her, too. What more could a girl ask? *To not laugh, that's what!* Emily closed her eyes at the memory. Because she *had* laughed. No, she had gone into a fit of giggling hysteria and couldn't quit.

They had gotten back to his place, he had poured them a glass of wine and put on a Michael Buble`CD, then he'd taken her hand and kissed each of her fingers. He kissed the back of her hand, kissed all the way up her arm to her shoulder, then nibbled on her neck and even blew in her ear.

He led her down the short hallway to his room and kissed her romantically while cupping her head in his hand. He undressed her slowly, and then undressed himself. And that's when it started. He stood there in all his naked glory, with his manly part listing to one side, and that's what caused Emily to burst into laughter. No matter how she tried to quash it, she simply couldn't. And Michael seemed to suffer worst of all. They had both dressed and he had driven her home. He hadn't bothered to call her again.

"Oh well, Em, I guess you're going to die a virgin," she said. "No, no, no! Lord, *please* don't let me die a virgin," she shouted, looking Heavenward.

"Hmm, I guess you didn't hear me," Nick said with a grin.

Emily whirled around and felt her cheeks coloring. "H-h-how long have you been standing there?"

"Long enough to know that you do pray." Nick's grin grew wider even as Emily's cheeks stained a deeper color of red.

Emily glared at him. "I was, well, it was… oh, never mind! What do you want anyway?"

"I came to tell you there's problems with some of the horses and we need to go into town to pick up medicine for them."

"Is it serious?"

"I hope not. I hope I caught it early enough that they'll recover quickly. We need to get some bag balm for the cows, too. They haven't been milked regularly and that can cause problems with their teats. They can get plugged up and it causes them a great deal of pain." Nick saw the concern in Emily's eyes and was glad of it. At least he knew she was serious about making a go of the ranch.

"All right, give me an hour to get showered and changed," Emily told him.

"No problem," Nick said and went back through the kitchen to the door.

Yeah, no problem at all, he thought as he gritted his teeth. Except that she'd told him she was going to take a shower. He could imagine her every move, no matter how he tried not too.

"Then you need to think of something else, you idiot," Nick berated himself.

If he didn't find a way to stop thinking of Emily, he was going to have to live in the shower with icy cold spray raining down on his heated skin.

~ * ~

"Did you live in Phoenix all your life?" Emily turned the Jeep onto the main road and headed toward Billings.

"Not until my mom got sick and we had to be near doctors and the hospital," Nick answered, looking out the window.

"Oh," Emily said, feeling badly for causing him to bring up his mother. "So, did you grow up in Arizona or somewhere else?"

"I was raised in a small town called White River on the Fort Apache Reservation. My mother's people were there and helped her take care of me when I was a child."

"I didn't know your mother was Indian, too." Emily glanced over at him.

"Yep, she was raised in Fort Apache, my father was from the San Carlos Reservation and lived in a town called Clifton. They met at a pow-wow and then," Emily heard him sigh, "then I was born."

"At least you had your mother's family. Did you know your father's family at all?"

Nick nodded. "I was their only grandson, so they were there on birthdays and Christmas and I visited them in the summer. My Grandmother Blade liked to tell me about my father, liked to show me pictures. And he did show up occasionally."

"I always liked him," Emily said.

"I don't know if I did or not." Nick looked at her. "It seems you knew him better than I did."

Emily was glad the feed store wasn't all the way into Billings, but sat on the county road a couple of miles from town. She felt like her attempt at friendly conversation had gone terribly awry, and had only succeeded in up-setting Nick. She was glad when she turned onto the paved parking lot so she could change the subject.

They bought the necessary medicine Nick said was needed, plus some antibiotics and feed. Emily followed Nick through the store allowing him to get whatever he thought necessary without saying a word. When they brought the items to the checkout counter, Emily told the cashier to put it on the *N Bar C Ranch* account, and then she told them to add Nick's name to those allowed to make purchases on the account.

"You didn't have to do that," he said when they were driving back toward the ranch.

"I only authorized you to purchase items so you can do your job. You don't need to come to me every time you need something, and this way you can come and go as need be."

Nick didn't answer. He stared out the window and watched the scenery slip quickly past as he thought of Emily. She asked more questions than any person he'd ever known before, but she seemed to be genuinely concerned and not asking out of nosiness. He thought she had an innocent quality about her, and he knew she was unassuming and not in the least pretentious.

She was clean and fresh and perfectly suited for this open land that could make a person feel alone and swallowed up by it. And she seemed perfectly suited for Nick Blade, which made Nick feel just a little bit uncomfortable. Of course, it was nothing Emily had said, or done, or even implied. It was just Nick. And he didn't have a clue as to why he would think of her the way he was now. He took a deep breath and blew it out, relieved they were back at the ranch and he had work to do.

Nick jumped out of the Jeep and went to the back to unload what they'd bought at the feed store.

"Supper's in an hour," Emily said as she shut her door.

Nick looked up at her and nodded as he hefted a bag of feed onto his shoulder, and tried not to watch the gentle sway of her hips as she walked to the house.

Nick muttered as he carried the feed to the barn.

~ * ~

Nick and Emily's working relationship went smoothly over the next few weeks. Nick worked hard bringing the ranch back into working order and that allowed little time for him and Emily to be alone together. He only had to see her at mealtime, and lately he had been skipping the mid-day meal telling her he had too much work to do. He really just couldn't spend so much time with her. He dreamed of her every night as it was, and whenever he caught sight of her hanging laundry on the line, or weeding the flowerbeds she planted beneath the kitchen window, it only served to fuel his dreams more intensely.

He knew he had to get himself under control where Emily was concerned. He didn't know why he felt the way he did about her when he had never had this reaction to any other woman he'd ever known. Not that he'd known all that many in his twenty-six years, but the ones he had known certainly hadn't had this effect on him. Maybe it was because he hadn't been with a woman since his mother had gotten so ill she couldn't get out of bed a year before she died.

"Crap," he muttered as it occurred to him how long it had been since he'd had a date. "No wonder I'm having this reaction to her." He shook his head and set the feed sack down.

Anyone who had been under the stress and pressure Nick had endured while his mother lay slowly dying day after day, would be having a reaction to Emily. Especially a man who couldn't even clearly remember what the last woman he'd been with looked like. He was just in need of a night out. A club in town where the music was loud, the drinks were strong, and the women were willing. And it was Friday night. He'd been at the ranch for just over a month now, looking at Emily day after day, and it was driving him crazy. Maybe he'd just take a little ride into Billings and see what he could see. He felt a lot better now. He finished his chores and washed up for supper.

~ * ~

"This is good," Nick said as he shoveled another bite of lasagna into his mouth.

"Thank you," Emily said, smiling as she watched him eat.

His mood had changed dramatically from the way it had been over the past few weeks, but Emily couldn't fig-ure out what might have happened to cheer him up. The past week or so he had been especially surly and she felt as if he was trying to avoid her altogether. But now he seemed to be in a much lighter mood, and Emily's heart did a flip every time he smiled at her.

~ * ~

"I'm going into town for a while tonight," he told her, swallowing the last of the wine in his glass.

"Is there a problem with the animals?"

"No." He shook his head and served himself another piece of lasagna. "I just thought I'd check things out in town, maybe go dancing, have a couple of drinks."

"Oh," Emily said and wondered why he hadn't asked her to go along. But maybe he wanted to be alone, she thought, even though she still felt a little put off. "Well then, have fun. I'll see you when you get back."

She stood and picked up her plate even though she hadn't finished her meal.

Nick scraped the last bite from his plate and swallowed it as he carried his plate to the sink. "Thanks, Em, that was great. I might not make it back till tomorrow, so don't worry about breakfast in the morning," he said with a grin and left the house.

Emily stood with her mouth opening and closing as he left. She didn't know why she suddenly wanted to throw the cup she held at him, but it took all of her resolve not to. Emily fumed while she cleared the table and washed the dishes.

He was going out on the town, just like that, and she was seething as she plunged another plate into the soapy water. They had basically lived together for over a month now and she thought they had become friends. Apparently Nick only considered her his boss and not his friend. She knew she shouldn't be mad at him—after all he was a single man. A single available man. A sexy man. A single, available, sexy man! And he made it very clear what his intentions were—he was going to pick up some bimbo and spend the night with her! Had he not noticed there was an available woman right here in front of him?

"Well," Emily said and slammed the cupboard door.

She stomped all the way down the hallway when she heard Nick's truck start up and drive away.

Emily slammed the door back when she went into her room and jerked open the closet door. "Fine," she gritted through clenched teeth, "I can go out on the town too." There was no reason for her to stay home on a Friday night, no reason at all. She pushed the hangers aside one after the other, then suddenly her hand smoothed down the little black dress she'd bought for a special occasion, but had never gotten to wear.

It was perfect with its thin spaghetti straps, the deep "V" that showed so much of her cleavage it left little to the imagination. It draped over her body like a second skin and thin wispy pieces of sheer black fabric hung from the hem of the dress half way down her claves. It had little silver threads that ran through it and caught the light every time she moved.

She kicked off her Nikes and stripped out of her jeans and shirt, then jumped into the shower. When she was dry, she smoothed scented lotion all over her body, then slipped the little black dress over her head and wriggled her body until the dress was hugging her, clinging to her just like it was supposed to. She bent forward and fluffed her breasts to their full advantage, then put on her make-up, and fixed her hair. Or, she thought, at least she fixed the light brown ringlets as best she could since they seemed to have a mind of their own, and there was really very little else she could do with them.

She chose a pair of black high-heels with an ankle strap and open toes, then sat on the foot of the bed to put them on. She stood in front of the full-length mirror and turned side to side, then turned her back to it and looked over her shoulder at her reflection and ran her hands over her bottom. She smiled. That was as good as it would get and she was a knock out.

~ TWENTY-EIGHT ~

Emily grabbed her black beaded bag, stuck her ID and some money inside and went out to the Jeep. Butterflies took flight as she started the engine and drove to town. Emily wasn't the clubbing type, though she'd gone with friends in L.A. She preferred one-on-one dates in a quiet restaurant, and she preferred dancing to something slow and soft instead of loud and rocking, but this outing was to prove a point.

She didn't care what Nick Blade did, she didn't care where he did it, and she didn't care who he did it to. So what if he was gorgeous enough to make any girl think twice about him? Or to have one or two dreams about him, okay numerous dreams? Or to fantasize he wanted her, too? It meant nothing. Nothing at all. She had been looking at Nick Blade for over a month now, and she was used to him. He was just a ranch hand. Nothing more. She could go out and have fun and not think about him even once. She'd prove it, too.

She didn't know exactly where to go since she'd never been clubbing in Billings, so she drove around a little while and spotted a place that reminded her of a club she'd gone to in L.A. She parked the Jeep and slid her long legs out of the vehicle and smoothed her dress as she locked the door.

Inside the music was pumping and bodies were packed on the dance floor. Emily made her way to the bar and sat on a stool. She smiled at the bartender when he winked at her, then ordered an appletini. She looked around the room and felt like running right back to the ranch. She was overdressed and feeling out of place, but the bartender placed the drink in front of her and told her it was on the house.

Single ladies drank free from seven to nine on Friday nights. Emily didn't know it, but the club had discovered if they gave away the drinks, by nine the ladies were all very happy and the men began pouring in looking for Ms. Right. Then the price of drinks was nine bucks apiece, and the club raked in the cash until two in the morning.

Emily swallowed her drink in two big gulps and ordered another. "New in town," a voice beside her said, and Emily turned to see a man's grinning face.

"Yes," Emily nodded. "Does it show?"

"Just a little," the man chuckled. "I'm Dan." He held out his hand and Emily shook it.

"Emily," she said

"Where you from?'

"L.A. I've only been here a few weeks."

"You look like a city girl." Dan grinned charmingly. "But it looks good on you." Emily didn't miss his gaze running from one end of her to the other. "Would you like to dance?"

Emily caught her bottom lip between her teeth and thought of saying no, but she'd come to have fun, hadn't she? She grinned and slipped off the barstool. Dan caught Emily's hand in his and led her to the floor.

She was glad the music was loud and fast so they didn't have to be too close to one another. She wasn't looking to be picked up on, and she was sure that was exactly what Dan *was* looking for. When the music faded, Emily smiled and hurried off the dance floor back to her barstool.

She finished the rest of her drink and picked up her bag. *This was a bad idea*, Emily thought. She was here because she'd gotten mad at Nick for no real reason. It wasn't as if they were anything but co-workers on the ranch. Emily couldn't think of herself as Nick's employer, or of Nick as an employee. She thought of them as equals at the ranch and it didn't matter to her that she owned it all. She felt as of she were acting like a child. Nick deserved a night out. And Emily wasn't comfortable sitting on a barstool, but before she could slip out, Dan blocked her way.

"Are you leaving?"

"Yes," Emily nodded. "I have to get back home, but thank you for the dance and the drink. Nice meeting you, Dan." Emily tried to slip around him, but he wouldn't let her pass. "Excuse me, Dan," Emily tried to be polite.

"There's no need to rush off, Emily. I thought we could get to know each other."

"Maybe some other time, Dan, but I'm leaving now." Emily wasn't smiling anymore.

Dan took her arm and she kicked him in the shin. "What was that?" Dan bellowed.

Emily felt a wave of panic skitter through her, but then a voice behind her said, "Is there a problem here?"

Emily turned to see the bartender, and sighed with relief. "I told this man I was leaving and he won't leave me alone."

The bartender looked at Dan. "Is that right? You need to leave, sir."

"I'm staying right here." Dan glared at Emily, then at the bartender. The bartender raised his hand above his head and suddenly two very large men who looked like weight lifters appeared on either side of Dan.

"Sir, we'll see you to the door," one of the bouncers said. Dan slammed his glass down on the bar and with a last menacing look at Emily, he walked toward the door with the bouncers following him.

"Sorry about that," the bartender said and slid another drink in front of her. "Sometimes the jerks think they can get away with crap like that, but we don't allow it in here. You drink that on me, doll, and give Romeo there enough time to get on down the road."

"Thank you," Emily said and picked up the drink, surprised her hand was shaking.

It was her third drink and she rarely drank more than two because she was a lightweight and new her limit-ations. And since she had to drive, she didn't want to drink too much, but her hands were still shaking slightly from the encounter with Dan, and Emily finished the drink quickly. The bartender was at the other end of the bar when Emily slipped off her stool and walked toward the door. She could feel the alcohol swimming in her blood-stream, and she was feeling a little dizzy. She decided to sit in the Jeep for a little while to let the alcohol dissipate before she drove, then walked outside into the warm night air.

She looked around, and other than a few people coming and going from the club, she didn't see Dan anywhere. She walked down the sidewalk, turned at the corner, and then walked across the street to where she'd parked her car. There was no one about on this side of the building and Emily glanced nervously around as she put the key in the lock. Her hands were unsteady from the alcohol and nerves, and it took her a few moments to fit the key in the lock. She turned the key and pulled the door handle and just as the door opened, a hand grasped hers.

"Well Emily, it looks as if we were destined to be together," Dan said.

Emily jumped when he grabbed her. He held her in his grip even as she twisted her arm and tried to break free. "Let go of me," she demanded.

"I'll let go of you," he whispered as his finger cares-sed her cheek and she jerked her head back, "just as soon as I get you back to my place."

"I'm not going anywhere with you!" Emily lifted her knee to his crotch, but he blocked her just before she made contact.

"Witch!" Dan twisted her arm hard and had her back against his front with her arm caught hard against him. "Now, walk!"

Emily screamed then and rammed her other elbow into his rib cage, and suddenly she was pitched forward against the side of the Jeep, but Dan was no longer touching her. She turned in time to see Dan fly face first into the street and Nick Blade landed on top of him in an instant. He caught one of his hands in Dan's hair and pulled his head back, then smashed his face into the asphalt, once, twice, and when he pulled Dan's head back the third time, Emily was beside them.

She grabbed Nick's shoulder and shouted, "Nick, let him go! Nick, you have to let him go. Now!"

Nick looked at her and Emily had never seen anyone look so dangerous, so cold, or so deadly. His eyes were flat and cold, and there was no expression on his face. She felt as if the air had suddenly dropped twenty degrees and Emily shivered against it.

"Nick," she said softly. "Let him go."

Nick dropped Dan and stood to his full height. He glared at Emily, looked her up and down, then grabbed her by her arm and practically dragged her to the Jeep.

"Get in," he commanded, jerking the Jeep's door open and pushing her into the seat. "Go home. I will be right behind you. Go straight home, Emily," he commanded her through clenched teeth. He slammed the door, turned on the heel of his boot and stalked off.

Emily started the engine and put the vehicle in gear. She was so stunned by what had just happened, she hadn't even thought to argue with Nick until she was nearly back to the ranch. Nick had followed her the entire way, Emily noticed. And as she pulled to a stop in the driveway, she could only think of how relieved she was to be home.

She climbed out of the Jeep and walked to the house, opened the door and threw her keys on the kitchen counter. She walked to the threshold of the living room and braced one hand on the wall, and used the other to unbuckle the straps around her ankles, then kicked her high-heels off and started down the hall.

"Stop right there," Nick shouted.

Emily spun around. "Nick, I'm going to bed. We'll talk about this tomorrow."

"No, we'll talk about it now," he said, taking long strides toward her. He grasped her wrist and hauled her back to the living room and sat her down on the sofa.

"Nick, I know I haven't said thank you to you for rescuing me, but it's been a rough night," Emily began.

"Shut up, Emily," Nick said without emotion. Emily stopped with her mouth open and then shut it as she stared at him. "What do you think you were doing?"

"What *I* was doing? Who do *you* think you are?" Emily looked incredulously at him.

"I think I'm the one who just saved you from being raped, or worse," Nick thundered and came to his feet. "I want to know what you were doing out by yourself dressed like that?"

Emily came to her feet as well, and with her hands fisted on her hips she glared at him. "I am a grown wo-man, you big, stupid jerk! I am as free to go out to clubs as you are. So don't even think you can lecture me on what I do or where I go. Or who I do it with. Now get out of my way, I'm going to bed." She shoved at him as she stormed past him to go to her room.

He caught her by one arm and spun her around to face him. "We're not through," Nick said softly, his voice belying the fury on his face.

"Oh, yes we are," she said and tried twisting free of his grip but he just looked at her. "Fine!" She ground out after realizing she wasn't able to break free. Emily went to the sofa with Nick still holding her wrist.

Nick sat on the sofa with some space between them and released Emily's hand. He folded his together, leaned forward and rested his elbows on his knees. "Emily, what were you doing out tonight?"

"None..."

Nick looked at her. "Emily, just answer me."

"You went out, what's the difference?"

"So you went out because I did?"

"Well," she pushed at her cuticles, "you just seemed so happy to be going and made it quite clear what you were planning on doing all night. I guess I just, well, I just figured a night out would do me as much good as it would you."

"You thought I was going out to find a woman for the night," he sighed, "so you were going to pick up on some guy?"

"Well, weren't you going out to find a woman?"

"That's none of your business," he retorted quickly.

"So what you do is none of my business, but what I do is your business? I don't think so. And I'm tired of this conversation. I'm going to bed," Emily said wearily and stood.

She hadn't taken three steps when Nick had her by the hand and spun her around again. He pulled her up against his muscled chest and wrapped his arms around her. She looked up at him and licked her lips nervously. Nick lowered his head slowly until their lips were a breath apart, but Emily didn't try to stop him and he pressed his lips to hers.

The blood in Nick's body raced through him like hot oil heating every part of him. His heart slammed against his chest and the world around him seemed to fade to black. He could only feel Emily, hear Emily, as she seeped into his bloodstream and her scent assaulted his senses. This... her... Emily was all he needed. Ever.

~ TWENTY-NINE ~

Emily didn't recognize the feelings flooding her body. Her blood hummed and her heart pounded in her ears, while the taste of Nick on her tongue drugged her. She felt the sensations, like an electrical shock, as they moved through when their lips met, and it shot through her to every nerve in her body. The heat moved through her, balled in her stomach, became a living thing and roared through her body like a freight train. Her hands became restless, moved over Nick's body, down his back and found their way beneath his shirt. She raked her nails over his skin and Emily felt her knees give.

Nick held her, picked her up in his arms and carried her down the hallway to the last door and pushed it open with his elbow. He carried her to the old iron-framed bed and set her on her feet. His hands slipped into her hair, tangled in the tight curls and tilted her head back so her lips were angled up at him. He kissed her again, skimmed his lips over hers, grazed his teeth over her lips, sucked her bottom lip into his mouth, and then he sealed his lips over hers. He kissed her, and kissed her, continued drawing the kiss out. A long, fluid kiss that rocked them both.

Nick pulled back, looked into her liquid gold eyes and was lost. He licked her lips, kissed her cheeks. Kissed her nose. Kissed her eyelids. Kissed her forehead. He moved back to her mouth, then kissed her again. Their tongues mated, the flavor of her spread over his tongue, and slid deep inside of him.

His hands moved from her hair, his fingers lingered at the nape of her neck and slid lightly over her shoulders. Hooking his thumbs beneath the thin straps of her dress, he pulled them over her skin, down her arms, and then pushed the fabric over her stomach and hips. It floated down her legs and landed in a pool at her feet. She was exquisite, he thought. Simply the most stunning woman he'd ever seen.

The fear that ran through him when he saw Emily being attacked was like ice water in his veins. Never had he been so scared in his life, nor had he ever felt panic rise like bile in the back of his throat before. The desire to kill the man with his bare hands was overwhelming, just as the feelings of possessiveness, anger, and fear were. But it was at that moment he knew he just wasn't falling in love with her, he *was* in love with her.

Now, as he gazed into Emily's eyes, the candlelight made her skin glow, her eyes reflected iridescently in the dim light, and her hair shimmered like gold in sunlight.

Emily was devastated by him, stunned by him, and just a little bit afraid. He was like a Greek God, so well sculpted was his body, and Emily quivered uncontrollably when he touched her. And he did touch her, on every level. Emily tentively reached for him, smoothed the palm of her hand over his chest and down his stomach, and felt his muscles twitch beneath her touch.

He watched her every movement. Watched her eyes glow with desire. Watched her hands tremble as she touched him. Watched her watching him. All of this was new to her, he knew, and it excited him that much more to know that he would be her first. She had never loved a man, not physically, not emotionally, not with her heart and soul, and he would be her first everything.

"Are you all right?"

"Hmm," she sighed. "I'm perfect."

He gathered her close, nuzzled her ear, and said, "Yes, you are. Absolutely perfect."

She turned to look at him. "So are you."

~ * ~

They woke late the next morning and Emily stretched lazily, then curled into the warmth of Nick's body. She didn't want to get out of bed just yet, she wanted the feelings that started last night to continue on in the light of day. She glanced up at Nick's sleeping face and hoped he wanted the same thing. Hoped he wouldn't regret what had happened between them. She had worried needlessly because Nick's arms came around her then and he pulled her on top of him.

"Good morning," he said.

"Good morning," Emily said. "Are you hungry?"

"Definitely."

Nick grinned wolfishly and pulled her mouth to his. Then Emily got out of bed and went into the kitchen to make coffee and fix breakfast.

They sat at the table together eating waffles with strawberries and whipped cream off the same plate, drinking coffee and talking about the ranch. Emily shared with him what she hoped to accomplish, and smiled as he told her his many ideas. He knew so much about horses and training them. He was perfect for her in every way.

"My great-grandmother, many times great," Emily told him as she licked whipped cream from her fingers, "began this ranch sometime in the early 1870's. Her husband was thought to be dead and he'd always wanted to have a horse ranch where he could stay at home rather than being gone all the time. It seems he was some kind of liaison for the Army with the Indians back then and it kept him away a lot. Anyway, she thought he was dead and moved from Indian Territory with their four children and bought this place and started raising horses. Then my great-grandfather came back, arriving here one Christmas night in the middle of a blizzard, and I guess you could say they lived happily ever after.

"I'd just like to see this place as successful as they say Noah and Carrie were here. They had some kind of deal with the Army and sold most of their horses to them for the Calvary. It's been handed down generation after generation, and since my father didn't want to live out here, I inherited the place."

"That's cool you know so much about your family history. My family handed the stories down by word of mouth from generation to generation. I had a great-grandfather who was famous in his day, or at least he was well known. He was an Apache chief and during the Indian Wars he caused a lot of headaches for the Army. He refused to go to the reservation and he continued making raids on white settlers and the Calvary units that came on Apache land. But in the end, sometime in the 1870's, he was killed in a battle with the Army, and the Apache's wound up on the reservations anyway. We've lived there ever since."

"That's an interesting story," Emily said. "Would you like to see the journal written by Noah's and Carrie's daughter? She wrote the entire story out for her kids and it's been passed down to each generation with this house." Emily went into the den and opened the old chest. She pulled out the journal, and then she and Nick went back to the bedroom. Nick lay back on the pillows as Emily began to read.

After a while, Nick took over reading but a few pages through, he stopped and looked at Emily, then back at the journal. He read silently over the next few pages then passed it to Emily.

"You aren't going to believe this," he said, sounding amazed.

"What is it?" Emily asked as she picked up the journal and read over the pages Nick had just been reading.

"Read that part out loud," Nick said and pointed to a paragraph and Emily began reading.

"'*His mother was a* senorita *from south of the border, a captive his father had kept for some time, and though the real story might never be known, it was said that after Bear Killer's birth, his father killed his mother and then tried to drown the boy in the river. The story went that a female bear had found the wet and starving babe on the banks of the White River and raised him as her own. And when he was twelve and food was nowhere to be found, he killed the female bear, roasted her meat and used her fur as clothing. Then he went looking for his father, and when he found him several years later, he slit the old man's throat while looking him in the eye and telling him who he was.'* That part?" Emily looked up at Nick.

"Yeah," Nick said, his voice thick. "That's my great-grandfather. I was raised on that story."

"Really?"

"Really." Nick nodded.

"There's more about him later on," she told him and flipped through the journal until she found the rest of the story about Bear Killer.

Reading aloud, Emily then handed him the journal and he read it again to himself.

"I can't believe our grandfather's knew each other," Nick said. "We have always known the stories about Bear Killer, and about the man the Indians called Dark Horse. He was the only man outside of our tribe Bear Killer had respected and considered a friend. And he was your grand-father."

Emily looked at him and said softly, "I wish your father had known. It's strange to think our families have been connected for all these years."

"Yeah," Nick said and set the journal on the bedside table. He pulled Emily to him and kissed her softly. "I know this is sudden Emily, but I'm not willing to let any more time go by without telling you that I love you."

Nick continued looking into her golden eyes and waited, hoping she'd not throw it back in his face, hoping he'd not just made a fool out of himself.

"Really," Emily said, amazed. "You love me?"

257

"I love you, Emily." Nick smiled slightly and waited.

"Oh, Nick." Emily threw her arms around him. "I love you, Nick. I think I fell in love with you the first time I saw you."

"I know it's when I fell in love with you, Emily. And I want to marry you and live happily ever after with you. Will you marry me?"

"Yes, Nick. Yes, I'll marry you!"

Nick kissed her deeply and passionately. Neither Nick nor Emily noticed the two figures standing in the doorway of the bedroom. The man was tall with long, curly, black hair and golden eyes, and the woman was smiling, wiping tears from her green eyes as the man bent down to kiss her. Then both disappeared. They had not noticed the Indian either, a fierce looking man with eyes as black as night and a face that closely resembled Nick's as he looked at the pair on the bed, then nodded his head, satisfied with what he saw. The Indian became a mist that vanished as if he had never been there at all.

~ * ~

Nick Blade led a horse by the reins and looked up when his son laughed with delight. A son, he thought with pride, made from the love he and Emily shared. Then he looked at his wife, who held her hands over her very round stomach, and smiled as she blew him a kiss and waved to their son. Nick couldn't believe how his life had become one filled with such love and happiness, and all because of a letter his mother had saved.

Emily moved her hand over her stomach as the babies kicked inside her womb. She wiped a tear from her eye as she watched her husband and son in the coral, and thought of the twins that would be born in just three short months.

She'd written a book about her family from the journal left by Sarah Mosely-Washington all those years ago and it had been a best seller. Now sitting in the family history section of libraries, as well as in the romance section, the book was a favorite among the Apache Tribe at the Fort Apache Reservation. Emily's parents had acted like she was the first person to ever write a book.

Emily was still amazed how much her life had changed from the one she thought she would live when she was in L.A. But then again, it also seemed to be exactly how things were meant to be. And every now and then, from the corner of her eye, she sometimes thought she saw a man and woman smiling at her when she was in their bedroom alone.

Maybe it was Noah and Carrie, or maybe it was Sarah and Amos, Emily didn't know, but she knew they were happy to share their home with the family that lived here now.

Emily watched Nick lift their Noah from the horse and set him on the ground. He ran to his mother, his golden eyes sparkling as he shouted to her about the horse he'd ridden. Emily lifted him in her arms and kissed him, then set him on his feet. Nick wrapped his arm around her and kissed her as he rubbed his hand over her evergrowing stomach.

"I love you," Nick said. "I love all of you so much."

Emily looked up at him as they walked to the house for dinner. "I love you, too, Nick," she said and kissed him.

They went inside and shut the door to the house where love continued to live.

~END~

About The Author

Marie McGaha is an ordained minister, a speaker, author and editor. She is the owner of Dancing With Bear Publishing, which is named in remembrance of her late husband, Bear. She is a wife, mother, and Nana, belongs to the Patriot Guard Riders and is the chaplain of 18Wheels Chapter 580South M/A.

You can visit Marie at www.mariemcgaha.com or contact her at dancingwithbear@gmail.com

Other books by Marie from:

www.dancingwithbearpublishing.com

Dancing With Bear: A Love Story
When God Talks, It's Time To Listen
Comfort & Joy book one: forgiveness